KEEPING THE FAITH

A. M. Leibowitz

Supposed Crimes LLC • Matthews, North Carolina

Published in the United States.

ISBN: 978-1-944591-27-4

www.supposedcrimes.com

This book is typeset in Goudy Old Style.

For Ben
(1980-2007)

CHAPTER ONE

BLESSED ARE THOSE WHO MOURN

THUNK. THE last of the items for donation landed in the bin, and Micah snapped the lid on. He dragged the bin to the door and left it. For a moment, he stood there staring at it, hands on hips and lips pressed into a thin line. He was proud of himself; not usually one for getting rid of things, he'd managed to successfully clean out nearly three years' worth of junk in a single weekend without any help.

He stepped away from the bin and retreated to the back of the house. There was only one more room, and it was the one he didn't want to think about. There wasn't much in there anyway, other than a bed, a desk, and some empty shelves. He'd cleared most of it out as soon as possible—he knew it's what his spouse would've wanted. Cat had never liked clutter, and he'd made his wishes known repeatedly that Micah wasn't to keep his things around just to hold onto him.

For the most part, Micah had obeyed the command. He'd thrown out or donated everything he could. There were a few things, though, he hadn't wanted to let go of. Cat's extensive shoe collection—twenty-two pairs of Converse, two pairs of work boots, a pair of black lace-up calf-high boots, and a pair of grubby sneakers—still sat in neat rows in the spare room closet. His cello was there, too, as were several kits full of tools in pristine condition. The nightstand contained a few of Cat's random personal effects in the bottom drawer. The top drawer was full of sex toys Micah hadn't been able to look at, let alone remove—not to mention those weren't exactly the sort of thing one took to Goodwill.

Everything else was gone. Micah stepped inside once more, hoping this time he'd be able to give away or toss those last few items. After all, what good were twenty-six pairs of shoes two sizes too small for him? He stopped before he reached the closet and sat down on the bed. It would probably be easier to go through the sex toys than the other items. He reevaluated donating them. Concordia was a progressive, queer-friendly town; maybe the local Goodwill would take them after all.

While he was contemplating, his eyes traveled the room and lit on something peeking out from underneath a shelf. Puzzled, he stood up and went over to it. He reached down and dragged it out, only to find a wave of raw emotion washing over him. It was an unopened package of the medical tubing Cat used to use to inject his meds through his central access port.

"Shit," Micah said and sat back down on the bed, wiping his eyes.

For the most part, the intervening years had cleared away the heaviest part of Micah's grief. It was white noise now rather than the constant clanging of the early days after his death. Micah was never sure whether knowing ahead that it would happen had been better or worse; he alternated depending on the day. Still, he'd managed to get through it with the support of their friends. Every now and again, however, something popped up that brought it all rushing to the surface again. The surgical supplies was one of them.

Micah set the package on the nightstand. He would need to ask someone if there was a place to take unused tubing, especially of the kind Cat used. Grief superseded his desire to clean, and he picked up the only things he didn't have so much sentimental attachment to: the tool kits. As quickly as he could, he backed out of the room and closed the door before more emotions could swell up. It wasn't that he didn't want to feel; he'd been down that road, and it wasn't worth it. Cat had shown him that much. It was that he didn't want to spend time dwelling in a pit of sadness because for him, it could spiral out of control far too easily.

He returned to the entryway, paused, and headed for the stairs instead. He climbed two flights to the attic and deposited the tools there. He'd moved them around the house three times already, closer to parting with them each successive time. One day, he'd find a use for them, but not today. He returned downstairs. With a deep breath, he picked up the first bin of his own junk and began hauling things to the car for a trip into town.

Micah sat at his sister-in-law's kitchen table, spooning food into his nephew's open mouth. About fifty percent of it made it—hopefully—to Robbie's stomach; the other half landed on his chin, the tray in front of him, and Micah's hand. Robbie giggled and blew a raspberry, resulting in flecks of pureed squash landing on Micah's cheek.

LR glanced over. "You really don't have to do that. He can eat Cheerios until I finish the dishes."

"I don't mind."

Never having wanted his own children, Micah nevertheless loved the ones belonging to other people. Good thing, or he wouldn't have made a very good teacher. It had surprised him—and Cat—that Micah had taken so readily to babies, though. Robbie was number four and the third unplanned surprise. LR swore he was the last.

Micah finished feeding the baby and stepped to the sink for a cloth to clean himself, Robbie, and anything in a ten-foot radius of the high chair. LR glanced at him and choked on a laugh.

"Got some in your hair," she said.

"Gross," Micah remarked. He reached up with the damp cloth and wiped at it.

While he cleaned up, he contemplated what he wanted to say to LR. He wasn't sure how to explain. They were close, made possible in large part because LR lived next door to him. Cat had moved in with Micah, and the house, which technically she'd owned anyway, had become hers. It was a good thing, too—she and Jamal had barely been married five minutes when she officially announced she was pregnant. Only Cat and Micah had known before the wedding.

"Can I talk to you about something?" Micah asked, lifting Robbie from the high chair.

"Of course," LR replied. She accepted Robbie into her arms and carted him to the living room, where she plopped him down with some toys. He promptly dropped into crawl mode and scooted away, dragging a stuffed bunny by the ear.

Micah fidgeted a little. "I don't know how to say this, but... I can't clean out his room. I just can't."

LR frowned. "I thought you already had."

"Mostly, yeah. But I've got his shoes and his cello and some of his clothes, plus an attic full of his old tools." He drew in a deep breath, holding it together. "I need to move on, but I feel so stuck."

"There's no time limit, you know. It hasn't even been three years. Take however long you need. I don't know what you think moving on looks like, but you seem to me like you're doing fine." LR rested her hand on his arm.

He shook his head, his knee bouncing. "I'm not, though. I don't know... I need something to put all this extra energy into. Maybe then I can bring myself to do the one thing he asked me to."

"Which was?"

"He asked me to empty my life of him so I wouldn't waste my time in mourning." Micah allowed exactly one tear to escape before furiously brushing at his eyes.

"My brother was an absolute ass sometimes," LR remarked, shaking her head. "How could he ask you to do that?"

"He knew me better than anyone, and I think he might have been right. He didn't say I should get rid of pictures or things he gave me. He wanted me not to keep all his things around, looking at them all the time and losing myself in grief. Even you remember what I was like the summer we met."

"I do," LR confirmed. "But you've come a long way since then."

"I know." He clenched his teeth as though that might help him shove his overflowing emotions back where they belonged. "I found some of his medical tubing, and I almost lost it. Stupid shit like that keeps popping up."

"It's not stupid, Micah. It happens to me too, all the time." She put her arms around him and squeezed. After a moment, she said, "I think I have an idea."

"Oh?" Micah pulled away.

"Yeah. You know that new community center they remodeled?"

"Of course."

"I know a couple of people who are coordinating volunteers to teach some classes. How about I give them a call? They can contact you with whatever they need, and maybe you can help out. That'll give you something to focus on for a while." She smiled. "It's something Cat would've loved."

"He would have," Micah agreed. "Though he'd have been a lot more fun than I am." He kissed her cheek. "All right. Thanks."

"Any time."

A crash and a yelp from the kitchen propelled Micah to his feet. In a flash, he scooped up a crying Robbie and set the chair he'd pulled over back on its legs. He inspected Robbie head to toe, but there wasn't a scratch on him. Relieved, Micah turned around with the baby in his arms and nearly collided with LR.

"Thank you," she said, her shoulders relaxing.

"No problem." Micah toted Robbie back out to the living room and kept hold of him when he sat back down, tickling Robbie's toes and making him squirm while LR examined him for injuries. His tears transformed into giggles. Micah looked up at LR as she sank down next to them.

"Do you ever worry about him?" he nodded his chin at Robbie.

"Clearly not enough," LR muttered. Louder, she said, "Sometimes. I try not to, but it's hard." She sighed. "I don't want to make the same mistakes my parents did, but I'm not sure how else to do things. At least he doesn't appear to be prone to the same sorts of problems Cat had."

"Robbie does seem to be generally pretty healthy."

"Healthy and with the energy of all the rest combined."

On cue, Robbie wriggled and kicked, so Micah set him back on the floor. He scooted off, and both Micah and LR watched him go in silence. Like his uncle, Robbie had hemophilia, but his brother did not. They hadn't yet had the girls tested to find out if they carried the gene.

Micah turned back to LR. "You'll figure it out."

She closed her eyes briefly. "I know. But I wish Cat were here to tell me what I should do."

LR rested her head on Micah's shoulder, and he put his arm around her. There didn't seem to be anything else to say. Eventually, LR squeezed his hand and sat up again. They stood, and she rescued Robbie from nearly falling off the recliner he'd decided to scale before walking Micah to the door. He bent and planted a kiss on Robbie's head then stepped out for the short walk next door.

The weather turned slightly cooler and wet. With a week left until school began, Micah had enough to keep his mind occupied during the day. He parked behind his school in the faculty lot and carried his box of supplies into the building. He paused in the dim entryway to absorb the pre-season quiet. Almost no one was in the building yet.

Micah shifted the box to one arm so he could wave to the secretary on the way past. She looked up from her computer screen, phone cradled between her ear and shoulder, and smiled as he passed. He carted his things down the hallway to the sixth grade classrooms, around the corner from the music rooms.

Inside, he set the box on his desk and turned in a slow circle. This had been his room for nine of the ten years since the school expanded. He'd spent his first two years with the district in the temporary classrooms, which had been replaced by the permanent addition to the building. In the dozen years he'd lived in Concordia, the only year he hadn't worked for the school was when he'd taken a leave of absence to care for Cat and grieve his death.

It felt good to be back after the summer off. Micah had spent most of his free time completing his fifteenth book and sending it off to his publisher. She'd recently expanded into young adult literature, and he'd jumped at the opportunity. His contribution to the new label was a collection of short stories. He hadn't heard back yet, but he didn't anticipate she would say no.

Micah opened the box and shuffled through the contents. He pulled out his laptop, plugged it in, and turned on some music to keep him company. Whistling along, he unrolled his usual motivational posters and began tacking them up in strategic locations around the room. While he worked, he turned over a few new ideas for writing workshops with his students.

The light, cheerful taps on his door startled him, and he looked down from the chair he was standing on. A young person stood in his doorway. They were dressed in neatly pressed trousers and a collared shirt with the top three buttons undone and the sleeves rolled up. They had very short hair gelled into spikes, wire-framed glasses, and shoes with a bit of extra shine. The person was slim but curvy in the hips and chest. They were smiling but seemed a little nervous.

Micah hopped down from the chair and turned off the music. "Hey there," he said. "What can I do for you?"

They stuck out a hand. "I'm Jude Lily. I just moved in." They laughed, their voice a warm alto. "In many ways. I'm the new general music teacher."

"Micah Forbes. Sixth grade language arts." He took their hand and noticed the slight hesitation and the smallest slip of the smile.

Recovering, Jude accepted the handshake. "I saw your light on, so I figured I'd see who at least one of my neighbors will be."

"I knew they'd hired someone, but I wasn't on the committee. I think I remember seeing your name on the staff list, though. This your first job?"

Jude nodded. "How'd you guess?"

"You're overdressed to get your classroom in order, for one thing."

Cringing, Jude replied, "This is how I always dress."

Micah studied them for a moment. "Fair enough. So where did you do your studies?"

"Got my undergrad from Roberts Wesleyan, and just finished my master's at Eastman."

Micah's eyebrows shot up, and then he chuckled. "I wasn't expecting that answer. Well, Eastman, maybe."

"Wait, you've heard of both schools?"

Micah laughed harder. "I'm originally from Rochester. I wasn't allowed to go to Roberts. My father thought it was too liberal."

Jude joined in. "Oh, god! Yeah, I almost wasn't either, but my parents knew it was the only way they'd get me to go to a Christian school. Once, when my parents attended a concert, they checked out the student exhibit in the art gallery. It was all on the theme of diversity. I thought my father was going to have a fit when he saw one celebrating same-sex couples. I had to promise him the school wasn't that liberal—which is mainly true. I didn't tell him about a few of my professors with rainbow stickers on their doors or the campus LGBT group."

"They have an LGBT group?" Micah stared at Jude.

"Sure do. They have for a while. I don't think it's heavily advertised."

"I can imagine it's not."

While they talked, Micah went back to sorting things in his supply box and putting them away in his room. Jude intrigued him, and he wanted to know more. So far, he hadn't met too many people in town from a religious background similar to his, and definitely no one from his home town. There were a few conservative families remaining from Concordia's less welcoming days, but they mostly left people alone. None of them had children young enough to be Micah's students.

"How in the world did you end up in this tiny town?"

Jude looked thoughtful. "It promised to be welcoming."

"Welcoming?" he repeated, although he was fairly sure he knew the meaning.

"I did my research. Concordia is LGBT-friendly."

"It is," Micah agreed. Moving on, he said, "How would you like to be addressed in front of your students? I'd like to know for when I need to refer to you professionally."

Jude relaxed visibly. "Ms. Lily, not Miss, and definitely not Mrs."

"You'll love it here," Micah told her. "I've lived in town for nearly twelve years, and we're our own little rainbow paradise on the lake. Probably a bit more small-town sheltered than most queer-friendly places, but it works for us. Pretty touristy in the summer, if you can handle that sort of thing."

"Wow," Jude said. Her expression was touched with a bit of sadness for a moment before her cheerful demeanor returned. "Well, I can't wait to learn more. I don't know anyone here yet—I meant it when I said I just moved, and not only to my classroom."

"I should introduce you to a few people," Micah said without thinking. He could have kicked himself. Surely someone as young and vivacious as Jude didn't want to hang around with people twice her age.

Jude didn't seem to be bothered. "Sure, that would be great." She grinned. "Just so you know, though, I don't date men or coworkers."

Taken aback, Micah snorted a laugh. "Well, you're in luck, because while I do date men—mostly—I'm in complete agreement about coworkers."

"Mostly?" Jude arched an eyebrow.

A wave of sorrow passed over Micah, and he swallowed heavily. "My wi—hus—spouse was gender...something. Queer. He always said he didn't have a good word for himself."

"Was?" Jude paused. "Oh. Oh, I'm so sorry," she said, catching on.

"It's all right. Nearly three years." He managed a weak smile.

"Hey, listen, I should probably let you—" Jude waved a hand around the room. "Or...um...I could help?"

"You know, I think I'd like the company. Then maybe I can return the favor."

Jude smiled again, full of sunshine and enthusiasm. She picked up a stack of folders from the box. "Just tell me where to put everything."

CHAPTER TWO

I Stand at the Door and Knock

The cat showed up the day before school started.

It was an orange tabby, strikingly handsome and as cool as you please when he perched on the stoop staring up at the open door with his unblinking green eyes. Micah had only gone to retrieve the mail, but there was the beast. It opened its mouth and offered a meow in greeting.

Amused, Micah replied, "Hello to you too."

He reached down to see if the cat had a collar and was rewarded with a *whap* of the cat's paw. Fortunately, the thing kept its claws retracted. Micah straightened up and crossed his arms, glowering down at the cat.

"No need to be so touchy. Not going to let me see who you belong to, then? Fine. Maybe if I feed you. Wait here."

He retreated inside the house and went to the kitchen. Inside, he pulled out a bowl and rooted through the fridge to see if there was anything cat-friendly. The most he found there was last night's leftover casserole, which didn't seem appealing for his guest. He finally located a can of tuna in the pantry and dumped the whole thing into the bowl. As he turned around to cart it back to the stoop, he nearly dropped it when the cat leaped up on the counter next to him, purring.

"Jesus fuck, you scared me," Micah muttered at him. "Thought I closed the door. Please, feel free to make yourself at home." He nudged the cat, who jumped off the counter and wound himself around Micah's leg.

Micah set the bowl down, and the cat began eating. At last Micah could see if the damn thing had a collar and tag. Unfortunately, he had neither. Micah scratched him a little behind his ears. Poor thing looked like he hadn't had a decent meal in a while—he was on the scrawny side. Friendly, though, so he must have come from a family at some point. Micah would need to ask around to see if anyone had lost their pet.

When the cat finished eating, he rubbed up against Micah's shin, stretching and purring. Micah chuckled softly. Mr. Whiskers had certainly made it clear he intended to stay a while. No harm in that; he would be well cared-for until Micah located his real owner.

He started for the living room, and the cat followed, hopping into Micah's lap the moment he settled down in his chair to flip on the television. Micah put his feet up, and the cat curled against his stomach, rumbling away. As Micah stroked his fur, he thought about how nice it was to have a warm body in the house again. He loved living next door to his sister-in-law, and her kids kept him busy. But it wasn't the same as having another soul around all the time.

"Wish I knew your name," Micah said to the cat. "I can't just call you Cat." He swallowed the lump in his throat and fought the tears pricking his eyes. Every little thing, it seemed, brought up his long-gone spouse these days.

The cat placed his paw on Micah's cheek where the tear tracked its way down. He head-butted Micah, still purring. Sorrow turned to laughter as the cat's whiskers tickled Micah's chin before the animal settled back down with his tail curled around him. Keeping one hand on the cat's back, Micah flipped channels to find something— anything—which would take his mind off his grief even for a little while. Before he knew it, both he and the cat were fast asleep.

When Micah woke, the house was completely dark except for

the television. The cat was gone from his lap. This was the time of day he hated most, always had. In his younger years, he'd passed the crushing nighttime hours with excessive alcohol and mind-and-body-numbing sex with strangers. At nearly fifty, neither of those options appealed anymore. In fact, they hadn't in years. All the things he'd learned, both from a good therapist and a good spouse, were usually enough to get him through the most painful part of the day. Tonight, though, everything weighed heavily on him.

Despite the nervous joy of starting a new school year, he felt off somehow in a way he hadn't for a long time. Too many things lately seemed to be conspiring against him to break open his grief. From cleaning out his own junk to meeting his new coworker and taking in the stray tabby, he couldn't suppress the sorrow he'd kept down to a dull roar. Standing and stretching, he forced himself to focus on getting ready for bed. Once he was beneath the blankets, he could let it out and sleep off the fuzziness afterward.

He hurried to brush his teeth and change into pajamas, wondering where the cat had gone off to. He hadn't seen him since falling asleep earlier, not even after he rose from the chair. Shrugging, Micah assumed Mr. Whiskers—or whatever his name really was—had made himself comfortable in a corner somewhere. That, or he was in search of critters to chase. He would turn back up when he wanted something.

Micah trudged up the stairs and flung back the covers. He flopped onto the bed and lay staring at the ceiling. Some nights, he gave in and let his memories of making love with Cat in this very room take over, stroking himself to orgasm over the images. Others, all he wanted was a good, hard cry. Tonight, he needed both.

By the time he'd sobbed his way through a less-than-thrilling climax, he was exhausted. He cleaned up and rolled over, nestling down under the sheets. Hugging a pillow which no longer held Cat's scent, he allowed his mind and body to shut down and sleep to overtake him.

Early in the morning—much too early—something woke Micah out of a strange dream involving Cat, Micah's new coworker Jude, a power drill, and thirty Kindergartners singing the National Anthem off-key. He groaned and sat up, rubbing his eyes and wondering what had awakened him at such an ungodly hour. It wasn't even fully light yet.

"Meow."

Micah snarled and flopped back down, flinging an arm over his eyes. "Damn cat," he muttered, but he couldn't keep the affection out of his voice.

The cat knew it, too. He pounced, kneading Micah's chest through the blankets and purring so loud Micah wondered why the neighbors weren't calling. He stroked the cat's head, and the thing paused to turn his jewel-green eyes in Micah's direction.

"Meow."

"All right, already."

Micah sat up more slowly, and the cat hopped off the bed. He stood there waiting until Micah was up and running a hand through his messy salt-and-pepper curls. The cat stalked out, sashaying his rump and swishing his tail.

"Drama queen," Micah called after him before making the bed and following the cat out of the bedroom.

They ate breakfast together, Micah nibbling on a couple of pieces of whole wheat toast with strawberry jam and the cat finishing off the tuna from the night before. Micah scrolled through his emails, marking things he needed to take care of later when he had a planning period. The cat leaped onto his lap, sticking his tuna-scented nose right into Micah's face. Micah cringed, but then he laughed.

"You're a pain, you know that?" He scratched the cat's ears. He was already falling for the obnoxious beast, even knowing he couldn't keep someone else's pet forever. "Wish I knew your name. I definitely can't continue calling you Cat." He paused, waiting for the painful lump to appear, but the sorrow was less sharp today. Instead, he smiled. "I don't think Mr. Whiskers really suits you either."

The cat didn't seem interested. He jumped down again and wandered off, probably looking for a place to lick his butt in private. Later, Micah would need to invest in some supplies, such as a litter box and some real cat food. He would put in a call to a veterinarian, too. For now, he would need to figure out a way to let the cat come and go as he pleased or risk having his carpet ruined.

Micah finished the last of his coffee and toast and headed back up the stairs to shower. No sense in wasting the extra time, especially on the first day of school. He didn't need to be in the building early, not after so many years of being well-prepared to greet a new class. Instead, he would check in on Jude and see if she needed anything from him.

As he reached for his towel to dry off, he spotted the cat peering up at him from the bath mat. Micah jumped and rushed to cover himself before rolling his eyes at his own misplaced modesty. It wasn't as though the cat had been trying to catch a glimpse of naked, wet man. Micah was still chuckling to himself when he grabbed his razor. He looked down at the cat, and for half a second, he was certain the thing was smirking at him. Shaking his head, he turned back to his task.

Back in the bedroom, he whistled as he pulled out his work clothes. The cat blinked at him from his position in the center of the bed, and Micah grinned. For no good reason, he felt as though this year was already off to a good start.

"Mr. Forbes?"

Micah glanced up, startled by the PA system piping into his room. "Yes?"

"Sorry to bother you, but there's someone here to see you. Do you have a minute?" the secretary asked.

"Is it a parent?" Micah frowned and looked at the clock. He usually tried to make time for parents, but he was anxious to get home and talk more to LR about the community center idea. He wanted to ask if she'd heard anything yet.

"No, I don't think so."

"All right. I'll be out in a moment." Micah pushed the papers he'd been grading into a neat stack and left everything on his desk.

Out in the main foyer, a short, bald man in business casual attire was talking with the secretary. As Micah approached, he noticed the man wasn't entirely bald after all—only on top, and he'd shaved everything else. He turned around and looked at Micah, his earrings winking in the foyer's fluorescent lights.

"Mr. Forbes, right?" he asked.

"Uh...yes. You can call me Micah. And you are?" Micah approached and extended a hand.

"Chris Sharpe. I'm the associate pastor at the inter-denominational church on the north end of town—Unity."

"Oh. Uh...oh," was all Micah managed. That had been Cat's church. He took several breaths to steady himself. Chris looked vaguely familiar, but Micah couldn't be sure; he'd only been to church with Cat a handful of times, and he hadn't gone at all after Cat's funeral.

"I'm sorry. I assumed this would be the best way to find you. I'm still getting reacquainted with life in a small town after living in the city for so long." Chris smiled.

"No problem. You're right, this is probably easier than showing up on my doorstep." Micah let out a shaky laugh.

Chris chuckled too. "Right. Well, I was hoping to talk to you for a moment."

"We can go to my classroom," Micah suggested.

They wound their way back to the sixth grade wing of the elementary school to Micah's room. Inside, he offered Chris a seat at a long table then sat across from him.

"Now. What can I do for you?" Micah asked.

"I'm one of the lead volunteers on the community center's continuing education program. I got a call from another leader that you might be interested in helping us out." Chris folded his hands on top of the table.

"Oh! Right," Micah said. "My sister-in-law"—his throat pinched painfully—"thought I might be interested. I, uh, asked her if she knew of something going on around town where I could volunteer."

"That's great! We could definitely use all the help we can get. Mainly our purpose is to provide general skills training, such as basic household and auto maintenance, cooking, sewing, and the like. I did talk to the other leader, and he seemed to think you'd still be able to teach a class or two, depending on the subject." Chris's mouth moved as though he was trying not to smile. "I guess your sister-in-law suggested you're not well-suited for the other classes."

Micah laughed. "You're being polite. She's absolutely right — I'm not handy at all. That was my—" He cut himself off, not wanting to continue. He'd reached the point where he could talk about Cat with family and his closest friends, but he drew the line at opening up with complete strangers.

Chris tilted his head, peering at Micah while he let the words hang. When it was clear Micah wasn't going to finish the sentence, Chris said, "That's fine. What sorts of things might you be able to teach?"

"Well, I could offer homework help, but I'd be no good at working through advanced math and science, so that might not be terribly useful. I'm a language arts teacher."

"We'll be offering high school equivalency classes, so that's a possibility. We're also considering a few classes just for fun. You mentioned teaching language arts. Are you any good at creative writing?"

Micah almost laughed again but realized Chris wouldn't understand what was so funny. "I'm actually a published author. I don't use my real name for that—too many awkward questions from parents."

Chris's eyebrows rose. "Interesting. What do you write that would make it awkward?"

"Uh-hm." Micah's face was hot. "Romance." He didn't add the small detail that his pairings were of a variety of genders and sexual orientations.

The expression on Chris's face was priceless—somewhere between amused, surprised, and curious. "I see. Well, as long as you're open to giving students freedom of expression, I don't see a problem."

"No worries in that regard," Micah said. "Could be fun." He grinned. "I'll keep it clean."

Chris relaxed, laughing. "I sure hope so. How long have you been writing romance?"

"About fifteen years. I wrote the first one on a dare, and it ended up being a lot more popular than I expected. A few years later, I was cleaning out my house, and—" He stopped again and shook his head, feeling his smile slip. "Anyway, I've written roughly one novel a year and a number of short stories since then."

A tiny frown creased Chris's brow. For a moment, Micah was sure he would ask about cleaning the house and why Micah had stopped, but the frown disappeared as quickly as it had formed. "It definitely sounds like you'd be a great asset. I'll let you know when we're ready to create a list of class offerings." He rose from his seat.

Micah remained sitting. As much as he wanted to be part of the new community center, he didn't want to wait to help. He wondered what else he could offer before then. A thought occurred to him, and it would accomplish two purposes. "Wait," he said.

Chris stopped. "Yes?"

"Um...are you in need of anything for the life skills classes? Like, say, tools or supplies?" He almost choked up on the last words.

Tilting his head, Chris replied, "Well, we could always use that stuff. Why?"

Micah looked down, collecting himself, then back up at Chris. "My spouse..." He trailed off, taking a moment to compose himself. He cleared his throat. "My spouse passed away a few years ago. He left me boxes full of tools I have no idea how to use." A faint smile worked its way forward when he thought about the way Cat always made fun of his extreme inability to so much as use a screwdriver.

For a moment, Chris didn't say anything. When he spoke, his voice was quiet and soothing. "I'm so sorry for your loss. If you want to donate his things, that's fine, but it's really up to you."

Micah nodded then asked the question that had been playing on his mind. "Did you know him?"

"Your spouse? I'm not sure. Why?"

"You're a pastor at his church, that's all. Though now I think of it, I don't recall you being there for his funeral. It was kind of a blur, and I didn't really know anyone from the church." Micah shrugged, assuming he'd been mistaken.

"Oh!" Chris exclaimed. "It must have been his death Pastor Maryann spoke of. She said the former associate left right after. I've only been back for a year."

"Ah." For no good reason, it disappointed Micah. He supposed maybe he'd wanted one last link to Cat through the church.

"Wait a moment," Chris said. "I did my internship at that

church too, years ago. Who was your spouse?"

"Ca—Becket Rowland. Most people called him Cat."

Chris's mouth dropped open. "My God," he murmured. "I am so, so sorry." He sat back down. "Yes, I knew Cat. What a gentle soul."

"He was," Micah agreed, feeling the familiar lump rise in his throat.

"And you," Chris continued. "I remember you, too. Just barely, but you were there the summer I was an intern." He shook his head, smiling. "We met on the beach—my dog found you."

The sorrow dissipated, and Micah grinned. "I remember that. It was an awful summer, but that was a pretty nice moment. I won't say you were solely responsible for convincing me not to give up on Cat, but you did give me a lot to think about."

"So you married him. I'm glad—he deserved such happiness." Chris reached across the table to squeeze Micah's hand. "I'm sorry again that he's gone."

Micah nodded. "Me too, but he'd been sick for a long time. I won't call it a 'gift' or a 'blessing.' It certainly wasn't for me. I'm glad he's not suffering, though."

Chris let go of Micah's hand. "If you still feel you can donate his things, that would be appreciated. I have the sense he'd have liked that."

"I do, too."

"Maybe..." Chris tapped his lips. "I know you said you're not handy, but maybe you'd like to try out a couple of our classes, learn how to use the tools. You could think about it before donating everything to us."

Micah chuckled. "That doesn't sound too bad. I'll consider it."

"In the meantime, why don't you stop by this weekend to meet the team and help us put the finishing touches on the community center? I promise, it's nothing to do with building things. We're arranging the rooms now the furniture and supplies have arrived."

"All right," Micah agreed, his mouth moving before his brain had a chance to disagree.

"See you then." Chris shook his hand again.

They stood, and Micah showed Chris to the door. When he was

gone, Micah sat back down at his desk. Giving Cat's things a home made his chest ache, but it also carried a sense of peace he hadn't had in a long time. With luck, it would work out to everyone's benefit.

CHAPTER THREE

The Harvest Is Plentiful

MUCH EARLIER on Saturday than he would have liked, Micah woke to prepare for his day. He would start with volunteering at the community center and go from there. Chris had said they were arranging the rooms, so at least it wasn't anything too far out of his skill set. Still, the idea of a building full of strangers intimidated him. Being around so many unfamiliar people always set him on edge.

The cat, whom Micah had begun calling Thomas, jumped up on the bed the minute Micah stirred. He shoved his face into Micah's and meowed loudly before bopping him on the nose. Micah chuckled and rubbed Thomas' ears.

"Rascal. C'mon, let's get breakfast. I probably need a whole pot of coffee for this day."

Micah pushed the covers back, displacing Thomas from his chest. The cat hopped off the bed, looking back at Micah with a disdainful expression. Micah rolled his eyes and ignored him while he made the bed. He followed Thomas downstairs and dumped food in the cat's bowl before putting on the coffee pot. Thomas sniffed the food, twitched his tail, and stalked off.

As snooty as Thomas could be, Micah enjoyed having the company. He'd never considered having a pet before. It seemed to him about as much work as having a child, and before Cat, he'd had enough trouble remembering his own basic needs. He and Cat had never had any furry companions. Now, Micah was grateful for Thomas' presence in the house. He liked Thomas, even if he was stubborn and finicky and several shades of irritating on mornings Micah would have preferred to sleep longer.

He gave Thomas his cream cheese knife to lick, earning a pleased chirrup and a head-butt. Micah left him to it and went upstairs to shower and dress. He let the hot water relax him, reminding himself that even if he didn't know anyone, at least he'd met Chris before. A nervous tingle fluttered in his belly, but Micah discovered it wasn't entirely unpleasant. Chris had been warm and friendly, and Micah looked forward to seeing him again. It had been a while since making new friends, and in the span of less than two weeks, he'd now made two.

En route to town, the anticipation of talking to Chris gave way to Micah's anxiety. He repeated to himself words of safety and comfort as he drove. He was glad to be alone for the time being. No one but Cat knew all the small things he'd learned to do over the years, not even Micah's best friend, Zayne. Cat had always treated it as being the same as when he took his meds, simply something Micah needed to do in order to function the same way Cat needed to infuse clotting factor. Everything with him had been matter-of-fact.

Having gotten distracted with thoughts of Cat, Micah almost missed the turn for the new center. He applied the brakes quickly and made a sharp right into the parking lot. There were already several cars there, but he couldn't tell how many people might be inside. He parked and got out, standing beside the car for a few minutes before heading for the building.

Inside, he heard voices and unidentifiable clattering. He stepped through a second set of doors, propped open, into the main part of the building. Looking around, he imagined the place must once have been some kind of medical facility. There was a desk right up front, and behind it stretched two long hallways of rooms. The remodeling had transformed it into a bright, cheerful place, with murals along the walls and autumn decorations at the main desk. Micah approached, seeing a group of people standing there with paper cups of coffee and tea in their hands.

"Excuse me?" he said.

A plump woman whose brown hair was streaked with white-blond smiled at him. "Morning! What can we do for you?"

"I'm looking for Chris Sharpe."

A young woman poked her head around the plump woman. "Oh, hey, Micah," she said.

"Jude! What are you doing here?"

She grinned. "A bunch of us from school are here. Where are you going to be working?"

"I don't know yet. Chris said you're moving furniture, and he promised we'd find a way I could help that didn't involve building anything."

Jude snorted. "I can relate. Some of us are setting up classrooms, and others are taking inventory and stocking rooms."

"I could probably manage those tasks, at least."

Before they could continue, Chris showed up. He was dressed more casually than the day before, wearing faded jeans and a worn T-shirt. His beard was a little scruffier than it had been the other day, and he'd taken out the earrings. Micah missed the earrings, but he thought Chris looked good this way. When Chris glanced over and smiled, heat rose to Micah's ears. He was sure he'd been caught staring and enjoying the view, even though there wasn't anything more to it than appreciation.

"Hello, Micah," Chris said. "I see you've met the welcoming committee." He turned to the others. "Did you all at least offer him some coffee?"

Micah laughed. "They didn't, but I've had plenty. You don't want to see what would happen if I had any more."

"I might," Jude piped up. She grinned wickedly.

Ignoring her, Micah said, "I hear we're arranging classrooms and stocking shelves. I've got years of experience with those tasks, so I'm all yours for the day."

Chris smiled again, and something in it sent warm ripples

through Micah's chest. "Yes, that's correct. Everything's been delivered, but we haven't set it up. I was planning to start with taking inventory in the stock rooms, and then we'll begin distributing supplies where they're needed."

"Sounds good," Micah said. "Point the way, and I'll join you."

"Mind if I come?" Jude asked.

"Sure," Chris told her. "Follow me."

He led them down one of the hallways, and Micah peeked in the rooms along the way. Most of the rooms were empty except for desks and chairs stacked along the walls. There were shelves, but they were bare. The rooms appeared to be color-coded, and Micah wondered what everything meant. He supposed he would find out soon enough. His earlier impression of the building's original use faded, as he noticed the rooms were the wrong size for a hospital or clinic.

"What was this place?" Micah asked.

Chris glanced over his shoulder. "Used to be a skilled nursing facility, and before that, I think it was a psychiatric hospital. They've knocked out some of the walls between rooms and removed the bathrooms. They constructed a whole new set for public use on each side of the building."

They entered a room which seemed to be closer to the original size. There were boxes upon boxes stacked there and empty shelves from floor to ceiling. At the far end, there was a step ladder. Chris took a clipboard from a nail in the wall.

"We need to go through the boxes and figure out what we have and what we still need. This is the classroom end of the building, so it's the same types of things you'd find in a school. The other end has the practical skills rooms, with a completely different set of supplies."

Micah took the lid off a box and discovered it was full of markers, pens, and pencils. "Did you buy all this?"

"No," Chris said. "A lot of what we have has been donated by families and local businesses. Some things may be incomplete, so we'll need to indicate that as we go."

Nodding, Micah thought about the tool boxes in his attic. If the other end of the building was the same way, he would have no trouble unloading the tools on the center for use with their classes. He might have other items in his attic he'd forgotten, since he hadn't gone through it with his most recent cleaning frenzy.

Chris interrupted his thoughts by opening another bin, this time full of laminated signs. "All right, let's get started. You two count, I'll write, and then we'll all label and load the shelves."

Micah was tired and sweaty when he returned home late in the afternoon. He offered Thomas more food—which he rejected, although he had eventually eaten what Micah left in the morning—then went to shower. When he descended the stairs again and went into the kitchen to make dinner, Jamal was already there waiting for him.

"Is that your cat?" he asked, pointing down to Thomas, who was making his best effort to leave his entire ginger coat on Jamal's trousers.

"Sort of." Micah grinned. "He showed up one day. Kind of like you right now. What's going on?"

"Nothing. Came to see if you wanted to join us for dinner."

His words and tone were casual, but Micah saw through it. LR had obviously said something to him, and they were both convinced Micah needed them to be more direct about checking in on him. Regardless of their motivation, Micah wasn't going to turn down someone else cooking dinner and a chance to spend more time with his nieces and nephews.

"Sure," he told Jamal.

Thomas gave one last twitch of his tail and hopped up on the counter. He stared at Micah, challenging him to shoo him off. Micah ignored him; there was no point, since Thomas would be up on the counter again the minute they were gone. Grabbing his keys on the way out, Micah followed Jamal next door.

Inside the house, it was utter chaos. Langston, the seven-year-old, was chasing Emily, his five-year-old sister, with a stick. He was wearing what looked like a graduation gown, which was so big on him he kept tripping on the hem. Emily didn't seem bothered by it. She was giggling and playing along with whatever it was. Four-year-old Maya, the quiet one, was coloring at the kitchen table. Micah didn't see Robbie, but chances were high that with everyone else occupied, he was up to no good. He was a wily one.

LR was at the sink, rinsing greens. Micah waited until Lang made another dash past him then stepped over to greet LR with a kiss on her cheek. She set the greens in the colander and handed him a knife.

"Cut the peppers, will you?"

"Sure."

Jamal disappeared and returned a moment later with Robbie giggling in his arms. "Rescued this rascal from scaling the baby gate again."

"We don't need a gate. We need a wall," LR replied.

Micah laughed. "He would find a way to get over that, too."

"Point," LR said, nodding.

Balancing Robbie with one arm, Jamal stirred something in a pot on the stove and then reached into the cupboard for the dishes. He hollered for the big kids to come help set the table. Lang arrived first, waving his stick at the stack of plates. LR glanced over her shoulder and rolled her eyes.

"Jamal's been reading Harry Potter to them," she explained. "They're a little...enthusiastic."

"Obsessed," Jamal corrected. "Not that I mind."

That explained the stick Lang was still waving. Micah put a hand on his shoulder. "Maybe you should try using your hands until you get the hang of that spell, okay?"

Lang gave Micah a half-hearted scowl before stepping away from him to take the plates from Jamal. Micah held out his hands, and Jamal deposited Robbie into them so he could help Emily with the silverware.

Less than fifteen minutes later, all seven of them were seated around the dining room table. They didn't say grace, really, but Jamal always offered a few words of thankfulness for the good gifts they had. The adults and Lang served food to the younger ones.

"So, Micah," Jamal began. "Tell us about your cat."

Micah almost choked, hastily grabbing his water glass and taking a sip. LR's eyebrows shot up, and the kids turned to Micah with interest.

"Uncle Mike has a cat?" Lang asked.

"What kind?" Emily wanted to know.

"An orange tabby, and he showed up at my house right before school started." Micah shrugged. "I named him Thomas."

"As in Thomas O'Malley?" Lang bounced excitedly. Micah had forgotten his nephew was as keen on Disney films as he was on Harry Potter.

"Um ... no." Micah flushed. "As in Thomas à Becket, the archbishop of Canterbury."

LR's mouth dropped open, and Jamal leaned over to gently press a finger to the underside of her chin. When she had recovered, she said, "Why?"

Micah sighed. "He didn't have a tag, and I couldn't keep calling him Cat. But he reminds me of—" He stopped.

Understanding passed between Micah and LR. She nodded. "That's fair. I like it."

Changing the subject, Micah said, "I took your advice, by the way. Spent the day down at the remodeled community center, doing some inventory. Some of my coworkers were there, too." For no good reason, Micah didn't feel comfortable saying he'd mostly spent the time with Jude and Chris. Their friendships were too new. He didn't want to talk about it, as though that might somehow jinx it.

"That's great! I can't wait to see what they do with it. We've needed something like this for a long time. The old center wasn't enough with the growth the town has seen."

"I was told they're going to offer basic household maintenance classes. You know, everyday practical skills. I guess they'll have high school equivalency too, and I've been asked to possibly teach creative writing."

LR grinned. "That's fantastic!"

Conversation moved on to the new building and the programs offered there. Micah relaxed, glad for family after the long day. They finished their meal, and after helping to clear up, Micah bid them goodnight and returned next door.

Thomas was waiting for him, and after checking to see that he had indeed eaten his dinner, Micah settled down in the living room with a book and his headphones. He put on some soft music and stretched out on the couch. Thomas hopped up and staked his claim on Micah's belly. With one hand, Micah absently stroked his back.

His thoughts wandered to the day at the community center, and he couldn't help smiling to himself. He enjoyed Jude's company, but there was something compelling him to find out more about Chris. He'd been curious since recalling their brief meeting years before, but he hesitated. Chris was a minister, which meant he was probably more traditionally religious than Cat had been. Cat sometimes referred to himself as a "feral believer" because he'd been so unorthodox. Chris didn't strike Micah as the type of person who would jerk off while praying the rosary.

That last thought startled Micah. He hadn't been thinking about Chris in such a way at all, but there it was, out on the table. He had no business putting Chris in the same context as Cat, and certainly not in a sexual way. Embarrassed, Micah turned his attention back to his book. In a few minutes, he was deeply absorbed in the story, the music, and the cat purring happily under his hand, all thoughts of Chris buried beneath the words on the page in front of Micah.

Inside the cafe, Micah waved to his mother-in-law when he saw her peek at him from the kitchen. Audrey stepped out and came around to give him a hug. Now in her sixties, her hair had gone from deep red to a soft almost white-blond. She still kept it long, piled into a loose bun and covered with a net for work. The scent of her shampoo, so similar to the one Cat had used, tickled Micah's nose as he pressed his cheek to the top of her head. He let her go and bent to kiss her cheek.

"How are you doing?" she asked. It never failed; she'd been through it all herself, but she always asked after Micah's well-being.

"Not bad. Meeting a friend here today for brunch. Reid."

"Ah, yes." She smiled. "What would you like? We have some apple cinnamon pastries, and our caramel vanilla coffee is on special today."

"That sounds amazing. Both, please."

Audrey disappeared into the back, and Micah spoke quietly to the cashier. He wanted to pay for it before Audrey noticed. She would try to give it to him for free otherwise, and he didn't want to have that conversation again. She wouldn't know he'd paid, which would make them both happier.

Once Micah had coffee and pastries for himself and Reid, he carried the tray to a table in the corner and waited until Reid showed up. He breezed in a few minutes later, looking good as ever. Reid had always had a polished, professional air about him, and he'd only become more attractive as he got older. While Micah wasn't necessarily bothered by the fact that he was only a few months away from fifty, he did fuss a little over his crow's feet and graying hair. Somehow, Reid seemed to wear his age much better.

Micah stood up to greet him and was rewarded with a kiss on the mouth. Reid had never been shy. He gave Micah a naughty smile as they sat down. Micah shook his head, but he didn't mind how forward Reid was with him. They had a colorful history, and Reid was the only person who could get away with it.

Reid took a bite of the pastry Micah pushed across the table to him. "That's good. Audrey's outdone herself." He polished it off in a couple more bites. "You going to eat yours?"

"Hm?" Micah looked down at his plate. He'd been watching Reid eat and had forgotten he had his own. "Did you want it?"

"Can I?"

Micah laughed. "Yeah, whatever." He passed over the other plate.

"Here, you can have a bite first." Reid held it out so Micah could taste it.

The pastry was good, light and delicate with a cool, sweet-tart filling. A little of it dribbled onto Micah's lip, and he poked his tongue out to lick it. Reid raised an eyebrow, and Micah flushed, realizing what he'd done.

"Don't tempt me," Reid said.

Micah scowled, even though he knew Reid wasn't serious. Or not entirely, anyway. "Wasn't trying to."

Reid blew on his coffee. "So, tell me. How's it going these days?"

"Not too bad. The kids this year are all right so far. There's always one or two, though." It was easy to forget in a picturesque town built on tourism that not every family benefited from it. Micah already had some students he was keeping an eye on.

"Good, good." Reid drained his coffee cup and glanced over his shoulder. "You want anything? I think I'm going to get another cup and maybe something less sticky to eat."

"Sure. Another one of those tarts, please. Since you ate all my damn pastries."

"You said I could!"

Reid returned shortly with another tray and passed Micah's food to him. While they ate, Reid kept Micah entertained with stories about some of his more interesting clients. Less fascinating was his assessment of the housing market in Watkins Glen, but Micah tolerated listening for the sake of their friendship.

"Listen to me, going on," Reid remarked. "Sorry about that. I get a little excited. Not that you're not always quiet, but you seem distracted today. Everything all right?" He leaned in and said more quietly, "You need to come over later and let us take care of you?"

Micah knew what he was referring to. Reid was in a relationship—or rather several—in a house full of men. Micah wasn't exactly sure how it all worked for them, and he wasn't bold enough to ask for specifics. Reid had never been the monogamous sort, but he'd spent years trying out relationships and both breaking hearts and having his own squashed. Now he was with three other guys who loved and cared for each other, and they'd been together for about five years.

They weren't entirely exclusive. They'd found Reid because he'd been invited in to play, and he'd stayed. It was the open nature of their household about which Reid was now speaking. Micah flushed a little, remembering the first time. He still felt guilty. The day after Cat's funeral, Micah had spent his time in bed, sobbing uncontrollably but refusing to call anyone. Reid had come to check up on him and brought him back to his house. He and his partners had looked after Micah for a few days, which included a lot of intimate touch and sex. The guilt was less over allowing them to care for him and more about how much he'd wanted it.

Micah sighed. "I don't think so." It was tempting, but he wasn't in a state of shock or grief with a need to feel protected, nor was he in need of company and relief.

"All right. You know you can call me if you do, right?"

"I know." Micah reached across the table to grip Reid's arm briefly. "I promise, I'll let you know if I need you."

"So, what's on your mind, then?"

Where to start? "I'm trying something different. Volunteering at the new community center."

Reid gave him an incredulous look. "Isn't that like cooking and home repair classes and shit? What could you possibly be doing there?"

Micah chuckled. "Helping them get the building set up and then maybe teaching some creative writing classes."

"Oh yeah? Wait, you're not trying to build prepackaged furniture again, are you?" Even Reid knew how pathetic Micah's skills were with anything handy.

"Of course not! I'm helping inventory stock and arrange desks."

"Good. I was worried they might try to give you a screwdriver. Now, if it had been Cat—shit. I'm sorry."

Same song, different lyrics. Everyone was afraid to mention his name. Not that Micah could blame them. He'd never held the door open, and he tried not to talk about Cat himself. He suspected his reasons might be different from theirs.

"Don't worry about it." Micah paused, waiting for the bubble of grief, but the shadow passed. "You're right. He'd have been much better than I would be. Though I did manage to live on my own for fifteen years before we met, you know."

Reid's expression relaxed into an easy smile, and he laughed. "Good point. I assumed you hired out."

Micah shoved Reid's foot with his own. "Whatever."

They finished their meal, and Reid stood up. When Micah followed him, Reid wrapped him in a hug and told him not to be a stranger. He was leaving open the invitation to return to be cared for by Reid and his partners, but Micah didn't think he would need to. His mind drifted to Chris and Jude and the work at the community center, and he knew he had enough to keep him occupied for the time being.

He threw out his trash and bid Audrey goodbye. Time to go home and clean out the attic, looking for anything he might donate. He still might take a class or three, but he couldn't see hanging onto Cat's things anyway. Surely once he was free of the items he no longer needed, he could also be free of the shadows that clung to him. He would do exactly as Cat asked, once and for all.

CHAPTER FOUR

WRITE, THEREFORE, WHAT YOU HAVE SEEN

MICAH SET his laptop on the kitchen table and opened it. He already had a document up, a blank page for a new chapter of his latest novel. So far, with the exception of the year after Cat died, he'd managed to put out roughly one novel a year. Because of his leave of absence, he'd spent the months after Cat was gone pouring his attention into writing and had delivered three to his publisher.

He had notes and the beginning chapters of the one he'd been working on over the summer after finishing the anthology. For no good reason he could fathom, he hadn't been able to get any further with this new one. He hated everything he had so far and wished he could start over. More than likely, his publisher would have something to say about his lack of respect for deadlines. He would need to be persuasive in asking for an extension. This project had priority over an erotic lesbian retelling of the tortoise and the hare he'd outlined, but he was tempted to work on that one instead.

With his fingers poised over the keys, he hesitated. What he'd written felt both too personal and yet somehow not intimate enough. For years, Micah's brand of romance had been rooted mainly in the complexities of established couples rather than meeting and falling in love. His publisher was putting out a series of bittersweet stories, and he'd planned to write one about an older couple at the end of their lives. Only it felt all wrong every time he tried to write it, as though he was missing some key ingredient. He had experience with a lover's terminal illness, but it wasn't translating to the page in any meaningful way.

Micah sighed heavily and rose from the table. He almost tripped before realizing it was Thomas, blocking his exit. The cat wound around his legs and meowed, lashing his tail. Micah reached down to scratch his ears. He'd fed him before retrieving his laptop, so he knew Thomas wasn't hungry. Thomas looked up at him then turned around, twitching his rump. Micah snorted, but he followed when Thomas led him out of the room.

They ascended the stairs, and at the top, Thomas stopped by the door to the attic. Micah pulled it open, and the cat dashed up the steps. Curious, Micah followed. He didn't go up there often, only when he needed something out of storage or to find yet another storage space for his deceased spouse's tools. The holiday decorations were up there, as were some artifacts he'd kept from when his parents had owned the house. There were photo albums and a handful of other random items, but that was it.

There was a possibility Thomas was only curious about the room Micah hadn't let him in, but something told Micah the cat wanted him up there for a reason. Micah climbed more slowly than Thomas had. The weather was still warm, and the room was stuffy. Sunlight filtered in through the narrow windows, illuminating the dust Thomas had stirred up with his paws. Micah pulled the chain on the light and watched Thomas leap up onto a trunk.

Frowning, Micah followed him over. He hadn't noticed that particular trunk the last time he'd been up here. As he approached, Thomas stretched and jumped down. Micah flicked the latches and opened the lid. Inside, there were perhaps two dozen old-style composition books. Along with them, Micah found several spiral-bound books of musical score sheets, a stack of photo albums, a packet of letters, and a small box.

Micah withdrew one of the spiral-bound music books and opened it. On the inside cover, in a child's script—too precise and yet somehow sloppy—was Cat's full name. Micah flipped through the pages and saw some of Cat's earliest compositions. He set that one aside and thumbed through a couple more, noting the dates and the progressive complexity of the music. In the years he and Micah were together, Cat had always used modern technology for his scores. Micah had saved those, although he hadn't done anything with them. He gathered that Cat had, at one time, been a serious musician, but Cat had never wanted to talk about that part of his life. It was before they met, and he had only continued composing for his own amusement rather than to publish. Micah had considered publishing them in his name, but he hadn't done it.

He set the music back in the trunk and pulled out one of the black and white composition books. These, too, dated from a much earlier time. The first one listed the year as 1997. Micah read a few pages, realizing quickly these were Cat's journals. He'd never known Cat kept any. The one time he'd seen Cat do any writing, it was when he'd sat in Micah's lap and messed up his manuscript with a few horrible lines of sexual innuendo. The memory made Micah both laugh and flush. Cat had inspired him to make one of his characters bisexual.

Micah skimmed a story about the time Cat had played Mary in his church Christmas pageant. It didn't surprise Micah, but he did wonder how it got approved by a strict Catholic Sunday school teacher. When he reached the end of the story, Micah discovered Cat had swapped roles with a friend at the last minute. Leave it to Cat to go about things in an unorthodox way.

That was Cat all over, of course. Micah stared down at the journal in his hands. He wasn't sure if he'd been meant to find them. Cat had never mentioned keeping them, and in fact, he'd implied he wasn't much on writing. Yet here they were, and Cat was not. Micah had an opportunity to know more about the person he'd loved. He hesitated, contemplating reading more, but he wasn't ready. He set aside the composition books and picked up one of the photo albums.

As companions to the other books, these provided Micah a visual history of Cat's life. He wondered if LR or Cat's parents would want any of what was in the trunk. After flipping through an album of Cat's early childhood, Micah put that in the growing pile next to him and lifted out the letters.

These were different. They were written more recently. Micah went through the envelopes, his mouth dropping open in surprise. Cat had written them all during the time after he'd become ill. He'd known then he was dying; it had been his choice not to take drastic measures to alter the course of his long illness. It had taken five months almost to the day for him to finally acquiesce to the effects of multiple organ failure on his body. The final month had been agony, and Cat hadn't been lucid enough in that time to compose any more letters. The last one was dated about five weeks before he died.

The only thing left in the trunk was the small box. Micah took it out and examined it. The box was metal and had a lock, but there was no key. Micah searched the bottom of the now-empty trunk, but there was nothing inside. He shook the box and heard the items rattle. There might be a way to pick the lock, but he wasn't any kind of expert. He set the box with the letters, promising himself to find someone who could open it.

He placed the albums, the composition books, and the musical scores back in the trunk. The only things he kept out were the letters and lock box. Closing the lid on the trunk, he carted the items downstairs. Thomas, who had been watching from a perch on top of a box of Christmas decorations, hopped down and followed him. Micah shut the attic door once he was sure Thomas had gotten down.

Back in the kitchen, Micah sorted the letters by date. He'd been down this road once before, the year he moved into the house. Among other items, he'd discovered a box of love letters exchanged between his mother and her neighbor, a woman who still lived a couple houses down from Micah. It was never clear to Micah whether his mother's suicide was connected directly to the affair or not, but those letters were his last link to her. He'd saved them too, in a different bin in the attic, sheathed in acid-free page protectors in an album.

Micah opened the first letter. Inside, he found the key to the lock box and a folded piece of paper. He withdrew both and set the key on top of the box. Slowly, he unfolded the letter and read the greeting. He only got as far as *Dearest Micah* when he let the paper fall from his fingers. His immediate urge was to shove it back into the envelope and never open it again nor any of the others.

His head swam; he wasn't ready for this. What secrets was Cat going to reveal in death that he hadn't shared in life? It was as though Cat spoke his name right from the page, and it tore open the wound of his death. Micah's eyes burned as he struggled to hold back an ocean of raw grief. Unable to continue for the moment, Micah let it take him, covering his face and sobbing.

It took a moment for him to realize that something was nudging him, and he fought to regain control. Opening his eyes, he found Thomas in his lap, trying to press close to Micah's chest. Thomas' head rubbed under Micah's chin, and the cat purred. The rumbles soothed Micah, and his crying slowed. He took a deep breath.

He could do this. He could read Cat's letters and not fall apart. Cat had trusted him to do so eventually, and Thomas was here to comfort him. Micah wiped his eyes and nose and picked the letter up again. He closed his eyes and went through the steps to calm his anxiety before looking back at the page and trying again.

Dearest Micah,

I'm starting these letters because it feels to me like I have a lifetime of things I want to tell you before I go. Which is weird, maybe, since we talk a lot. What else could I possibly have to say? Except I do have things. Things I want to write down so I remember them. I might get too sick to recall stuff like our wedding day.

It's funny. I told you not to hold onto me, but here I am trying to do exactly that. I'm not as good a writer as you, so maybe I won't get the details right. A long time ago, you told me you weren't afraid to write queer stories anymore because you'd been writing your own. That night, you told me you loved me for the first time. Maybe I'm hopelessly sappy, but that was one of the best moments of my life.

You've written a lot of queer stories since then. And I would know, since you made me read them all to see if they were good enough. The first one you gave me is my favorite, though. I still get hot reading it.

My point is this: You've written a lot of other people's stories. Why not do for us what you do for them? We were pretty good together, honey. So as crappy a writer as I am, I'm giving you a start. Maybe then you can let go of us and move on with your life. What do you say? Write about us, and then do one last thing for me. Give it to someone. You can't keep me, but maybe someone else can.

I've left you the box and the key. Read the letters and then burn them. I don't want to sit on your shelf collecting dust and sadness.

All my love,

Cat

Micah read the letter three times. He couldn't fathom what Cat had been thinking, putting their entire history into a series of letters. He definitely didn't want to read them. Why revisit the past? Hadn't Cat asked him not to sit on his grief that way? Micah should burn them now, without reading them.

Except curiosity had hold of him. He needed to know what memories Cat specifically thought were important enough to write down. He'd been right. Although he remained lucid for a long time, by the end he barely remembered who Micah was. It had been painful to watch as his whole body shut down, leaving him with frightening symptoms of the effects on his brain. He must have written the letters near the beginning of his illness, before the worst of it set in.

Micah tore his thoughts away from those memories. He didn't want to think about Cat in his last days. Hell, he didn't want to think about Cat before then, either. Cat hadn't intended him to dwell on the past. He'd said it over and over. What Micah had never understood was why he'd been so insistent. Yet now he was commanding Micah to write their story. How could he put into words the nine years he'd spent loving Cat? What could he possibly say that would communicate the beautiful brilliance of the person he'd adored?

Against his will, dozens of images passed through his mind, all the ways in which being with Cat had made him a better person. He was a different man now, stronger and more capable of facing the world. It wasn't only Cat, of course. Micah never would have survived his death without the others, people he knew and trusted because of Cat. He thought about waiting until he had a moment with LR or possibly calling Zayne instead. But if Cat had left something private for him, it would only embarrass LR, and Zayne couldn't take time away from her boutique just to watch him open letters. It was up to him to draw on the strength he'd developed to do it on his own.

Slowly, hands shaking, he opened the second letter and withdrew it. In spite of the tears threatening, he chuckled when he started reading.

Dearest Micah,

Remember how we met? I'll bet you don't know what a wreck I was that summer. Holy shit. I wanted you so bad. I was like a teenager with his first crush. I did everything I could to be near you, even though I was sure we could never make it work. This one time, I waited in my living room just so I could watch you get the mail. I might even be able to excuse it if I was looking at your ass or something, which is what I tried to tell myself I was doing. And don't you dare pretend you weren't ogling mine because I caught you at it all the time. Anyway, nope. I wanted to see things like, did you look through the pile first and pick out the good stuff? Or did you take the whole stack inside without peeking? I tried to imagine you putting it on your table and opening it one by one, and I wondered which ones would be most important. Did you know you can tell a lot about a guy by how he sorts his mail?

I'm not sure I learned anything that day except that I was lying to myself. I pretended I only wanted to peek because you were hot and I was curious. Except that's when I figured out I wanted more than to fantasize about you opening your mail. Wait...that sounds bad, but I think you know what I mean. I wanted all of you, and it scared the piss out of me.

The letter was long, and Cat shared with Micah things he'd

never said out loud. He'd talked about why he was afraid to get attached, but he'd never mentioned the little details of his internal dialog as they slowly made their way toward each other. It was strange and yet somehow not to see the events through Cat's eyes. His words brought back all of Micah's memories of that summer.

By the time he was done reading, Micah was laughing and crying at the same time. This seemed to confuse Thomas, who chirruped and hopped off Micah's lap to go find a less emotional sleeping spot. Micah set aside the letter and picked up the key to insert it into the lock box.

The latch sprang open, and he lifted the lid. Micah stared at the contents. There lay Cat's most personal and intimate belongings, items Micah had either not known about or had searched for before assuming LR had them. Cat's rosary, his MedicAlert tags, an old-fashioned metronome, his pot leaf earring with its mate he never wore and magnetic ear cuffs, and a pair of sunset orange lacy bikini underwear. The last one made Micah blush, laugh, and choke up, in that order.

He closed the lid and his eyes, leaning back in his chair. For several minutes, he didn't move, allowing himself to absorb everything he'd seen and read over the last half hour. When he opened his eyes again, he knew what he was going to do. A slow smile spread across his face as he turned it over in his mind, knowing exactly how he wanted to craft the story.

His laptop was still sitting on the table, and he pulled it closer. He closed the project he was working on and started a new one. His fingers hovered as he contemplated a title, but he couldn't think of anything that fit, so he simply typed, *Love Letters*. For a moment, he hesitated, and then he began to type.

A certain man held a fine estate in the lower country…

CHAPTER FIVE

THE SALT OF THE EARTH

WHEN MICAH arrived at the community center on Saturday, he picked up the sounds of conversation from inside. He entered the building and went straight to the desk in the center. Chris looked up from where he was bent over a stack of papers, and his face broke into a wide smile.

"Morning, Micah!" he called.

It was warmer than the previous weekend, with temperatures in the low seventies. Chris had on a gray t-shirt and a pair of grungy jeans. Micah happened to glance down and see his shoes when he came from behind the desk, and he almost laughed. They were faded rainbow, and they looked like they'd seen better days. A weird feeling like double vision passed through Micah. Cat would have loved the shoes, but he never would have let them get into such a state. Something about them simultaneously appealed to and repelled Micah in a way he couldn't make sense of.

Jude appeared from the kitchen area with a cup of tea in hand. She greeted Micah and offered to show him where everything was so he could make himself some coffee. Once he had his drink, he joined the group back at the desk dividing up tasks for the day.

Chris ran a finger down the list. "We're nearly there. Good thing, since classes start next week. Micah, are you still going to run that creative writing class?"

"If you want me to."

"I do." Chris gave him a crooked smile. "I might even take it myself. Could be good for writing sermons."

Micah had to breathe slowly for a moment, both at the thought of Chris sitting in on his class and about the sermons. The same split sensation he'd had earlier returned. He wanted Chris to make sense to him—to be either like Cat or not, instead of having painful similarities and yet being so different. He shook his head and internally scolded himself for being so hung up on it.

"I was thinking about taking a couple of the classes myself," Micah said. "I've told you how useless I am around the house."

"Yes, so you've said." Chris's eyes twinkled. "I can schedule you for the same night, if you prefer. The auto maintenance and cooking classes are long, so they'll be on Saturdays. But the basic household skills and sewing classes will be offered on a few nights during the week, as will the secondary completion classes. What are you taking?"

"I already know how to sew, thanks to my friend Zayne and her mom. I'm taking the home repairs and cooking classes." Micah turned to Jude. "What about you? Are you teaching or taking classes?"

"I'm going to finally learn how to change my own oil," Jude replied, laughing. "I can cook and sew just fine. I'm teaching some music classes, maybe private lessons too."

"Voice?" Micah asked.

"Yes, and I also play the cello and most other strings. I only teach general music because the school already has a strings teacher. I'd have to go back home to get my cello, but it might be worth it."

Another jolt went through Micah. Cat had never believed in coincidences, and Micah hadn't been able to convince him otherwise. For a moment, he was torn, and once again caught in that space between what had been and what currently was. He spoke before he could change his mind.

"I...might have a cello you can use. Or have."

Jude stared at him for a moment, long enough Micah thought he'd said the wrong thing. At last she said, "Wow. That would be great, thanks."

"I'll bring it to school." He had to swallow to keep from letting his emotions get the better of him.

Fortunately, Chris spared him by telling everyone it was time to work. They separated into groups, and this time, Micah, Chris, and Jude were joined by the woman with the blond highlights. She approached Micah and held out her hand.

"I'm Hope," she said. "I have a child in your class."

Micah wracked his brain, trying to come up with whose parent she was. "I'm sorry—" He cut himself off, realizing she'd said *child* and not *son* or *daughter*. "Raven's mom, right?"

"Yes, that's right." Hope smiled.

Raven had attached themself to Micah right from day one. They were a gentle, serious student, and Micah had sensed there was something else going on behind the scenes. Raven didn't talk much about family, though Micah had a standing weekly lunch appointment with Raven for extra help. They struggled with reading and were often annoyed by the kinds of books at their level, feeling they were too "babyish," in their words.

"Good to meet you. Coming with us to stock classrooms?"

"Sure."

Micah and Hope followed the others back to the rooms they hadn't done yet. As they arrived, Micah smacked his forehead. "I'm sorry. I did bring some of the tools for the workshop, but I left them all in my car."

Chris nodded to Hope and Jude. "Can you two get started with labeling the shelves in the work room? Micah, I'll give you a hand with your stuff."

Out at the car, Micah lifted the tote out of his trunk. Chris peeked in, checking out the supplies. Micah could have done it himself, but it was nice to have help. Chris took one end, and Micah took the other. Together, they hauled the bin back into the community center.

They returned to the room, and Jude began pulling the supplies out of the bin. She reached in and frowned, her hand emerging with the lock box Micah had forgotten he'd thrown in when he carried it to the car. He'd intended to stop off at the cafe and ask Audrey if she wanted any of the items, but he'd accidentally left it in the tote instead of setting it aside. As much as he wanted to snatch it away from Jude, he also didn't want to answer questions about it that his behavior would surely raise.

"Here," Jude said, handing the box to Micah. "This doesn't look like it goes with the other stuff."

"What is it?" Hope asked.

"Nothing," Micah told her. "Just a box that I meant to leave in the car and forgot about."

"Ooh, mysterious," Hope teased, giggling.

Micah scowled. "Not terribly. It isn't important anyway. Old junk." He felt guilty speaking about Cat's belongings that way, but he didn't want to talk about it.

Something must have been off in the way he responded because Chris said, "Are you all right?"

Micah set the box on one of the desks. "Never mind. I'll take it home later. Let's get this done."

Tension hung in the air, but the others resumed their work without questioning Micah. After a while, they relaxed. Jude and Hope were having an animated conversation about some of the new things Jude had her students working on. Micah listened to them while he and Chris worked side by side. Chris glanced at Micah every so often, but he didn't say much.

When they stopped for lunch, Chris collected their donations to cover the boxed lunches the crew had ordered. He returned to the room with their food, and they sat in a circle on the floor. Micah was distracted, the contents of the lock box still at the forefront of his mind. He chewed thoughtfully on his sandwich.

Chris nudged him. "What's up?"

"Nothing, I—" Micah looked around at the others. He couldn't explain it, but something in him wanted to confess to these three near-strangers what was in his lock box. He took a steadying breath. "The box Jude found. It has personal items belonging to my dead spouse in it."

"Really?" Hope's eyebrows rose. "Why did you have it in your car?"

Micah shrugged. "I was going to stop by and ask his mom if she wanted them." Micah reached into his pocket for his keys and pulled them out. He held up the small one for the lock box. "Before he died, he was very sick for months. He wrote me a whole bunch of letters and put a few things in here for me to find after he was gone. I'm not sure why he didn't give them to me while he was alive."

The others were all still for a moment. Jude broke the bubble. "Maybe he thought this would be easier."

"I suppose. He told me to read the letters and then burn them, but I don't know what purpose that would serve. I haven't finished reading the letters yet."

Hope tilted her head. "It sounds like he had something he still wanted to say to you."

"I don't know if I want to hear it." A confession Micah couldn't even make to LR, whom he had yet to tell about the box.

Chris's hand on Micah's was warm, and it tingled where their skin touched. "That's understandable."

Micah wasn't ready to tell them what he'd begun doing. It was enough to talk to them about what Cat had left. Wanting to end the awkward silence, he meant to suggest they get back to work. What came out instead was, "I miss him."

He tried to stop himself from crying—again—and almost succeeded. He kept it to a short sniffle and a swipe of his wrist over his wet eyes. Embarrassed, he stood up and silently went to one of the shelves to unload the bin he'd brought. He regained control, though he could still feel the tension in the room. Movement behind him made him half turn around to look. Hope was there, her hand reaching for but not quite touching his shoulder.

"My husband," she said. "Last year. It's why it's been so hard on Raven." She let her fingers rest briefly on Micah's upper arm.

He nodded. "I'm sorry."

Hope grabbed her purse from the floor and pulled out her phone. "This is him." She showed Micah a photo of a handsome man with brown hair and a dimpled smile. He looked a lot like Raven.

Micah pulled his phone out of his back pocket and brought up a picture of Cat. "Here."

Jude and Chris stepped closer to have a look. Jude said, "He's adorable."

"Yeah, he was. Even into his thirties, he always looked so young."

Micah stared at Cat's sweet smile then looked up at the others. "He would have liked this," he said. "All of us working together on the community center."

"I'm sure he would," Chris agreed.

They returned to their task without saying anything more about either Cat or Hope's husband. While the atmosphere was a little less cheerful than before lunch, somehow Micah felt more at ease than he had when he arrived.

After class, Micah emerged from the workshop and walked to the other end of the building. He now knew how to change a doorknob, but he wasn't sure what use he might put that information to. All the knobs in his house had been replaced within six years. Cat had gone on a frenzy after he wasn't able to work anymore, throwing his rage into various projects which didn't really need to be accomplished. He'd never made peace with either his constant exhaustion or with being a stay-at-home spouse.

Micah set his bag down on the desk and pulled things out. He plugged in his laptop and turned it on. It was his third class, and he'd given his students an assignment the last time to bring in a piece of writing to share. He had one of his previously published works with him. Old habits die hard, and even though he didn't expect to run into much bigotry, he'd chosen something which felt safer: his first novel, the one he'd written on a dare from Zayne.

By now he knew everyone's name, and he greeted them as they came in. Jude, Chris, and Hope all sat together in a cluster on the left side of the room. Two of Reid's partners sat all the way in the back, and the owner of the town's most popular tattoo and piercing shop took the middle with his daughters. There were a few students from the community college as well. All of them were familiar, friendly faces except for one of the college guys. His name was Dyl, and he had a perpetual scowl which twisted his otherwise handsome face into something more unpleasant. Micah remembered teaching him years before, and he wondered why Dyl was there in the first place if he wasn't enjoying it.

"Did everyone bring a sample of your writing?" Micah asked.

Everyone's heads bobbed in response, including the young man in the front, which surprised Micah. He walked around the room collecting them. He brought them to his desk, shuffled them, and set them aside for the moment.

"One of the most helpful things to do is read your work out loud. There are a lot of reasons why, and we'll go over them later. For now, I'll keep your work anonymous, but I'll pick a few to read to you. Is there anyone who would rather I not share your work with the class?" A couple of hands went up. "All right. We probably won't get to all of them anyway, but I'll be sure not to read yours."

Micah went through the stack, reading and offering tips for making the writing stronger. Other students chimed in with their opinions, and Micah directed them gently in how to offer the most useful feedback. He was reaching for the next page on the stack when Dyl waved his hand.

"Yes?" Micah answered him.

"You're making us do this, but I don't see you volunteering your work for us to analyze."

"That's fair. I did bring something to share with you at the end for that purpose." He held up his copy of the book.

Dyl eyed it. "You wrote that?" He tilted his chin at the book. "It's not your name on the cover."

"I was writing under a different pen name at the time. This is about fifteen years old, from when I'd just started out. That's why I brought it."

"Uh huh," Dyl said. "Well, you didn't bring us anything you're working on now, did you?"

Micah's cheeks burned. Of course he hadn't. His work in progress about Cat was too private and too new to share it with them, wasn't it? "No, I didn't," he told Dyl.

Carlie, one of the college students, asked, "Why not? Don't you have anything?"

"I do, but—"

"You expect us to share our unedited work, but you don't need to do the same?" Dyl challenged him.

Micah wanted to ask if Dyl had been this much of a pain to his former teachers, but he knew the answer. "Are you saying you think it's not fair? Most teachers don't provide samples of what they're doing outside of class."

"Yeah, but this isn't, like, real school," another one of the college women, Maricela, said. "We're here for fun. I think we could learn a lot from seeing your process."

Dyl arched an eyebrow at Micah, who relented with a sigh. "All right. It's rough, though. I'm still drafting. I'll tell you what. I was going to have you choose whether to continue what you've already done or pick a new project for the term of the class. We'll still do that, and if you keep up your end of the bargain—working on it in between classes—I'll let you in on what I'm doing. Fair?"

Most of the class nodded. Dyl folded his arms, his eyes narrowed. "And we get to critique it?"

Micah counted to five before answering. "Yes, all right. I'm sure my editor will be thrilled at having less work to do. Now. Shall we get back to what we were doing?"

He continued reading bits of the students' work, all the while his gut churning. He'd promised to read part of his to them at the end, and now he was faced with having to share from his work in progress rather than his old novel. It distracted him. He needed to pull himself together or else get it over with so he could concentrate on making recommendations to the others. Dyl's huff broke through his rattling thoughts.

"Hm?" Micah asked.

"I said, do you think I should expand the part about the auto mechanic a bit?"

"Oh." Micah looked back down at the page in front of him. "No, not at this stage. If you give too much of his history now, you'll lose your readers." He made eye contact. "That was why I wanted to read from my first novel—it's one of the mistakes I made."

Dyl smirked. "So you're not perfect."

"Good grief," Micah said, then almost clamped his hand over his mouth. He let out a breath slowly, expelling his irritation along with it. "I never said I was perfect. Will it help if we move on and I show you what I've got?"

He didn't wait for an answer, afraid Dyl was going to be a sarcastic smartass about it. There was a good chance he would be anyhow, but Micah was out of patience. His fingers trembled as he pulled up the file on his laptop. He glanced at the class and saw all eyes were focused on him.

Micah cleared his throat and began to read. "'A certain man held a fine estate in the lower country. He had three sons: the eldest was wise, the second shrewd, and the youngest generous. The man esteemed his first two sons yet reviled the third. Upon his death, he left to them each an inheritance.'"

He read half a page of the opening chapter before looking up at the class. Micah knew his writing at this stage was rough, but he had obviously shocked his students into silence. No one so much as shuffled in their seat. Even Dyl was quiet. Micah frowned.

"Go on," Maricela said. "I want to know what happens to the unfortunate youngest son."

Hope nodded. "I do too. It's like a fairy tale. How does he get out of the mess he's in?"

Micah stared at them. "Is that all?" he asked. "I thought you wanted to critique it. This is a first draft."

Dyl scoffed. "I'll start. Nobody's life is that shitty. And even if it were, no one goes from that deep in it to some magical happy ever after. Why are all supposed fairy tales like that?"

A couple of people flinched, but Micah said, "Sometimes life is, in fact, shitty. And sometimes it's wonderful." He locked gazes with Dyl, challenging him to deny it.

Instead of remaining hard as Micah expected, he saw the smallest flicker of something else in the way Dyl's eyes crinkled. For a moment, neither of them moved, and then Dyl nodded and looked away. Micah let the tension out of his shoulders and addressed the whole group.

"We're out of time for this week." He picked up the stack of papers from his desk. "Come get your work from me, and bring in another part next class."

The students filed out, taking their papers as they passed Micah.

He closed his laptop and began packing things away. He looked up when someone paused by the desk.

"Great class, Micah," Chris said.

His smile nearly took Micah's breath away. "Glad you're enjoying it. Did you find anything helpful for your sermons?"

Chris chuckled. "Not yet, but I'll get there. I liked the style of your story, by the way."

"Thanks." Micah zipped his bag, trying to keep his hand steady. "It's different from what I usually write, but it seemed to fit." He hadn't told Chris how it was connected to the letters, but he wondered if he'd guessed.

"I get the sense there's more to this than writing a new story." That answered Micah's unspoken question.

"In a way." Micah shouldered his bag, hoping to send the message he didn't want to discuss it further.

Chris got the hint, but he surprised Micah with the next thing he said. "Would you like to get a drink sometime?"

Micah's breath caught. He hesitated, apparently too long because Chris looked like he was about to take it back. Micah stopped him. "I would, but I don't drink." He might as well be honest. "I've been sober for most of the last twenty years."

"Doesn't have to be alcohol," Chris said. "Coffee?"

"All right," Micah replied before he could stop himself.

Chris's smile made it worthwhile. "Great. Maybe this weekend."

"I'm free after the cooking class on Saturday."

"I'll see you then," Chris promised.

He slipped out the door, and Micah watched him go before gathering the rest of his things and following him out. He wasn't sure what he'd agreed to, but it wasn't anything serious. Just coffee between friends, that was all. It didn't have to mean more. In any case, Micah had three days to figure out how to let Chris down gently and tell him he didn't date, ever. If only it didn't feel so much like one, and if only something long-buried inside Micah wasn't hoping it was after all.

CHAPTER SIX

NOT THE HEALTHY BUT THE SICK

EVENINGS HAD begun to feel less like lonely darkness settling in and more like a chance to unwind. On weeknights he wasn't at the community center, Micah filled his time with grading papers and then pulling up his latest novel to work on. Reading the letters was a mix of grief and joy. He loved going over Cat's words, imagining them in his voice. At the same time, he was peeling back the protective layers he'd created. Things he'd tried to forget for Cat's sake surfaced.

After the first time, Thomas wasn't so bothered by Micah's mood swings. He curled up on the desk next to the computer, occasionally poking his head around the monitor or stalking across the keyboard and typing his opinion as he went. It reminded Micah of the times Cat would lie on their bed, reading while Micah worked. For the life of him, Micah couldn't figure out why Cat liked the most poorly written heterosexual erotica, but about half the time, that's what he had on hand. The rest of the time he split between equally cheesy gay romance and whatever Micah's latest novel happened to be. Cat always said he liked Micah's best, but Micah wasn't sure how much of that was Cat being a dutiful spouse.

When Cat got bored, he would distract Micah, teasing him by stripping naked and stretching out on top of the covers or by wriggling into Micah's lap and typing a few lines of nonsense text. There was almost never a time when he couldn't entice Micah into a break. On nights when lovemaking was too much for Micah, they rolled around on the bed, laughing and kissing until they and the covers were a rumpled mess. However he chose to do it, Cat wasn't one for leaving Micah uninterrupted. It was a wonder he'd ever completed a novel while they were married.

Thomas's throaty meow, twitching tail, and penchant for demanding attention brought Micah back to the present. While he skimmed last night's writing to see where he needed to pick back up, Thomas leaped into his lap and purred. Micah rubbed between his ears.

"Here to help?"

Turning his head, Thomas fastened his gaze on Micah. He batted his chin and settled down in his lap. For a long time, Micah ran his hand along Thomas's back, staring at the screen. He was distracted, thinking about his upcoming maybe-date with Chris. Micah didn't know much about him other than that he was a pastor and had only lived in Concordia for a year or so. Chris didn't talk much about his life before moving there, outside of a few mentions of friends or family.

Surely the church had a web site where Micah could at least find a brief bio. He paused before typing in the name of Cat's church. It felt strange, as though he were intruding not on Chris's privacy but on Cat's. Micah hadn't attended outside of the occasional holiday, and he wasn't looking to go there now. He shivered, once again slipping into the unfamiliar space between his life then and his life now.

Micah pulled up the church web site and clicked on the staff profiles. They were arranged alphabetically rather than by hierarchy, which interested Micah. The caretaker—the sexton, the web site called her—was listed first. Micah scrolled until he came to Chris Sharpe. The only giveaway that the picture wasn't new was that Chris had slightly more hair. Otherwise, he had the same neatly trimmed beard, the same dark eyes, and the same laid-back smile.

Micah clicked the link next to the photo.

"Chris Sharpe grew up in a liberal Christian denomination in the northeast. He always knew he wanted to go into ministry, but he didn't act on his goals until he was in his thirties. Before becoming ordained, Chris worked in LGBTQIA youth advocacy. He is formerly the associate pastor of Faith Dimensions in Syracuse, NY, where he led the youth ministry and initiated the church's transgender advocacy project. He is an activist who has done work to prevent anti-trans laws in vulnerable areas. In his spare time, Chris studies queer theology and provides education for lay leaders in social justice. He is the co-director of the Concordia Community Center."

It made sense, mostly. Chris was mild-mannered, but he was outgoing and excelled at leadership, evidenced by how smoothly he'd handled the community center project. It wasn't surprising to find he'd done other types of organizing. Micah exhaled and ran his hand over his face, trying to collect his thoughts. His brain was stuck on the idea of "queer theology," whatever that was. He supposed it fit with his assessment of Chris as being more traditional in his religious practice, but Micah wouldn't necessarily have associated those concepts with each other.

He wished he could ask Cat, who might have known what it meant. Thinking about Cat reminded Micah he hadn't yet written anything. He needed new inspiration. He reached for the box of letters and removed the next one in line.

Dearest Micah,

You always worried that it would get too hard for me to stay with you. I'll be honest, sometimes you scared me. Is that okay to say? I don't know. There was the time you took off, going out in a thunderstorm. I didn't know if you were coming back. When we found you, I'd never seen you like that, locked up so tight none of us could reach you.

Is that how you felt when it was me? I used to worry you'd get tired of taking care of me, too. You never did, or at least you never let on, not during all those times you took me to the hospital or bathed me or held me while I puked my guts out. I remember telling you after I had heart surgery that I wanted to go back to normal. You asked me what I meant, and you said, "There is no normal. There's only what is." It made sense, I guess. I didn't want to hear it at the time because I was so angry about another thing my body was doing wrong.

You do all these little things that make it okay. You touch my joints or kiss me right where my mediport is instead of pretending they're not there. Did I at least get that right with you? Remember the first time I prayed for you? You'd been so deeply hurt by people claiming to speak for God.

Micah did remember, and all the times after as well. Praying with Cat had been a strangely erotic experience. Whether that was intentional or not, Micah couldn't recall a time when prayer hadn't led to the bedroom. Or hallway, bathroom, kitchen...wherever they'd found a place. Cat had never used prayer as a means of breaking Micah's will and coercing him into sex. He'd only ever done it when he sensed Micah needed to expel some unholy part of his past.

Carefully, Micah slid the letter back in the envelope and set it aside. He rested his fingers on the keyboard then began to type, transforming memories into story.

~ ** ~

After Micah's appointment with his therapist, he came home and beelined for the bathroom, shutting Cat out. He needed to cut himself off from everything for a while. All the things he couldn't make sense of in his life pushed their way to the surface, and he expelled them via his tears and vomit.

He rinsed his mouth and sat on the cold floor, leaning his back against the door. It had been years since he'd felt so powerless he wanted to die. Here he sat, gripping his head with his hands, terrified to move but wishing God would strike him dead. Before he could formulate a plan, he heard Cat's gentle voice through the door. Little of what he said made sense, but it didn't matter. The sound anchored Micah.

Slowly he came back to himself, listening to Cat sing to him and pray his way around the rosary. It wasn't meant to be arousing, but because of their history and Cat's intent, it was. Micah didn't stop to question what they were doing. He let their sensuality guide him back from the brink, half undressing so he could touch himself and knowing Cat was on the other side of the door doing the same.

When they had both reached completion, Micah dragged his pants back on and emerged from the bathroom at last. Cat suggested cleaning up and having dinner; he hadn't made it to taking his clothes off while they pleasured themselves together. They made their way up to the bedroom, Micah appreciating the view of Cat's ass in his yoga pants. When Cat glanced over his shoulder and twitched his hips a tiny bit, Micah was caught between fresh tears and laughter. Such a small thing, yet it said so much.

In the upstairs hallway, Micah pulled Cat in and kissed him, long and deep. He slid his hands down to cup Cat's perfect ass, lifting him so Cat could wrap his long legs around Micah's waist. Cat usually didn't like to do anything which could leave him injured, but he didn't object when Micah leaned him up against the wall and pressed kiss after kiss to his lips. Despite Cat's sexy yoga pants and the hungry, devouring way they were making out, it had still been too soon since they both came. Cat tore his mouth away, panting.

"Hon, please let me get out of these clothes. I feel so gross, and I'm messing up your work pants."

Micah chuckled and set Cat down gently. "I managed to do that on my own already. Shower?"

"Yeah. Damn it! I wore these so you could get me out of them, and now we've done it all ass-backwards." Cat shook his head, but he was smiling.

"I can still get you out of them. Sorry about that." Micah gave him a rueful look.

Cat touched his cheek. "Oh, honey, no. I'm sorry. You needed it, and it doesn't matter. I'll wear them for you again another time." He brushed his lips against Micah's stubbled chin.

They lingered, peeling out of their clothes and washing up together, taking time to simply be in the moment. Micah was glad; he had something he knew he needed to tell Cat, and this gave him a chance to work out how. They took pleasure again, this time coming with their hands and mouths on each other.

Out of the shower, they descended the stairs to the kitchen. Cat enlisted Micah's help making dinner, and in no time, the kitchen was full of good smells. Food had always been functional for Micah—half the time, he forgot meals when he'd lived alone, especially at grade entry time. When he lived in Rochester, Zayne had come over more times than he could count to bring him easy casseroles for the freezer. If she hadn't, he'd have ended up sick. Being with Cat, Micah had learned that food, like sex, required focus on the present to be enjoyed. Cat's senses were heightened in every way, and he loved food, despite all his restrictions. Every now and again, Micah would have sworn Cat was having a full-on orgasm from something he was eating.

Thinking about all that, and his own history of slacking off, reminded Micah of what he needed to say to Cat. He'd always had a low-grade unhealthy relationship with the world in general—food, sex, alcohol, religion, his body, friendships, family—he'd never known which parts were in his nature and which were the product of his hellish childhood. They were interconnected, and it was this which had brought Micah to his knees, sobbing and vomiting because it was both a relief and terrifying to uncover the truth.

He pulled himself out of his own head long enough to help put the meal on the table and sit down across from Cat. Now was the time to lay it all in the open, but when Micah opened his mouth, no words came out.

Cat tapped his wrist to get his attention. "I know it was a really rough day with your appointment. You don't have to tell me now, but if it will help, I'm here."

Micah nodded. "Right. Well, I probably should." He set his napkin down, thought better of it, and picked it back up so as to have something in his hands. "Dr. Alberti originally agreed that I was dealing with religious trauma, and you know he's since revised it to say it doesn't matter where the trauma came from—it's still essentially complex PTSD." Micah sighed. "He added depression and anxiety—separate from the PTSD—to the list, which I could have told him, I guess. I've probably had those both for as long as I can remember, except my family never believed in treating them. Dr. Alberti wants me to see someone who can prescribe meds. But he wanted to have a full picture of what he suspected first."

"That's probably a good move," Cat said. "Kind of like how I have my GP and my hematologist."

"A bit, yeah." Micah relaxed; Cat was pretty good at knowing how to frame things with the least judgment possible. He might be less generous after Micah's next admission, though. "He suggested I should have it confirmed, but…" Micah paused, collecting himself. "He said I have a personality disorder." Micah put his elbow on the table and rested his forehead on his palm. "He says I have features of both emotional disregulatory and obsessive-compulsive types, but not enough of either for a diagnosis. So he called it 'not otherwise specified.' Pretty much who I am is so fucked up he's not even sure what to label it."

"Oh, honey." Cat reached for him, but Micah withdrew from his touch.

"Don't," he said. "Don't pity me." He looked up at Cat. "What if…what if my father was right after all? Maybe this caused me to be a fag. Maybe I should've let them cast demons out of me after all."

Cat flinched at the hateful word. He set down his fork and sat silently looking at Micah for a minute. His voice was so soft Micah almost didn't hear when he said, "Do you think my genetics made me queer?"

"What?" Micah asked. "You mean is being queer something you can inherit? I don't know."

"No," Cat said, still quiet. "My hemophilia is linked to my sex chromosomes. Do you think having a fucked up X made me queer?"

Micah frowned. "No. Why would it? If it did, wouldn't all people with hemophilia be queer? And anyway, why does it even matter?"

Cat shrugged. "Maybe it's demons, then. Maybe I should find a church that will do ritual exorcism on me, hm? Cure me of being a *fag*—" he spat the word "—and my hemophilia. Is that what you think?"

"God! God no!" Micah gaped at him, horrified at what he was suggesting.

"So then what makes you believe a personality disorder or an imaginary evil spirit made you something other than straight or that it matters if it did?"

"I don't know!" Micah threw his hands up. "It just seemed like it might." He flopped back in his chair. "Aren't you upset?"

"No, not really," Cat said. "Should I be? It doesn't change anything except maybe you can have help that's more specific. It's no different from me. If they hadn't figured out what type of bleeding disorder I had, I'd be stuck with constant blood transfusions. You should have what you need too."

"I don't want to be like this!" Micah said. Rage bubbled inside him. "It's not something that can be fixed next week. None of it. I'm going to have to deal with all this for the rest of my life. What if—what if it really does kill me?"

Cat's eyes flashed. "Like me? How I live with this"—he gestured at his body—"all the time, every day? The difference is you get to hope yours doesn't kill you. I know mine will."

He stood up from the table and walked to the sink, keeping his back to Micah. It was good he hadn't left the room, though it wasn't much like Cat to hide himself away. He'd only done that when he wanted to protect Micah from the truth about the damage to his body. In all other ways, Cat was the type to face things head-on.

Micah twisted his napkin in his fingers and thought about what Cat had said. He cringed; Cat was right. His body was full of scars, and so much of the time, something hurt or got infected or simply didn't work the way most people's did. It wasn't unlike Micah's mind, fractured and with so many scars and bruises and ways in which he couldn't coax it to work the way he thought it should have.

But what was normal, anyway? If Dr. Alberti was right, Micah had lived most of his life with several different things which affected his brain's wiring. He'd learned to cope, and in itself, that was pretty amazing. Even if his family was right and he had demons, he was exorcising them all on his own.

He stood up and approached Cat from behind. "I'm sorry," he said. He leaned down and pressed a kiss to Cat's shoulder. "I know better than to say something so awful to you."

Cat turned around. "Yes, you do. But I wasn't being fair either. This is new for you." He reached up and ran a hand through Micah's still-damp curls. "You're not alone."

"I have you." Micah smiled.

"And all our friends. They love you too, silly."

Micah ran his fingers over the freckles on Cat's forearm then took his hand. "We've survived worse, haven't we?"

"We have." Cat stretched up to kiss him.

"I'm sorry again I was an ass. How about we go finish eating? Surviving is hard on an empty stomach."

"Definitely."

They sat back down, and conversation meandered to lighter things. Micah didn't know what he would do without Cat. His words from earlier sank in—that his condition would eventually claim his life. It didn't bear dwelling on, but Micah couldn't shake the low-level anxiety that hovered in the background. He made a decision in the moment which he hoped would work out in both their favor as long as he planned it right. Satisfied that they were both okay for the time being, Micah forced his attention away from his worries and concentrated on enjoying dinner with his love.

CHAPTER SEVEN

The Light of the World

FOR THE last fifteen minutes of the cooking class, Micah barely paid attention. He almost missed it when the timer went off on the oven. Fortunately, he caught it with a nudge from a classmate and was able to rescue the dinner rolls just in time. He gave the instructor credit; he'd never have been able to make them come out so well on his own with only a recipe.

As soon as he was sure he wasn't going to set anything on fire, he let his mind go back to circling around his maybe-date with Chris. He kept making leaps to the worst possible outcomes, from having it end badly to having it end well and then needing to tell other people. Why couldn't he be like everyone else and relax about the whole thing? Chris didn't seem like he was worried at all. He'd passed Micah in the corridor and checked in, making sure they were still meeting up after classes ended. Nothing in his posture suggested he was nervous in the least.

Micah helped the others clean up the kitchen then wrapped up his fresh rolls to take home. So far, he'd managed to follow the directions for three weeks running. The classes were paying off, and he was attempting to cook more sensibly. It was strange not having to work around anyone else's dietary needs, but at least what he was making was more edible than before and used more fresh ingredients.

As soon as he was out the door, he spotted Chris. He was leaning up against the wall, doing something on his phone. He looked up when the door opened, and he smiled when Micah started toward him. Shoving his phone into a pocket, he turned to face Micah.

"Hey," he said. "How's it going?"

Micah held up the foil-wrapped pan. "Made these. They turned out okay. No one will break a tooth on one, anyway." He laughed.

"Give yourself more credit than that," Chris replied. "Are you ready to go?"

"If you are."

As they walked out, Micah considered their options. It was only coffee, so the logical place to go would be Sweet Beans. Micah didn't want to go to his mother-in-law's cafe, though, so that was out. So was the Neanderthal. Gerri's daughter and son-in-law had taken it over, and Gerri wasn't there most of the time anymore, but there was still a high chance of running into people Micah knew. Not that it wasn't a risk anywhere in such a small town, but those two places had been closely associated with Cat.

Micah said, "I'm not sure where you had in mind, but there's a nice place on the waterfront. We could do a late lunch there."

Chris glanced over, but he was quiet for a moment before he finally said, "All right. I'll meet you there."

They parked side by side in one of the alley lots off Main Street and walked the short distance to the restaurant. Micah had to pause to collect himself before opening the door for Chris. It was the place Cat had taken him on their first not-a-date, when Micah had bought him dinner to thank him for his help restoring his house. Other than that, it had no special memories. It wasn't one of their regular spots.

Micah followed Chris inside. The room was dim, and the lighting had a faintly blue aura. There was hardly anyone there, long after the lunch crowds had filtered out but with time yet until the dinner rush. The hostess seated them, and Micah opened his menu as a buffer between himself and an awkward conversation. He was no good at small talk. Everything about the scenario suddenly felt both familiar and not, that eerie sense of seeing double again.

"I've never been here," Chris remarked. "When I was an intern, it wasn't in my budget. Since being back, I haven't had a lot of time."

Micah lowered his menu. "Work keeping you busy?"

"That and the community center. I meet up with a lot of people, but it's been in other settings." He scanned the menu. "What's good?"

"I don't know," Micah admitted. "I've lived here for over twelve years, and I hardly ever come to this restaurant."

Chris chuckled. "You seemed so certain about it."

"I was...nervous." He could at least admit that much. If Chris asked why, Micah's feelings about engaging socially with a pastor were probably safer than his anxiety about dating.

Chris's nod surprised Micah. "Me too. I'll be honest, I'd expected you to say no when I asked you."

Micah set his menu aside. He was about to answer when the server appeared with water and asked if they needed a moment. They both ordered coffee, and she disappeared. Micah sighed deeply and turned back to Chris.

"I wasn't going to say yes. I almost changed my mind afterward."

"Why didn't you?"

Micah's face heated. "I sort of looked you up on the church web site, and I wanted to know more about you." He hung his head, embarrassed.

Chris only grinned. "I'll take it as a compliment, especially since my bio didn't put you off, thinking I was some kind of political figure or something. I'm actually pretty tame, to be honest."

"I figured it was mostly the sort of stuff they want in there so it makes the org look good." Micah relaxed, finding familiar ground. "I've had to do teacher profiles for work, and it's the same thing. 'Had a ninety-four percent pass rate on state and local exams' sounds more important than 'his students didn't hate reading at the end of the year.'"

Chris's laughter warmed Micah's belly. "Exactly! I sent the original draft to the secretary, and she wanted to change it because I hadn't mentioned anything about being trans. I said fine and added the part about the project I did—very briefly, I might add—in Syracuse, and that's all I was willing to give her. I love my church, but holy crap, a few of them are fixated on public appearance. Mercifully, our senior pastor stops it."

Micah chuckled. "Good God. I don't think I'd last five minutes if my job practically hung a banner on the door about my presence. Though I'm hardly the only queer teacher in the building."

"It's not as though I am either. Half our church is. I guess it's not enough that Pastor Maryann is married to another woman. A few folks would like if our staff represented the entire rainbow." Chris shook his head, but he was still in a joking mood. "Well, I can represent two stripes, anyway."

Their coffee arrived, and they ordered lunch. Once the server was gone, Micah turned serious again. He was enjoying Chris's company, surprised to find he had more in common with him than he'd expected. Of course, he hadn't yet mentioned his lack of interest in matters of faith. He wondered if it would be a deal breaker.

Micah chose his next words carefully. He could easily excuse himself with his reservations about their different views on religion, but Chris deserved the truth, if Micah could get it out. "Look," he said. "As much as I'm enjoying this, I'm not sure—" he cut himself off, struggling with how to finish the statement.

"Not sure you're ready?" Chris completed his thought. "I know the feeling."

"You do?" Micah didn't know what to say. He leaned back in his seat and studied Chris. His honesty surprised Micah, but he appreciated it. "I don't wish to pry, but what do you mean?"

"I moved here as soon as my divorce was final. It took me a long time after the split to start dating again, and it was a real challenge back in Syracuse. It's the nature of life in ministry, having people think your private life should be public. Especially for me."

"Oh," Micah said. "I'm sorry."

Chris shrugged one shoulder. "It is what it is. My ex found it hard to be a pastor's wife, and a lot of other people don't want that responsibility either."

"Ex...wife." Micah said the words slowly, making sure he understood. "I've only had one relationship since my spouse died, and I wouldn't say we were dating. It was more like friends with benefits. She and I met in a grief and loss group." He hadn't mentioned her to anyone, not even Zayne. It felt right to explain it to Chris rather than having to go on at length about not caring what genders of people Chris had dated or what was under his clothes. The small smile assured Micah he'd said the right thing.

Chris turned serious again. "The truth is, I wasn't sure you'd agree to meeting up. You still seemed to be grieving. Something about you, though..." His eyes crinkled when the smile returned. "I had a feeling."

Micah laughed softly. "How do you know I'd be all right dating a minister?"

"I don't." Chris reached out and took Micah's hand on top of the table. "But I'm hoping."

Leaning in, Micah spoke low. "Is this a date, then?"

"I'd like if it were."

Micah froze, even though he'd expected Chris's answer. He wanted to take back the question, tell Chris what he'd originally planned—that he wasn't ready—and go back to the way things had been. Sure, it would be awkward at first, but they'd both move on. Chris would never need to know all the messy details of Micah's life or why he still needed time. None of those things were what came out of his mouth.

"So would I," he said.

By the time Micah returned home, the sun was sinking lower in the sky. He hadn't meant to stay out so long, but it had been some time since he'd enjoyed someone's company the way he did with Chris. As Micah unlocked the door, he glanced over to LR's house. A small bit of guilt niggled the back of his mind. He hadn't said anything to her about the possibility of dating someone new, and he wasn't sure how she would feel about it.

Inside, he fed Thomas, who didn't shun the food or the

companionship this time. As soon as the cat disappeared again, Micah stepped back outside to head two doors down. He could pretend he was only out for a late afternoon stroll, but Debbie would know he was really there to check in on her. It wasn't as though he had to hide it from her anyway. She wasn't the sort to passive-aggressively reject his offer of help while simultaneously expecting him to know when she needed it.

She was out in the yard, of course. Now in her eighties, she'd long since stopped being able to do the amount of landscaping she once had, but she still kept her own lawn tidy and bursting with color. When she looked up and saw Micah, she gave him a cheerful wave and beckoned him over.

"Come help me pull up these weeds, will you?" she called.

Micah joined her, and together they plucked the offending plants from around her shrubs. There wasn't any need to make small talk with Debbie. She was the closest thing Micah had to a mother, and she knew him well enough to read his signals. If she'd asked, he would gladly have told her about his day, but her warm silence was enough for now.

When they were through, the sun had turned golden red and was casting a fiery glow through the trees on the opposite side of the street. Debbie stood and stretched, and Micah followed her. He brushed the dirt and grass off his jeans, and she pulled off her wide-brimmed hat to wipe her forehead.

"Would you like to come in for a bit?" she offered.

"I'd love to."

Micah followed her in and sat at the kitchen table while she poured some iced tea. She offered him a plate of blueberry muffins. It was a private joke between them, a reference to the number of times Micah had gone to her with a need for a little TLC. She always said hers had magical properties, able to solve the most difficult of problems.

For a few minutes, Micah gave himself over to the taste and texture of the muffin. Even Cat hadn't been able to make them come out the same. He'd teased Micah about it, claiming he was making it up and that anyone could bake them. Micah would never tell him that it wasn't the recipe that made them special.

Debbie wrapped her fingers around Micah's and squeezed. "I can see the gears turning in there."

"Mm-hm," he replied, mouth full of muffin. He swallowed. "I went on a date today."

"Ah." She smiled. "And how did it go?"

"It was good." He paused. "Really good, in fact."

She let go of his hand and patted his arm. "But?"

"I feel guilty. I didn't tell anyone else I was considering it." He sighed. "What if they think I'm supposed to stay single? You know, stick to being the doting bachelor uncle and all that."

"You can't keep your eye on that bunch of rascals and also have someone else in your life?" Debbie arched an eyebrow.

"Well..." He trailed off. "You never remarried."

"I was divorced from a man I never wanted in the first place." She leaned closer when Micah eyed her, knowing that wasn't what he'd been referring to. "Just because I didn't get married doesn't mean I've never gone on a date before."

It was Micah's turn for surprise. "I thought you said you'd never found anyone after my mother."

Her smile was mysterious. "Look who thinks he knows everything. I didn't find what you might call true love, no. She was it for me. But I've found women who made me happy, even if it didn't become anything long-term."

"That's it, though. I've done that. I even had someone I was seeing briefly, but we both knew it was temporary. This feels different." He toyed with his fork, focusing his gaze on his hands instead of on Debbie's face. "I feel like I'm betraying everyone's trust."

"Because you want something different than I did?" Debbie's expression turned to one of incredulity. "I was young and foolish when I met your mother, and I bound my happiness in her. I wasn't out to anyone at that point, and I couldn't properly grieve for a married woman no one knew I'd been seeing. It was a different time and a different set of circumstances."

Micah remained silent, absorbing what she'd said. It seemed to him like there were always too many rules. Be sad, but not too much or for too long, and not over someone you weren't supposed to love in the first place. Eventually, he finished his glass of tea and set it back on the table.

"Chris seemed okay with taking things slowly," Micah told Debbie.

"Chris...the new minister? That Chris?"

Micah slid down in his seat and groaned, regretting telling Debbie who he'd been out with. He did find it mildly amusing that Chris had been there a year and was still the "new minister." He probably would have that title until he retired.

"He's the one. How do you know him? You don't even go to church."

The mysterious smile was back. "From the community center. Everyone knows it's his project."

"God. I'm dating a celebrity." Micah scowled.

"There, there, dear." Debbie patted his hand. "You'll manage. I won't breathe a word, but you'd probably better let your people know before the whole town learns about it and spills the beans."

"Small towns," Micah grumbled, but he smiled. "We're keeping it low-key for now. I think people realize we're friends, but no one has suggested anything else."

Debbie smiled back, but she looked tired to Micah. She was entitled, at her age, but he wondered how much longer she would be able to manage her house and her yard. He helped her out as much as he could, and so did their other neighbors. She'd taken care of them for years, and now it was time to return the favor. Still, she needed more help than a street full of people with full-time jobs—and some with children—could manage.

As if reading his thoughts, she said, "I'm fine. I'll make it an early night." She rose from the table.

Micah stood and kissed her cheek before saying goodnight to her. He strolled home, thinking about what she'd said and his date with Chris. Cat's demand, that Micah expunge him from existence, came back to him, but he was no closer to being rid of that part of his life than he had been before going out with Chris. Maybe an evening of reading Cat's letters and writing another bit of his new novel would help.

Inside the house, he gave Thomas a treat, heated a can of soup for himself—with a silent apology to Cat's memory for his pathetic dinner—and sat down with the next set of letters.

CHAPTER EIGHT

BLESSED ARE THE DEAD

MICAH FINISHED reading the weekly passage from his work in progress. He'd already gone over the exercises and allowed the students to give each other feedback. As promised, he was offering them the chance to discuss what he'd written. The process was unusual for him, not being in the habit of showing his drafts to anyone until they were complete and he'd been through them at least once.

When he was through, Dyl raised a hand. "So...the main characters. He'chatul has...seizures of some kind? And Benjamin sounds like he has ADD, and he's kind of—I don't know, anxious or scattered or something."

"Right. What we might call ADHD. The rest is what accompanies that. Since this is fantasy, I didn't use a specific term."

Dyl frowned. "Okay. But why didn't you make something up? Like a magical condition."

Micah tapped his pen against his leg. "You're right that many authors choose to create disabilities which would be unique to their world. This can work really well, in fact. I prefer to ground my fiction in reality. Many of us grow up reading about characters who don't look or talk or act like us or people we know. Instead, we end up reading about ourselves as magical or alien or mythical. It works for some people but not for others. It's good to have both."

Carlie blurted out, "I totally related to Benjamin." Her cheeks darkened at the light laughter which went around the room. "I have ADHD too. Sometimes it makes people uncomfortable, but I like being this way. I could help you write about it, if you want."

"I would love to talk to you more," Micah replied. "Stick around for a few after class, and we'll exchange contact info. Maybe you'd like to read those scenes after the first draft is done."

They continued the discussion for a few more minutes about the characters, and a couple of the students made suggestions, which Micah jotted down. He closed his laptop and dismissed the class. When he finished trading contacts with Carlie, he looked up to find Chris was still standing in the doorway. A thrill rushed to Micah's gut, and he grinned as he tucked his laptop back in its case.

"Hey, you," he said. "Enjoy tonight's session?"

"Very much. Want to go hang out for a bit?"

"Absolutely. Let me finish getting my stuff together."

They walked out to Micah's car, neither of them speaking. Instead of feeling awkward or searching for something to say, Micah enjoyed it. Although it made him feel a bit bad for doing so, he couldn't help comparing it to the way Cat had always been full of enthusiastic chatter. He wouldn't have been silent; he would've been asking Micah a thousand questions about the class. Micah stole a glance at Chris, catching him doing the same. They both chuckled.

"Where to?" Chris asked.

Micah thought about what Debbie had said. He wasn't ready to make an announcement, and he and Chris hadn't been on enough dates for that anyway. He did think it might be all right to bring him to Sweet Beans. At least then he could control what his mother-in-law was aware of.

"There's a nice little coffee shop on Main Street," he said. "Sweet Beans."

"I know the place. I'll meet you there."

Chris hesitated, looking like he wanted to say more. He gave a nod and turned toward his car. Micah watched him, wondering what he was thinking about. He climbed into his own car and sat for a moment before starting it and heading for town.

Sweet Beans smelled good as always, the combination of freshly ground coffee and cinnamon and sugar. Micah didn't spot Audrey immediately, so he assumed she was in the kitchen. A cheerful high schooler—one of Micah's former students—waved to him just as Chris stepped up behind him. The girl peered around Micah and gave Chris a friendly smile as well.

"Hi, Mr. Forbes, Pastor Chris. What can I get for you?"

Micah turned to Chris. "You want something?"

"Just a chai, thanks."

Micah finished ordering, including a couple of Audrey's perfect cinnamon rolls. They took everything to the far corner table. Micah never thought of it as "his" table, but it was his favorite spot. Until Cat was too sick, he'd worked there. On Saturdays, Micah would bring papers to grade or lessons to plan. He would sit in the corner and secretly watch Cat in between marking scores. Cat had known it, too. He'd taken delight in refilling Micah's coffee just for the purpose of twitching his ass on the way back to the kitchen.

Those days were long gone, and Micah's attention snapped back to the present. He and Chris sat opposite each other. Micah stirred sugar into his coffee, his mind full of the things he wanted to ask Chris. He thought it might be best to be upfront about his disinterest in religion or church, lest Chris think Micah was part of the flock. He wondered what the rules were on a minister dating someone who might be best described as an I-don't-care-ist.

He could ease into it. "So, how did you decide you wanted to be a minister? Was someone in your family one?"

Chris gave him a puzzled look. "No, no one else went into ministry. It's not really like inheriting the family business." His smile turned amused.

Micah wanted to tell him it was sometimes exactly like that, but he wasn't ready to explain his life in the tenth circle of hell yet. "Oh. Then how did you know you wanted to?"

"I grew up in church. Loved it from the time I was little—the music, the flow of the church service, the pastor's gentle sermons." Chris cleared his throat. "There was a lot of arguing in my house, and church was a refuge."

"I'm sorry."

Chris's cheery demeanor returned as quickly as it had faded. "I won't bore you with all the details. I didn't have an unhappy childhood, really. My parents loved me. They just didn't love each other."

They were interrupted by an older woman wearing a Sweet Beans apron and holding a pot of coffee. "Evening, fellas. We're almost ready to close up for the night. Either of you want to help finish off this pot of coffee?"

Micah looked up at Audrey's business partner. He was undecided whether he was relieved or disappointed Audrey wasn't there. "I'm all set, thanks."

"Pastor Chris?" she said, holding up the pot.

"None for me, but thank you for the offer. How are you doing?"

"Great." She beamed at him. "Are you working?" She laughed. "Maybe one of these days, you'll get Micah here to church."

Micah wanted to sink through the floor, but Chris only looked between them and covered a smile. He cleared his throat and gave Micah a glance.

"I'm sure if he wants to join us, he will. For now, we just finished up at the community center, teaching some classes."

The woman picked up their empty cups. "That's wonderful!" She nodded at the teenager ringing out the last of the customers. "My granddaughter was thinking about taking a couple next semester, when her schedule is a little easier."

Breathing easier now, Micah said, "We'll look forward to seeing her."

After the woman had left, Chris turned to Micah. "I'm sorry about that."

"You really do seem to know everyone." Micah shook his head. "Don't worry about it. We—Cat always—" He felt like he'd crossed the *things you don't say to your date* line. "Never mind. I'm used to it, anyway."

"That's...reassuring, I suppose. I'm not used to it at all yet."

Chris laughed.

Micah switched gears, trying to push past his mistake. "This place is closing, but it's a nice evening. You want to go for a walk?"

"Sure."

They stepped out into the cool, fragrant air. It had rained while they were inside, which made it damp and a little chilly, but the clouds were passing and the stars were out. As they headed down to the boardwalk, Micah was conscious of little details like how close their shoulders were and whether or not their hands brushed. Audrey's business partner wasn't gossipy, and she probably wouldn't care or remember that the two of them had been in Sweet Beans together. Micah couldn't say the same for other people around town, even though there weren't many out. It felt less like the awkward beginning of a new relationship and a lot more like being closeted again. He didn't enjoy the way it made his insides crawl or the sharp reminder he'd never had to hide anything with Cat.

After a few minutes, Micah said, "You never did tell me how you became a pastor."

Chris strolled beside him, his expression thoughtful. "Back when I was in college, I studied ministry. After I graduated, I'd planned to go to seminary right away. Instead, I spent the summer having a crisis of faith and coming out twice to my parents, first as trans and then as bi. Dad came out right after I did. Suddenly all the things my parents had been fighting about made sense. They finally got a divorce because Mom's not interested in women, although Dad is a lesbian."

Micah stopped walking. "You still call her Dad?"

"I just realized how what I said must have sounded. Yes, she asked me to because she said I'm the only person who will ever get to call her that." They resumed walking, and Chris continued, "My parents are a lot happier now. They've gotten to be friends again, even. I chose to wait until I'd decided how I wanted to handle my transition before going to seminary. So here I am, an ordained minister."

"You don't have brothers or sisters?"

"Nope," Chris replied. "Only child. How about you?"

"I have two older brothers. Both ministers. My father was too, and so was my grandfather." Micah clenched and released his fingers, trying to manage the tension spreading down his neck to his shoulders.

"Oh, no wonder you asked about that. But you're not in ministry."

Micah didn't respond right away. Chris had opened up to him about his life, but for Micah to talk about his family would blow the door off its hinges. He tried to organize in his head how much was appropriate to say and how much was best spoken in therapy sessions. He must've waited too long because Chris put a hand on his arm.

"You don't have to explain," he said.

"I'll give you the short version because if I give the long one, we'll still be here next week." Micah tried to joke, but he couldn't muster enough humor.

Chris's frown displayed his confusion. "All right."

"I was supposed to go into ministry like all the men in my family. Except not only was I not straight—I said gay at the time—but I wanted to be a teacher. I got permission for the second, but not the first. I was still supposed to go to seminary, provided I got 'help' for my problem. Didn't go so well. I hadn't spoken to my father in nearly fifteen years when he died, and I don't speak to one of my brothers now." He looked up at the sky and then over at Chris. "I don't do religion, not even if I'm seeing a minister."

He walked to the railing of the boardwalk and looked out over the lake and the moon's shimmering reflection. Maybe agreeing to two dates with Chris had been a bad idea. They wouldn't be able to get past this difference. Micah's tenuous recovery, which had taken a hit when Cat died, depended on not putting himself in situations which might do further damage. He couldn't see himself sitting in church week after week, dutifully on standby while Chris performed his responsibilities. He also couldn't see Chris quitting a job he loved.

Micah felt the warm press of Chris's shoulder against his as Chris leaned on the railing beside him. "What about your mother?"

"She...died." Micah took a deep breath. "Life was more than she could handle." He shrugged. "I know the feeling."

"All of that must have been awful for you. No wonder you—"

Micah cut him off. "Don't. I can't handle being in church, even now, nearly thirty years later. But that's not the only reason I stopped believing in anything. I simply never found a god more compelling than the hateful version I destroyed to get my soul back." Micah turned away from Chris, not wanting to look at him. He chose his next words carefully, echoing what he'd said to Cat years ago when he intended to give him one last chance to say no. "Being with me isn't easy. I understand if it's a deal-breaker. There's a lot you don't know about me."

"So, tell me then," Chris said. "Help me understand."

Without turning around, Micah replied, "I'm sick."

"Oh," Chris said. "Is it—is it serious?"

"Yes."

"Life-threatening?"

"It can be, yes."

Sick. It was the same word Cat had used so many years ago. Different setting, but the reason was more or less the same. He'd asked once why Cat said it, and all he'd answered was that it was true. It wasn't, though, not really until the end, and it wasn't true for Micah now. He slammed his hand on the railing and turned to face Chris.

"That's a lie," he said. "Or not exactly the truth. It's what Cat said when he wanted to pretend his hemophilia was something like a cold or the flu. It's what my father said when he wanted to pretend my mother hadn't taken half a bottle of pills and shot herself with his gun while the rest of us were at church." Micah laughed without humor. "Yeah, my minister father had a handgun. For protection, he said. I don't think it worked out the way he thought it would."

Judging by Chris's expression, he hadn't been anticipating that. Micah had reacted much the same way when Jeremiah finally broke down and told him the truth. Micah pressed his lips into a thin line to hold back any further confessions.

Chris shook his head. "So...you're not sick. I'm confused."

"It's not my body. It's my mind. Some of it is probably genetic, but the rest is the result of years' worth of trauma."

"Okay." Chris tilted his head. "I suppose I should've figured it out, given some of our conversation. What—"

"I could give you a list of my diagnoses," Micah said, scoffing. "Or you can come over and I'll show you all my meds." He tried to laugh, but it came out a little hysterical. "Other people have liquor cabinets. Cat and I had a locked medicine cabinet because between the two of us, we had almost a whole pharmacy going. He kept it all organized—color-coded, time-stamped, and shelved in order. For the first two years we lived together, he had the only key. So, what did you want to know?" His heart beat faster, and he was already feeling like he needed more air, despite being outside.

Very quietly, Chris said, "I was going to ask what would be the most helpful thing for me to say or do right now."

Micah startled; he hadn't been expecting that. He took a few calming breaths before responding. "I don't know," he admitted. "I figured finding out what was really going on might make you think twice about where this is headed. Maintaining my recovery means I can't be involved in church, and that's just about your entire world. You'd need to understand that finding the 'right' church isn't the fix for this. Cat—" He grimaced. "Fuck. Sorry. I'm not usually this honest, especially with someone I haven't known long."

"You trust me," Chris replied. He sounded surprised and pleased.

"You trusted me," Micah reminded him.

"I did." Chris slid his hand across the railing to grasp Micah's. "Do you want to talk about it more?"

"Maybe another time," Micah said. "I talk to my therapist. I talk to my psychiatrist. Sometimes I talk to my friend Zayne, but she's known me for almost forty years. I never had to talk to Cat—damn it, I'm sorry. Anyway, I don't discuss this shit with my other friends unless there's a reason."

They began walking back toward their cars. Micah had expected to feel drained by their conversation, but he felt lighter. When they arrived in the parking lot, Micah tried to come up with something to say. Chris hadn't walked away, which was good, but he hadn't given an indication he wanted their relationship to go any further.

Chris broke him out of his thoughts. "The story you're writing," he said quietly. "How much of it is true?"

Turning to face him, Micah said, "The details are different, but a lot of it is close to the truth. It's not exclusively about my hateful family, if that's what you mean. They're only part of the bigger story."

"And the rest?"

"Cat," Micah said. "It's about Cat."

"I see." Chris pursed his lips. "I like you, Micah. I'm not worried about your mental health, and I'm not bothered that you don't want to attend church. But you lost someone you loved, and I can tell you need to think about this. You've been half talking about him all night while trying really hard not to. Let's put things on hold for now." He smiled, but it only lifted one side of his mouth. "I haven't made a lot of friends yet, between my job and everything else. I could use another one. Is that okay?"

Micah wanted to say no. He wanted to persuade Chris, and maybe himself, that they were both wrong and everything would work out. It wasn't true, and the only thing on Micah's mind was that he hadn't tried hard enough to leave his life with Cat behind him. He sighed.

"Yes," he agreed. "It's fine. I should have known better, and I'm sorry."

"I shouldn't have pushed." Chris put a hand on Micah's arm and squeezed. "I had a good time, regardless. Goodnight, and I'll see you at the center."

He left Micah there, walking away and getting in his own car. Micah waited until Chris had gone from the parking lot to open his car door. He sat in the driver's seat for a long time, reviewing their conversation and trying to decide what part of it should have gone differently. When he couldn't find a single thing he would've changed, he turned over the engine and drove home.

CHAPTER NINE

The Spirit and the Bride Say Come

The letter Micah pulled off the top of the pile was stiff, as though there was something else inside it. He slit the top and pulled it out, laughing until the rest of his emotions caught up and his eyes misted over. It was a cardboard coaster from the Neanderthal. Cat had scrawled the date on it, and Micah traced the slightly indented pen strokes. He knew exactly when it was from.

The night he'd asked Cat to marry him. Micah had never thought he was the marrying type. It wasn't only the miserable way he'd spent his twenties, using the beds of other men to bury his father's shame. He also thought, once he'd begun to heal, that legal bonds meant still trying to fit himself into a tidy package his family might find acceptable. Not until Cat did he conclude the choice was his to make and not dependent on anyone else's approval. Cat made him want it all because Cat would never belong in anyone else's boxes.

Only Cat had said no, and not for the reasons Micah would've expected. The letter rustled as Micah's hand shook. He wondered what Cat had to say about the night represented by the coaster. Unfolding it, he began to read.

Dearest Micah,

Remember this? That's a silly question. Of course you do. What you probably don't remember is what happened after you proposed. Not right after, because I assume you remember we ate dinner and went home and had...dessert. Meaning, we stripped each other down and sucked each other's dicks like we were never getting another chance. God, I hope you don't show this to my mother.

No, I mean after-after. When I went to see LR and she called me a "complete dorkbutt" and told me if I didn't work out my drama, she was going to marry you herself on principle. I have no idea how she'd have managed that or even what the hell she meant. You should ask her sometime. She says the weirdest shit. Is she still doing that? She's going to fuck up her kids, and you can tell her I said so.

Micah paused, laughing. Living next door to LR, and later her family, had been a never-ending source of entertainment for him. Sometimes he ached with sadness that he'd never gotten to have what Cat and LR had, even if he and Jeremiah had made peace and kept in touch with each other. Other times, Micah counted his blessings that he didn't have a pesty younger sister.

He continued reading the letter.

LR might be a holy terror, but you know she's been pretty good to me. She said I needed to learn how to do for myself what you'd done so that I could see the numbers. She helped me, and we took care of it. I know you'd have gone with me to get it all done, but I needed to know I was going to be okay if something happened to you.

I put a lot of trust in you then, something I suck at doing. I don't regret a single second, honey. Not one.

Micah closed his eyes, smiling to himself as he pictured the whole thing.

~ ** ~

With a lot of help from their friends, they moved Cat from his house to Micah's. It had surprised Micah to learn the house Cat had been living in actually belonged to LR—she'd bought it from their grandparents. She'd allowed Cat to live there under the assumption she would eventually move in as well, as she was likely to become his caregiver as he got older and couldn't manage on his own. She already worried about leaving him alone in the event something happened. He always just rolled his eyes at her and insisted he was fine.

After feeding their friends dinner, they'd gone upstairs to unpack Cat's things. They hadn't gotten any further than the items to be stashed in the bedside drawer. Instead, they'd spent the rest of the evening reacquainting themselves with Cat's collection of toys, to which they'd added a few as a housewarming gift to each other. Cat seemed determined to drag things out as long as possible, and they took hours to make love.

When they were both sated and sleepy, Micah made a decision that he needed to look into a few things and possibly call Reid to ask if he had a friend in financial planning. He also needed to call his insurance company. There were so many what-ifs he couldn't possibly do it all on his own. Even so, he wanted to keep it all a secret from Cat. He fell asleep with a long to-do list scrolling in his head.

Nearly two weeks later, Micah insisted they needed to celebrate moving in together—in style. They'd finally unpacked everything, and Micah told Cat they should just go out and relax. Naturally, they went to the Neanderthal. He'd called Gerri ahead of time to tell her what he had in mind, and he'd practically been able to hear her grinning through the phone.

Despite the casual atmosphere, Micah told Cat to dress up. That wasn't a problem—Cat had an extensive wardrobe for which he required the entire guest room closet. Micah asked to be surprised. When Cat came out of the bedroom, he had on Micah's favorite black leather skirt and a sapphire-blue silk blouse. He usually wore his pot plant earring, but he'd exchanged it for a blue teardrop with a matching necklace. Obviously something of

Micah's goddaughter, Elle, had rubbed off on Cat because he'd used eye makeup—a rare thing for him, since he always said it itched. His lips shimmered faintly pink, and Micah wondered if he was wearing the candy cane lip gloss Micah had bought him for Christmas. If so, Micah wanted to lick it off him—Cat tasted so good when he wore it.

Banishing those thoughts before his brain's interest traveled down his body, Micah straightened his tie. They almost matched—Micah had on black trousers and a blue Oxford. His tie was black with a blue three-dimensional diamond pattern. He grinned at Cat's reaction—his flushed cheeks, his parted lips, and the spark of lust in his eyes. Of course, Micah knew he looked exactly the same.

"As much as I want to rip those off you and find a dozen new ways to make you come so hard you see stars, we need to go," Micah told him.

A small whine escaped Cat's lips before he replied, "Okay. But later, I think I may be the one making you scream."

"As long as we don't wake the neighbors."

"Fuck the neighbors."

"No, thanks. Only you."

Micah clasped Cat's hand and tugged him out the door to the car. When they arrived at the Neanderthal, Gerri met them and led them to a private table in a back room. Cat looked at Micah with raised eyebrows, but he said nothing. Gerri left them with menus and gave Micah a sly wink.

Cat hadn't missed it. "All right, what's going on?"

The plan had been to wait until after dinner, but Micah was too excited. "I've been doing some thinking."

"Yeah, I can tell." Cat smiled.

"I checked into a few things for us, and I went to a financial planner."

"Oh, god. I do not want to ruin our evening talking about investments." Cat laughed.

"Ass. I'm not talking about investments, actually. I went to find out what would happen if, um, something were to change. Like…we were to…" Micah had to stop, his breath coming in shallow gasps. His hands were sweating so badly he was afraid to pick up his water glass for fear of losing his grip.

"If we were to what?" Cat tilted his head and gave Micah a tiny smile.

He knew. He knew what Micah was going to ask. "If we were to get married," Micah said in a rush.

Cat's smile faltered. "Oh, honey."

Micah was taken aback. He'd thought Cat would be happy, but his change in demeanor puzzled Micah. "This is why I went to a financial planner. I also checked the health plan I get through work. If I go up to the next tier, which I can do in January, you're covered in full. In full, Cat. Later, I'll show you the papers they sent—it's pretty clear that blood and blood products are taken care of." He was talking fast, trying to get everything out before Cat could speak.

"I'll lose my benefits," Cat said quietly.

"Yeah, you will. But I earn enough for us, and for the first time ever, you can get paid for the work you do. Hell, you can accept payment in chickens if you want. Wait—no. I don't know what to do with chickens. Um, you can get paid in organic pasta?"

Cat laughed, but he choked a little and his eyes shimmered. "Oh…"

"Don't cry!" Micah exclaimed. "You're going to ruin those gorgeous eyes, and I want you looking like this later when I make good on my promise." He grinned. "I hope you're planning on reapplying that lip gloss. Is it the peppermint one?"

Cat nodded. "It is." His smile returned, but there was strain around his eyes.

Micah groaned. "Shit, you taste amazing when you wear it. I'm getting hard just thinking about kissing it off you."

"Why do you think I use it?" A low, heated chuckle rose from

Cat's throat. "You're going to make it difficult to get through dinner."

"Too late. Already there." Micah slid down off his chair and knelt beside Cat then took his hand. "What do you say? Marry me?"

Cat made no reply, which was answer in itself. Anxiety swelled in Micah's chest, and his breathing sped up. Why wasn't Cat saying anything? The floor was cold and hard underneath Micah's knees, and he silently begged for Cat to say something—anything.

"I can't," Cat told him.

"I don't understand." Micah sat back. When Cat didn't continue, he rose to his feet and slid back into his chair. He covered his panic and embarrassment with anger. "You were going to marry David," he accused. "What makes me different? Am I not good enough for you because I'm not him?"

Cat's mouth dropped open, and he stared at Micah for a full thirty seconds before he spoke. "How dare you."

"It's the truth. You said yourself you only talked to me because I look like him. What, only one true love in your life?"

"Fuck you," Cat whispered harshly. His nostrils flared, and his eyes were dark.

Micah slammed his hand down on the table, making Cat jump. "I did everything right. I made sure I looked into every possibility, but somehow, it wasn't enough. Maybe you could explain again how I'm not measuring up to your standards."

"Is that really what you think of me? Then you don't know me well enough for me to say yes to you." Cat stood up. "Enjoy dinner alone."

He walked away, leaving Micah floundering after yet another misunderstanding between them. He reflected that it was nothing new; their whole relationship had been a roller coaster of communication failures because of their traumatic histories. This was beyond anything Micah knew how to resolve. His confusion and hurt transferred to Gerri when she returned.

She looked from the empty chair to Micah's pained expression and frowned. "Is everything okay?"

Micah looked up at her. "No."

Uncharacteristically for her during working hours, she sat down and took Micah's hand. "He said no."

"Yeah." Micah swallowed, trying to find words to explain it to her. He took a deep breath. Things he'd learned in therapy about his own poor interpersonal skills came back to him. "I think I knew he would, but I wanted to believe I could convince him." At Gerri's gentle nod, he continued. "I need to talk to him and tell him it's okay that he said no. It doesn't change how much I love him." His eyes spilled over. "Or how much he loves me."

Micah squeezed her fingers, thanked her for listening, and stood up. He apologized for not staying, but she waved him off, and he bid her goodnight. Hoping Cat would be waiting for him at home, he exited the Neanderthal and looked up and down the quiet street.

Cat hadn't left. He was sitting on the stoop of the shop next door to the Neanderthal, his head resting against the door of the darkened building and his eyes closed. Micah watched him, thinking about how to approach without turning the conversation into another argument. This had been their first bad one in a while, and he didn't want to assume it was okay to talk yet. Before he made up his mind what to say, Cat opened his eyes and looked up at him.

"Hey, honey," he said.

Surprised, Micah walked over and sat down next to him. "Hey, beautiful," he said, and Cat gave him a tiny but genuine smile.

"I'm sorry," Cat said.

"Me too," Micah replied. "I knew how you would react, but I did it anyway."

Cat rested his head on Micah's shoulder. "It's not about the money," he said.

"You can tell me."

"I don't want to be dependent on you," he said, his voice almost too quiet to hear. "I've been independent since the day I told my parents I wanted to train as an electrician. I couldn't work full-time, but I did everything on my own." He lifted his head. "David and I weren't really going to get married. It wasn't legal back then anyway, so it was only wishful thinking. But even if it had been, we couldn't."

"Why not?" Micah asked.

"Because of my benefits. It's a nightmare when it comes to marriage because they look at the entire household to decide if you still need them. We also knew it would be a bad idea to risk things like him dying and leaving me with no means of support." Cat sighed.

"But that's not us," Micah said. "I'm capable of supporting us both." He didn't want to say what was on his mind, which was that they both knew he was going to outlive Cat.

"What if something did happen, though? I would be left without a safety net."

Micah took Cat's face in his hands and looked into his eyes. What he saw written there made him understand. It wasn't about money or benefits or the down side of being a "kept man." No matter how much they both wanted the fairytale, there would always be some risk for both of them. Micah would never be able to give the kind of assurance Cat required.

Bending forward, Micah rested his forehead against Cat's. He closed his eyes and let their breathing sync before he spoke. "This is the story I want, sweetheart. Every princess gets married at the end, right? I know there are so many reasons not to, but they all seem ridiculous when we can't see that far into the future. What matters to me is being able to belong to each other in every way, right down to our certificate of legal marriage." He placed a tender kiss on Cat's forehead.

"But—" Cat started, and Micah shut him up with a kiss.

He drew back and said, "There's more. This may be what I asked for, but if it's not what you need, it doesn't change anything any more than all the other things we know about each other. You still want me, even though I've been in pieces my whole adult life. I still want you, even though you think your body is too broken. This is good enough." He kissed Cat again.

For a few moments, they explored each other, and Micah let the cool taste of the peppermint lip gloss burst on his tongue. At last he stopped them, not wanting to get carried away on the doorstep of a shop on Main Street.

Cat took Micah's hands. "You're wrong," he said. "I do want to marry you—very much." His voice became small and sad. "I'm...scared."

It had taken everything he had to say it, and Micah pulled him close for comfort. "I know, beautiful. I know."

They held on for a long time, Micah stroking Cat's hair and rocking him. Around them, bits of conversation drifted to their ears on the late spring breeze, but no one else mattered. They let go and settled back against the door.

Cat took a deep breath and angled to face Micah. "If I said maybe we could figure it out, would you propose to me again?"

Micah swiped under his eyes. "Anything."

"Okay," Cat said. "Ask me again."

"Here?"

"Right here."

Micah got down on one knee, and Cat laughed, almost a giggle. At Micah's raised eyebrows, he calmed down and sat primly with his hands folded on his knees. Micah pulled the little velvet box out of his pocket.

"Becket Rowland, will you marry me?" He opened the box to reveal a ring with a flat setting for three tiny diamonds.

"Yes." The word was barely a whisper on Cat's lips.

He slid it carefully onto Cat's finger then stood, bending to draw Cat to his feet. Micah pulled him into his arms and captured

Cat's lips with his own. The sweetness of the last bit of lip gloss flooded his tongue, and he groaned.

"So sexy," he murmured. He pulled away and glanced at the ring. "Even more with that on your hand."

"Micah?" Cat asked.

"Hm?"

"I'm kind of hungry," Cat said, biting his lower lip.

Micah laughed, the sound echoing off the walls of the building. "Well, come on, then. I'm sure Gerri will let us back in."

Arm in arm, they returned to the Neanderthal. Gerri was at the bar, but when she saw them, she came out from behind it. She looked them over and clearly decided everything was all right because she dragged them both into a fierce hug. When she let go, Cat held out his hand to flash the ring.

"He said yes," Micah told her.

Gerri clapped her hands. "Dinner's on me. You deserve it." She gave them both another hug and dabbed at her eyes.

She led them to a table and set menus down for them before scuttling back up to the bar. When she'd gone, both Cat and Micah laughed. Micah opened the menu. "Well, what should we have?"

CHAPTER TEN

They Shall Be Comforted

When Micah returned home from school, he was surprised to find the front door unlocked. He'd always been in the habit of locking up, despite his many years on the outskirts of a small town. Frowning, he opened the door slowly and poked his head in, not sure what to expect. He glanced down when Thomas meowed.

"I don't suppose you unlocked the door," Micah replied before peeking into the living room. At the sight of the man sprawled on his couch, feet up and munching an apple, he let out a giant sigh and stepped all the way inside. "Make yourself at home, Cooper," Micah muttered. Louder he said, "You didn't have your own house to raid the fridge?" Turning to the woman on the recliner, Micah switched to polite mode. "Hey, Lucy. How are you feeling these days?"

Lucy's round face broke out in a grin. "Excellent." She patted her belly. "Baby's growing well."

Micah crossed the room and bent to give her a kiss on the cheek. "Glad to hear it." He straightened up and faced Cooper again, ditching the sweetness. "What the hell are you doing in my house, eating my food?"

"Job interview," Cooper replied, not taking his eyes off the recap of whatever baseball game he was interested in.

"Oh? I thought you liked living in Albany."

Cooper shrugged. "It's not that great. We'd both rather raise our kids somewhere closer to home. There's a position in Watkins Glen, and I have another interview on Tuesday up in Rochester. Thought we'd pop in and say hello on our way through."

"What does Elle think of it? You'll be farther away from her."

"No idea, but you know Elle. She and Henry are always traveling anyway, and they didn't live that close by. New York is still nearly a three-hour drive."

He was probably right, but Elle had always liked knowing someone was near. She wasn't as much of a homebody as Cooper, and Micah hadn't seen her in some time. Her work as a photographer for an arts magazine took her to some fascinating places, and her partner of three years, a journalist for the same magazine, often accompanied her. Micah understood why, with all the time spent away, she might appreciate having family within a few hours' drive.

"So, where is this place you interviewed?" Micah asked.

"A family practice office. They added two new positions for physician's assistants."

"Got it. I assume you two are staying for dinner. Are you spending the night, or are you heading up to Rochester right away?"

Cooper stood and stretched then turned off the television. "We'd love to stay. I told Mom and Zayne we'd be there tomorrow. You sure you don't mind? We can go into town instead."

Micah laughed. "You let yourself in, ate food out of my fridge, and watched the game, but you draw the line at presuming you can stay overnight? Of course you're welcome."

Grinning, Cooper said, "All right. You want a hand with dinner?" His pointed look spoke volumes.

"I'm taking a cooking class and can now manage not to burn things, but I'd love some help."

In the kitchen, Micah took out ingredients to throw something together. He was about to ask Cooper what he wanted to make and turned around to see Cooper studying the items Micah had left out on the table the night before. His laptop was closed, but there were the letters and the box of personal items. Micah had brought down the photo albums as well, wanting a visual of the memories in Cat's letters.

"What's all this?" Cooper asked.

Micah hesitated. He had only shared about the letters with Chris, Jude, and Hope. His students at the community center knew about the book he was working on, but they didn't know the letters had inspired it. Chris was the one person who knew both. Micah turned it over in his mind, deciding how much to say.

"Cat left me some letters."

Cooper didn't reply at first. He flipped open one of the albums, and a puzzled frown arose on his face. "When are these from? Wait...that's not you. He looks similar, though."

Micah nodded. "I know. Those are pictures of David Simms. Cat was in a relationship with him for a couple of years. I remember LR saying it was 'ages,' but it wasn't. David died from complications of hemophilia and I think some other health problems. This was about five or six years before I met Cat, and we didn't talk about the details."

"Neither of you ever said anything about him. It's weird how much like you he looks at first." Cooper had paused on the picture Cat had kept on his mantel when he and Micah first met. It was a shot of David on the boardwalk.

Micah looked over Cooper's shoulder at it. "It's the reason Cat talked to me when I came here. He thought I looked like David, and it made him curious. Cat hardly ever mentioned him after the first few months we were together. I wouldn't have cared if he had, but their relationship seemed like something Cat couldn't or didn't want to discuss."

"Are you going to do anything with them?" Cooper closed the book and opened the one of Micah and Cat's wedding.

"I was, yes." Micah stepped around Cooper to the fridge and pulled out some stew beef. "You want to come somewhere with me tomorrow?"

Cooper eyed him sideways. "Sure, I guess."

"Lucy too, if she's up to it. Otherwise, she can hang out with LR for a while if she wants.”

“Okay. I think she’d enjoy that.”

“LR probably has some shit she can give Lucy for the baby, too. You may have to loan it back to her, though. She swears Robbie is the last, but I’ll believe it when I see it. She practically just has to say the word ‘baby’ and she’s pregnant.” Micah glanced over his shoulder and saw all the color had gone out of Cooper’s face. “Ah, damn it. I’m sorry. I wasn’t thinking. I know it was rough for you two.”

“Don’t worry about it.” Cooper closed the album. Abruptly, his demeanor changed. “Here. Let me give you a hand with your meat.” He snickered.

“One step too far, Coop,” Micah said as they began working on dinner and the momentary tension faded away.

The following morning, Lucy headed next door to see LR. After she was gone, Micah changed his shirt three times, weighing the choice between casual and formal. In the end, he put on a collared button-down, but he didn’t wear a tie and left the top buttons undone. It seemed like a reasonable compromise for visiting with someone he’d never met. Cooper stuck to jeans, but he’d put on a polo shirt. Close up, Micah could tell he was wearing makeup, but he didn’t say anything. He assumed the person they were going to see wouldn’t have a problem. She’d known Cat, after all.

The longish drive to Horseheads was uneventful. Marion Simms lived in a relatively new assisted living facility. A young man in the main office let Micah and Cooper in and pointed them in the right direction. When Micah knocked on the door, a short, slim woman with elegantly styled white hair answered. She looked roughly the same age as Micah’s parents would have been. Older than Cat’s parents, younger—he thought—than Debbie.

“You must be Micah,” she said. She gave Cooper a once-over before her gaze returned to Micah.

“Yes, and this is my godson, Cooper.”

“Godson, hm?” The corner of her mouth twitched. “Well, come on in, then.”

They followed her past a tiny kitchen into the main room of her apartment. Off to one side, Micah saw a bathroom and a closed door he assumed was her bedroom. The apartment was tidy, with little furniture. The few items on the coffee table were neatly arranged, and there was no clutter anywhere. Micah wondered if Ms. Simms was always this organized or if she'd hidden everything behind the closed door. He suspected the former; even her clothes, casual but stylish, suggested she preferred order.

Micah sat on the edge of the couch, feeling formal and not yet at ease. Cooper sat next to him, looking much more relaxed than Micah. Ms. Simms carried a tray with three cups of tea, a sugar bowl, and a cream pitcher out to the living room and set it on the coffee table. She settled into a plush chair and crossed her legs. She raised an eyebrow at Micah.

"You seem a little uncomfortable," she remarked. "I promise, I don't bite."

Micah took a deep breath. "Maybe I would feel different if this were under other circumstances."

She nodded. "You said on the phone you wanted to speak to me about my son?"

"Yes and no," Micah replied. At her confused expression, he added, "More about your son's partner."

"Oh!" She sat up straighter and smiled fondly. "Cat?"

Micah swallowed thickly. "He is...was...my spouse."

"Was?"

To give his hands something to do, Micah picked up the tea and blew on it. He sipped, thinking about the proper way to tell this woman that the person who had almost been married to her son was gone. There was only one option.

"He passed away a few years ago."

Marion's shoulders sagged. "I am so sorry." She reached out for Micah's hand. "Are you doing all right?"

That was a question he couldn't safely answer with a stranger, so he replied, "As well as I can be. My apologies for not visiting sooner. I'm trying to get the last of his affairs in order." It sounded oddly formal, but Micah felt formal sitting in Ms. Simms's living room.

She squeezed his hand then let go. "I only knew him for a short time. I hadn't seen him in a very long while, although he did send me a Christmas card every year. At some point, he stopped, and I assumed he had decided to move on with his life." She tilted her head, studying Micah. "David's been gone for over twenty years. Why did you want to talk to me about him?"

"I didn't," Micah admitted. "Cat knew he was dying. He'd been sick for a long time. Before he died, he wrote me a series of letters. In the process of going through items in my attic, I found them, along with a trunk full of photo albums and such. There was one with a bunch of pictures of Cat and David." Micah held out the book in his hands. "I wasn't sure whether you wanted it."

Ms. Simms accepted the album and opened it. "Oh, my."

"Cat told me how he died but not much else. It was a chapter in his life which he kept closed. I didn't even know he was sending you cards." It gave Micah a pang to think his spouse had been keeping such a secret. Had he believed Micah would be angry or jealous? He'd never felt any such thing toward David. Was this why Cat kept telling him he would need to get rid of all traces after he was gone?

"You're wondering if he hid you from me, aren't you?" Ms. Simms guessed. Micah nodded, and she went on. "Not at all. He kept me up on his life. It was only a bit here or there, like when he met you, when you got married, and so on. It wasn't as though he wrote me long letters or any such thing. Why he didn't tell you about it is a mystery, and one we will apparently never solve. He hadn't sent me a card in—oh, five or six years, I suppose. Though that must've been only a couple years before he passed away."

Micah finished his tea and set the cup down. He was at a loss for how to proceed. Finding out Cat had kept connected shocked him into uncomfortable silence. There was so much he felt he'd never known or understood about Cat. Cooper glanced at him and gave a quick nod.

Addressing Ms. Simms, Cooper filled in for Micah. "Can you tell us anything about David or the two of them together?"

"I can do better than that."

She stood up and walked over to a bookshelf built into the wall. She ran her finger over the spines until she found what she wanted and pulled it out. Back in her chair, she handed a photo album of her own to Micah.

He opened it, the spine creaking a little from disuse. Cooper leaned forward to have a look as well. There were pictures of Cat and David, mostly posed but a few in which she'd caught them unaware. Some of the photos had people Micah thought might be David's siblings, for as much as they looked like him. There were children, too, and it made Micah smile to see Cat blowing bubbles for a little blond boy.

In one picture, Cat and David were in the yard of a cozy little house. David lay in the grass on his back, his ball cap on backwards. Cat was stretched out half on top of him, laughing, and their lips were inches apart. The angle of the sun made Cat's red-gold hair gleam. Micah touched the plastic covering on the photo with one finger, tracing the line of his spouse's body. Ms. Simms's voice broke through the stillness, startling Micah. He withdrew his hand.

"That was David's last summer." She flipped through the pages until she found another one, this time of David in the hospital. He looked slightly annoyed, probably because his mother had taken a picture of him in that state. "It's hard to say whether he knew he was dying, the way you said Cat did. David had been through a lot. I'm not sure how much Cat told you."

"Only that David died in a car accident, or that he'd had a stroke. LR—Cat's sister—told me David had hemophilia, like Cat."

Ms. Simms nodded. "That's true. David was older than Cat by a few years. In the early eighties, he had a blood transfusion." She stopped. "You don't really want a history lesson, do you?"

Micah shrugged. "It's all right. I assume you're going to tell me David had HIV. Cat shared that much with me in the context of talking about his own childhood. I grew up in a very religious home, and my father used to say that people with hemophilia and 'innocent' women and babies were collateral damage from God's punishment on gay men. Cat had never heard such a thing. His experience was more with pitying and nosy people asking him about his own status."

"The 'innocent children' thing didn't stop people from being hateful to us," Ms. Simms said. "I was a single mother with three children, and one of them was ill. It didn't take much for people to blame me. I tried to protect David from it, but there's only so much a parent can do."

"It must have been awful for him."

"He watched people die. We didn't have a lot of money, so we went wherever we could get treatment. We were sure he was going to die back then too. Anyway, the point in all that is to say both the HIV and some of the medications he was on—especially to keep his hepatitis in remission—were not good for his hemophilia. He had several small strokes over the years, and then one much bigger one."

"I'm sorry." There didn't seem to be anything else to say. Micah hadn't known any of that.

"I'm sorry about Cat. He was sweet. He took everything about David so easily. It was simply the kind of person he was. Accepting, loving, generous. I don't know a single soul who didn't love him once they'd met him." She smiled at Micah. "I'm glad he found you."

"It took him a long time," Micah said. "He thought he was destined to be alone because he both blamed himself for David's death and didn't want to burden anyone else with the same thing."

Ms. Simms laughed a little. "That does sound like something Cat would do. It used to exasperate David. Cat was much harder on himself than he ever was on anyone else."

Micah nodded, suddenly choking up and yet laughing along with her. "He was. He put up with a lot from me over the years. I'm..." He let the word die, thinking about how much to tell her. "I'm not a good person. Not the way Cat was."

Ms. Simms patted his knee. "You must be, or Cat never would have been with you."

"Maybe." Micah pulled himself together. "Cat didn't tell me whether I was supposed to contact David's siblings. Would you be able to tell them?"

"Of course. They didn't know Cat as well as I did. They're not nearby. My son lives on Long Island, and my daughter is down in Bethlehem, Pennsylvania. I'm not sure if their children even remember Cat. Did you two have kids?"

Micah chuckled. "No. Neither of us ever wanted any. But Cat's sister lives next door, and she and her husband have four of them.

The oldest is seven, almost eight."

"Do you have pictures?"

He pulled out his wallet and showed her the latest, a spring photo of their whole family. They were dressed in identical shirts and jeans, posed by a tree. Elle had taken the photo as a gift for them. Micah had the same photo in a frame over the fireplace, right between LR and Jamal's wedding photo and his own.

"Beautiful family," Ms. Simms said.

"Did you want the album I brought?" Micah asked.

"Oh, no, dear. You keep it. In fact..." She took back the album Micah had been looking through and pulled out the one of Cat and David in the sunny yard. "Here. Add this one to yours."

Micah tucked his wallet away and accepted the photo. He slid it into one of the pages. Standing up, he said, "I should go."

Ms. Simms stood as well. "Don't be a stranger. I'll be happy to have you visit any time." She turned to Cooper, who had also gotten to his feet. "It was nice meeting you." The faint flicker of a naughty smile was back.

"He really is my godson," Micah said. "That wasn't code."

She laughed. "Fair enough." She reached out to give him a gentle hug, and he held onto her for a few moments.

She showed them out, and after the door clicked shut, Micah stood staring at it. He didn't know if he felt as though he had any kind of resolution with David or if he'd only dragged things out. Cat was his only connection to this woman, and even he hadn't maintained an active relationship with her. Micah wondered if he'd been sending the cards out of guilt. Ms. Simms didn't seem to blame Cat in any way. Micah didn't know if he would visit her again, but he considered resuming the Christmas cards.

He turned around and walked away, Cooper at his side. "Thanks for coming with me," he said.

"Sure." Cooper eyed him. "You okay?"

"I am, yes." Micah paused and looked at the photo album in his hand. "You know, I think I'll give this to LR for the kids. They're going to want to know things about their uncle, and this should help."

"Not a bad idea." Cooper was quiet for a moment, but then he started chuckling.

"What?"

"She thought—oh, my god. I really can't believe she thought 'godson' was some kind of euphemism for...well, not the kind of relationship we have, at least."

Micah laughed. "She didn't seem to care. Sorry, Coop, but you're not my type."

Cooper elbowed him. "And you are way too old for me, even if we weren't practically related."

They were still laughing when they got to Micah's car and drove home.

CHAPTER ELEVEN

MY JOY IS NOW COMPLETE

AFTER COOPER and Lucy left, with a whole bag full of Micah's second successful attempt at dinner rolls, he stretched out on the couch. Thomas immediately staked his claim on Micah's stomach, causing him to grunt in surprise when Thomas landed heavily on top of him. Micah laughed as he stroked Thomas's ears, remembering all the times Cat had used him as a human pillow. Cat had needed so much physical contact, an almost constant craving. Micah hadn't minded, exactly, but he felt guilty now for the occasions he'd asked for his personal space. He'd gladly have taken Cat's warmth pressed up against him now.

Damn it to hell, Micah thought as his eyes welled up simultaneously with a hum of arousal. How long was he to keep cycling through painful memories like this? He closed his eyes and ran his hand over Thomas' fur. The warmth and the rumble of his purr soothed Micah, lulling him into a state somewhere between imagination and dreams.

What came to mind wasn't Cat. Instead, Micah's thoughts meandered to Chris and their failed efforts at moving past friendship. For the first time since Cat died, Micah had felt something he might label interest. It had seemed right at the time, but he hadn't wanted to talk too much about Cat and risk pushing Chris away. It was too bad he'd done exactly that.

In his half-awake state, Micah pictured all the things he hadn't let himself consider with anyone but Cat. Long talks late into the night and walking together on the pier and slow, heated kisses before bed. The last one caused Micah to sit up with a gasp, propelling Thomas onto the floor with a sour meow and a reproachful glare.

Micah's heart thudded. He had to get that image out of his brain. Chris had put things on hold, and Micah had agreed. There would be no entertaining thoughts of Chris's soft lips or the tickle of his beard or the heat of his tongue. Micah swore loudly and got up from the couch. Until he'd purged the last of his grief over Cat, he had no business having Chris in his head.

Out in the kitchen, Micah dumped food into a bowl for Thomas and then heated up some leftover stew for himself. He set the bowl to the side and turned on his laptop. Another letter, another chapter, another thing to pack away for good in his memory box. He opened the letter on the top of the pile.

Dearest Micah,

Today I was thinking about our wedding day. I used to figure maybe I was weird for imagining it when I was a kid, you know? Because boys aren't supposed to. It's not like I had these visions of a lacy white dress and a veil, but I used to think it would be so cool if I could get married too. I told my friends once, and they looked at me like I was stupid. One girl said, "You know boys can't marry boys" and left it at that. I was too crushed to tell her I wasn't technically a boy. After all, everyone else always saw me that way.

Remember the time I asked you about it? I don't know, maybe I was looking for you to tell me I wasn't so strange after all. You said you'd never pictured it. It was just assumed you'd marry some girl eventually, except you couldn't see it. You always said weddings made you feel weird, but you had to sit through them a lot, like those hospital visits you said your father took you on.

When we got married, you were so sure no one would come.

You said they'd all think it was silly, just like my friends used to. I gave up trying to convince you and said that if no one came, we'd haul people off the street to watch us say our vows and eat the catered food. It turned out we didn't have to, obviously.

It was really fun surprising you. Do you know how hard it was not to say anything about what I had planned for the ceremony? I covered it up by making you wait to see what I'd picked to wear, even though I really didn't care if you saw it or not. I think that shit is ridiculous. You saw my naked ass—a lot—but you couldn't see what you were gonna take off me on our wedding night? Seriously? It made a good excuse, though.

~ ** ~

They were married in May. The weather cooperated, dawning sunny and mild as the season shifted away from the cold of winter. The air was thick with the blossoms of spring trees floating away on the breeze, and everything smelled warm and green.

Cat had wanted something halfway between traditional and contemporary, so everything had an ethereal fairy tale quality to it. From the flowers to the elegant decorations to the soft beauty of the women's dresses, it was all floating and dream-like. Even the music they'd chosen reflected the quiet holiness of the moment.

Micah half expected Cat to wear a dress—perhaps something lacy and delicate. Cat had refused to give him any clue, saying it was bad luck for them to know what the other was going to wear. He wouldn't allow Micah to talk about what he'd chosen either, though Micah was sure he knew. Micah had picked out a soft, white linen suit with a jade green vest to match the greenery of their theme, and he couldn't wait for Cat to see the tie he'd selected, knowing it would bring his eyes to life.

Right after they'd gotten engaged, Micah had finally gone out and had his ears pierced. For their wedding, he'd chosen jade earrings and bought two pairs, and they both planned to wear them at the wedding. For his part, Cat had chosen the dresses for the women—pale green, calf-length with an empire waist. The skirts and sleeves were some kind of gauzy, soft material. The men—and Pam—had on white shirts and green ties that matched Micah's. Pam had a tan skirt, and the men had tan trousers.

Micah met Cat to walk down the aisle together. To his surprise, Cat hadn't worn a dress. Instead, he had a pair of white pants and a silk blouse, both billowy and flowing. The green of his sash matched their colors, and, to Micah's great delight, so did Cat's brand-new Converse. Only he would wear them with such a gorgeous outfit.

Just before they proceeded, Cat leaned in and murmured, "There's one more surprise waiting for you." The scent of his peppermint lip gloss wafted to Micah's nostrils.

There was no time to react; they had to start walking. Their attendants waited for them in a long line at the altar, which at first puzzled Micah until he realized they must be concealing something. As the two of them approached, the others parted, and Micah gasped. There, beside Cat's pastor, was Micah's brother Jeremiah. Micah hadn't even been certain he would attend the wedding, let alone consent to performing the ceremony. For a moment, Micah couldn't breathe or speak. He stood perfectly still, his mouth open.

Jeremiah strode forward and wrapped his arms around Micah, breaking into his shock. Unable to hold back, Micah returned the embrace, gasping a little to keep from sobbing. Jeremiah didn't even bother; he let his tears flow freely, and that was enough for Micah to let go as well. After a long moment, they drew apart, and Micah peeked over to see Cat both smiling and brushing delicately at his eyes with his thumb. A glance over his shoulder revealed that the entire assembly of guests were in the same state. There wasn't a dry eye anywhere.

They'd written their own vows, delivered in front of a hundred and ten guests. They almost hadn't been able to get through them between nerves and the fountain of emotions welling up in both of them. Micah lost it again when Jeremiah led them through the vows, saying it was his honor and privilege to do so.

When he and Cat finally kissed, Micah tasted the lip gloss, and it sent an electric prickle rolling down his spine. He let go of Cat quickly, not missing the half-grin and the sly wink. The moment was lost in the chaos of Jeremiah's pronouncement and the dash to the back of the church to greet their guests.

After standing in line and then the lengthy process of photographs, it was a relief to climb into the limousine for the twenty-minute drive to the reception. Before Micah could speak, Cat was straddling his lap and leaning in for a series of smoldering kisses, still tasting of the peppermint gloss. Their embrace quickly grew frantic.

Panting, Micah drew back. "You wore that damn lip gloss."

Almost in a purr, Cat murmured, "Of course I did."

"God," Micah half-moaned, half-laughed. "Want you so bad, but I don't want to make a mess in here."

Cat rolled his hips. "I have an idea."

He slithered off Micah's lap to kneel in front of him. When he looked up, there was heat and lust burning in his gaze. He moved swiftly to unfasten Micah's fly, drawing out his hard dick. Without any preamble, he bent forward to take it in his mouth. He licked and sucked and played his tongue on Micah until he was gripping his thighs, sure he couldn't take much more before he exploded. Cat gently used his teeth to scrape lightly, and that was Micah's undoing. He cried out and came hard over Cat's tongue.

Cat used his mouth to clean Micah, making needy sounds Micah knew meant he was holding back his own release. Micah felt Cat's shudder, indicating he was barely restraining his hand from frantically pumping out his climax. When he was through, he pulled away and sat up on the seat next to Micah. His pants were already undone and his hard length jutted up appealingly, his red-gold pubic hair peeking out enough to make Micah shiver with anticipation.

"Please, baby," Cat said. "I need it. Need you." He pinched the base of his erection and gasped.

Happy to oblige, Micah leaned over Cat's lap and repeated the same steps Cat had taken with him. He'd barely lowered his lips to kiss the tip of Cat's swollen penis when Cat moaned.

"Shit…it's not going to take much," he said, his voice shaking. "Too close."

Micah descended, engulfing his husband. Cat had been right; he gave only a couple of firm sucks and Cat gripped his hair, pulsing against Micah's palate. He swallowed then carefully licked until he'd gotten every bit. He straightened his back and leaned against the upholstery, dragging up his zipper and fastening the button on his trousers.

Cat tucked himself away and adjusted his fly. When they were properly dressed again, Cat reached for Micah's fingers, twining them with his own. He rolled his head to look at Micah.

"I think that'll get me through the rest of the day."

Micah chuckled. "If we're lucky."

Cat pressed a kiss to Micah's lips. "We're married. I'd say we're already lucky."

They kissed gently for a few more minutes until the limousine stopped. Micah pulled away and looked Cat over.

"Crap. You look exactly like we've been fucking in the limo."

Laughing, Cat replied, "You're no better. Here, let me fix that."

He threaded his fingers gently through Micah's curls, teasing and neatening them. Then he straightened Micah's tie and smoothed the fabric of his tux. When he was through, Micah took care of Cat. Before climbing out, they examined each other carefully for anything they'd missed. By that point, their flushed cheeks had returned to their natural color, and both of them had cooled off.

"Perfect," Cat said. He withdrew the tube of lip gloss from his pocket and expertly applied it, popping his lips and making a kissy face at Micah, who laughed. He made to open the door.

"Wait," Micah said, embarrassed heat rising in his face. "Um…here. You can spit it out if you can't drink it, but…you know." He pulled the open bottle of champagne from the ice bucket and handed it to Cat, who grinned and took a swig then passed it back. Micah tilted the bottle into his own mouth and swished before spitting it into the grass.

"Better." Cat laughed, and his gray-green eyes danced.

"Let's go, then," Micah urged. "Can't keep our people waiting."

They got out and threaded their fingers together, pausing to exchange one last—and much more chaste—kiss before they walked into the reception hall.

~**~

It was late by the time Micah finished writing about the memory. He stretched and stood, glancing at the bowl on the table and wondering when he'd eaten the contents. He'd been so wrapped up in getting out the next part of the story that he hadn't paid much attention to anything else. The evidence was in his stiff joints and the sudden realization he needed the bathroom. At least the chapter was done. After the hell he'd put his characters through, it had been nice to give them a romantic interlude. He would need to edit his reading for polite company when he shared it with his class, but it had felt good to put it all into words.

Later, as Micah lay in bed with Thomas curled up on the pillow on the empty side of the bed, he closed his eyes and let his mind scroll through the day's events. For the first time in a while, he felt naturally tired instead of drained with his brain's cogs still turning. He rolled over, wished Thomas goodnight—to which he got one eye cracked and a half-hearted, creaky meow—and drifted into a peaceful slumber.

CHAPTER TWELVE

EVERYONE WHO ASKS SHALL RECEIVE

THE ALARM clock on the nightstand buzzed, and Micah slapped at it until it stopped. He stretched, flexing his toes, and opened his eyes slowly. Thomas was still curled up next to him, or perhaps again since he'd probably gotten up to prowl overnight. Sleepily, Micah reached out and rubbed his head.

"Morning, beautiful," he mumbled.

When he realized what he'd just said, his eyes popped open all the way. He withdrew his hand and sat up, breathing slowly and waiting for the rush of sorrow and anxiety. It didn't show its face, and he relaxed. Something nagged at him, and he fished in his brain for it. Something about the way he'd let go enough to have a fleeting thought of Cat without needing to go sit in his old room, hoping to feel his presence. Micah wasn't sure he liked it.

There wasn't time to dwell on it. He had to be up and ready to go, off to spend his day molding the minds of eleven- and twelve-year-olds. He rose from the bed and stretched again. Thomas watched, but he made no move to get up or follow Micah to the bathroom as he sometimes did.

Thomas didn't join Micah again until breakfast. He haughtily ignored the clump of Salmon Dinner Supreme in his dish in favor of leaping up beside Micah and staring at the cream cheese on his bagel. Micah eyed him back.

"You're not very subtle, you know that?" He wasn't giving in. Not this time.

One pitiful meow later, and Thomas was happily licking cream cheese off the butter knife Micah set down for him. He stalked to his dish, took three licks of his cat food as if to say, "See? I'm eating it!" and escaped into the other room.

Micah watched him go, but when he saw where Thomas was headed, he paused with his bagel halfway to his mouth. He hadn't realized the door to Cat's room was open. He couldn't recall the last time he was in there, but he was sure he'd closed it all the way. Thomas shouldn't have been able to get in, and yet there he was. Micah contemplated kicking him out, making it clear to the damn thing he couldn't have it. And yet, somehow it seemed fitting he should take it over. It was on the shady side of the house in the afternoons, and it was a good deal warmer than the rest of the house on chilly days. There was a comfortable bed in there, too.

Slowly, a smile spread across Micah's face as he cleared the table. He could add a few things just for Thomas and make the room really his. He didn't think Cat would've minded at all.

Micah poked his head into Jude's classroom at the end of the day. She looked up from the drawer she was organizing and smiled, so he stepped all the way in.

"Hey," he said. "I'm sorry I've been lax about stopping by. How's everything going?"

"Good, good," she said, giving the drawer an expert shove with her hip. She dusted off her trousers and came over to where Micah stood.

"You've survived over a whole month. What do you think so far?"

Jude laughed. "School's great. I love the kids." Her smile slipped a little. "Everything else, though..."

"Oh, no. I'm sorry. Anything I can do?"

She sighed. "I shouldn't complain. I just don't feel like I've met too many people, um...my own age." She cringed visibly.

Micah was momentarily confused. "I thought you were attending the Baptist church. Aren't there people there?" Jude's cheeks reddened when she shook her head, and he understood. "I see. Trust me, you don't want me to play matchmaker for you, but I can definitely at least introduce you to a few people."

Jude's flush deepened. "It isn't that I haven't had opportunities before, but in such a small town, your business is everyone else's. I'm getting used to it, but all the grandmas at church have been trying to set me up with their grandkids. It's embarrassing! Also, it's weird, after growing up in my family. My mother's parents can't even say the word gay without choking. I never knew my father's parents, but with how he is, I doubt they'd have been any different."

"Ah, you need discretion. Okay, I can work with that. There's a place over in Watkins Glen that used to be a gay bar and is now inclusive of everyone. It's a fun place. If you're looking for something right in town that isn't necessarily to find someone to go home with, have you been to the Neanderthal?"

Jude giggled. "The what?"

"The Neanderthal." Micah grinned. "The original owner named it because she'd been groped too many times by, as she put it, 'cavemen in bars.' She, and now her kids, have always been good about keeping that sort out."

Tilting her head, Jude asked, "What about you? Surely you don't want to take me somewhere so you can sit in a corner watching me try pathetically to engage a hot woman in conversation."

Micah took a deep breath. "I don't mind. I'm not really looking, and I can always ask a few friends to meet us there so I'm not alone." An image of Chris came to mind, which he promptly banished. He couldn't imagine a minister in a place like Gerri's, even if there still had been something there between them. To cover his wandering thoughts, Micah added, "I'm a little too old to be your wingman anyway."

"You're not that old! Well, you've possibly solved one of my problems, at least. How about the rest of my sorry-ass life?"

"There's more?" Micah raised his eyebrows.

"My living situation isn't great either. I have two roommates, which is fine until they start either arguing or making out. I can't tell if they're actually a couple or what, but they are driving me out of my mind. They don't seem concerned with my work schedule or the fact that I don't want to constantly pick up after them or choose sides in their petty arguments."

"No wonder you spend so much time here," Micah remarked. "I might be able to help you out with that, too. Let me ask around, and I'll get back to you. One of my friends is in real estate."

"I'm not looking to buy a house just yet."

"No, but he may know of rental properties or have connections. Or…" Micah paused, thinking about Debbie, all alone in her house and in need of help. He might be able to solve both their problems if she was agreeable. He didn't want to let on until he'd talked to her. "Let me see, okay? I'll be able to tell you something in a couple of days."

Jude shrugged. "I've lived with it this long. I think I can manage to wait."

"Good. Hey, you want to get out of your roommates' hair and let them argue or whatever?"

"Sure, I guess. What did you have in mind?"

"I invited my sister-in-law and her family for dinner on Friday to practice my cooking. What's one more?" He gave her what he hoped was a winning smile.

Jude looked for a moment like she might laugh, but it passed. "Okay, sure. As long as you promise you won't send us all to the hospital."

"I'm not that terrible! Geez." Micah laughed. "I never was, and don't let my sister-in-law tell you otherwise. I'm just much better at it now, that's all."

"Whatever you say," Jude replied with a grin. "Sounds like a plan."

Micah ducked out of her room. On the way back to his own to gather his things, he contemplated talking to Chris after class at the community center and inviting him. They were friends, right? And this was a friendly dinner, nothing more. He decided to ask Debbie, too. Might as well let her and Jude get to know each other before proposing a housing arrangement. As an afterthought, he added his other neighbors' older daughter, Sienna, to the list. She was only a year or two younger than Jude, and Micah knew she was single and interested in women. All right, maybe he was matchmaking after all. Whistling, he packed up his things and headed home to put some practice into his developing skills in the kitchen.

The class at the community center paid rapt attention as Micah wrapped up his notes for them on creating characters and writing about people unlike themselves. He took them through an exercise in writing a brief biography.

"Tell me some places you might find a quick, maybe one paragraph, summary about a person," he said.

"An author bio," Carlie suggested.

"An award announcement," Jude said.

"Employee profile." That was Chris, and Micah smiled, remembering what he'd said about it.

"Cover letter for a job," Hope supplied.

Dyl said quietly, "An obituary."

Micah paused and waited to see if anyone else had an answer while he collected himself. "Right. Those are all good answers. Tonight, you're going to write one or two for your characters. If you're not writing fiction, you can do one for yourself or someone you know."

He gave them time to work on it, allowing an occasional comment but keeping an ear open so it didn't get out of hand. He opened his laptop and pulled up the section he'd prepared to read—naughty parts appropriately toned down. A few small tweaks later, he was ready to go after they wrapped up the weekly exercise.

Micah stood in front of the class. "All right. Who's ready to share theirs with us?"

Maricela offered to start. Her piece was a humorous obituary for a woman who seemed to have been the talk of her town for all her wild adventures. There were some hints at the sort of person she must have been, but Micah sensed something was missing. Instead of telling her that himself, he wanted to know if the others had picked up on it as well.

"Not bad," Micah told her. "Anyone want to offer suggestions?"

Hope said, "I feel like...there's something you're not telling us about her. You kept the tone light, which seems to fit the character, but it also sounds like you're holding back."

Maricela nodded. "I was. I mean, I know this class is pretty cool about stuff, and we've been listening to Mr. Forbes' story about two men. But..." She chewed her lip. "My family is really old-fashioned, and they were upset when my brother told them he was gay. They weren't a whole lot better with me, except they could still assume I'd marry a man and get over my phase or whatever. So I feel really weird writing a main character who..." She trailed off with a dismissive wave.

"Is bisexual or lesbian," Micah finished for her. "I'm supposing it's not really a secret that I'm—" He hesitated, almost defaulting to Cat's word, *queer*. "Bi," he finished. "For the longest time, I couldn't write LGBT characters. What's even funnier is that I was hiding being bi, too, and I wrote 'heterosexual' romance to cover it."

"Yes!" Maricela said. "It feels like I'm coming out all over again myself."

"Right," Micah agreed. "I suggest you don't hold back when you write, if you can find a way to do it safely and without worrying someone you don't trust will see it."

"I'll work on it." Maricela's smile was shy.

Several more students shared theirs, resulting in good discussion and critique. When they were through, Micah turned to his laptop. The class finished putting everything away, and when Micah looked up to begin, he saw that everyone had stopped shuffling. All eyes were on him. He almost laughed. It never would have occurred to him that his students would be so engaged in a simple fairytale written to expunge memories he'd rather not keep dwelling on.

He cleared his throat and read, "'On the last day of the spring gathering festival, He'chatul and Benjamin readied themselves in their separate tents...'"

At the end of the chapter, no one moved. Micah thought if it had been possible, they might not even have blinked. He waited for someone to say something. At last Dyl—of course—spoke up.

"I know this is fantasy, but did they really just have sex in the back of a caravan?" His expression was incredulous. "Who does that? Wouldn't someone, you know, notice?"

Several seats over, Hope's cheeks were flaming red. "We did," she muttered. Half the class turned to stare at her; the other half sank down in their seats. She said, "Our families were pretty strict, so we hadn't—you know—until we got married. And then we were in the limo, and it was going to be hours and hours until the hotel, and it was a long ride. So we kept ourselves busy."

Jude snickered. "Your family sounds like my parents. My father is a preacher, and boy did we ever hear it about keeping ourselves pure." She snorted.

Micah nodded. "I think it's familiar territory for many people. So, Dyl, you think it's unrealistic?"

He shrugged. "It sounds like teenagers going at it after prom, that's all. I didn't get the sense these two were exactly hands-off."

Carlie said, "The way the story goes, it seems like marriages are for political reasons, right? But these two had to overcome a lot to be together, and they really are in love. I don't think it's out of place. Kind of their way of defying expectations, maybe?"

"Plus all the unrest between the kingdoms," Maricela added. "They're going to have to fight Benjamin's violent family if they want to save He'chatul's home."

"It does make a nice break from the tension," Hope said with a giggle. "Are you going to make it more detailed or keep it fade-to-black?"

Micah tried to make his smile mysterious. "Wouldn't you like to know."

"Yes," Dyl answered, causing a ripple of laughter around the room.

"You'll just have to wait for the final version. Now, if no one has anything else to add, let's wrap this up and go home."

Everyone grabbed their things and headed out. As Micah packed away his laptop, he called out, "Hey, Chris. Hang on a sec."

Chris paused by the doorway. Micah slid the last of his papers away and zipped the case. Slinging it over his shoulder as he went, he joined Chris. The others had all gone except for Jude, who glanced back at them and waved.

"See you tomorrow!" she called before disappearing around the corner.

"I'd forgotten you work together," Chris remarked.

Micah didn't respond, too busy working through how to ask Chris to his house without making it seem momentous. "I wanted to ask you something."

"Okay." Chris tilted his head.

"I, uh, I'm having a few folks over on Friday. Nothing special," he added hastily. "I'm making dinner to practice what I'm learning in class."

Chris chuckled. "That's as good a reason as any."

"It'll be my sister-in-law and her family, Jude, and a couple of my neighbors. I was wondering if you'd like to join us too. That is, if you don't have plans and it's not too weird. I mean, my sister-in-law does have four kids, and—"

Chris cut him off. "It's fine. I don't have plans, it isn't too weird, and I love kids. Other people's, anyway."

"Isn't that the truth. Never wanted my own, but I do love my nieces and nephews." The ones he knew, anyway. Micah thought again about Elijah's kids and everything he'd missed out on over the years.

"Good. I'd love to come over. Can I bring anything?"

"How about something to drink? Anything is fine, but if you want wine or beer, you'll have to supply it. I don't keep it in my house."

"Is that all right with you?"

Micah nodded. "I don't drink at all, but I can be around people who do."

"Okay, then. I'll see you on Friday." Chris put his cool hand on Micah's arm and squeezed with light affection.

After he was gone, Micah sagged against the door frame, a little embarrassed at the way he'd babbled. Being around Chris made him feel half his age. There was something about him that felt different from the few people he'd hooked up with after Cat. There wasn't the raw, emotional sensuality of Reid and his roommates. Nor was it the same as his brief fling with the outgoing, lilac-haired woman from his grief group. When he tried to name the feeling, it was as though it slipped past him. The only thing he knew was that he wanted more of it.

Micah shouldered his bag, hit the lights, and pulled the door shut. He whistled softly to himself the whole way out to his car, enjoying the way the light, bubbly sensation lingered in his belly.

CHAPTER THIRTEEN

WHOEVER WELCOMES A CHILD

THERE WERE enough people at dinner on Friday that Micah had to put both extra leaves in the dining room table. He'd cleaned the house thoroughly and removed anything the baby might get into. He'd always considered his house to be mostly kid-proof, but it definitely wasn't Robbie-proof. Not much was these days, now that he was on the move.

LR and Jamal showed up early with their kids to lend a hand. Micah closed all the doors to the downstairs rooms, including the bathroom, while LR put up a temporary gate at the bottom of the stairs. Robbie could scale it, but with any luck, he'd find something more interesting to explore on the first floor. Thomas, displeased with being shut out of the rooms, turned into an orange streak and shot up the stairs to sulk in peace.

Jude and Sienna arrived at the same time. On her way past Micah with the salad she'd brought, Jude raised an eyebrow at him. *Really?* she mouthed. He shrugged and took the bowl from her hands. Sienna had brought a decadent cheesecake and some homemade chocolate chip cookies for the kids, courtesy of her father. She, too, gave Micah a look as she passed. By that point, Debbie had showed up.

"Hey," Micah greeted her, kissing her cheek and taking the basket of rolls from her hands. "I'd like you to meet someone." He beckoned to Jude.

"Oh? I think I'm a little too old for you to be setting me up." She winked.

"Not you, apparently," Jude said. "Me, judging by the woman over there trying to keep the kids out of the cookies before dinner. Hi, I'm Jude, and I apparently have no filter. Sorry." She extended a hand.

"Lucky for you, I like people who don't hold back. I'm Debbie, Micah's neighbor from two houses down."

"Ah, she of the blueberry muffins?" Jude asked, turning to Micah.

"That's not all she does!" Micah laughed. "Sorry, Deb. I brought some to work one day, and now that seems to be what you're famous for."

Debbie shook her head, but she was smiling. She patted Micah's cheek. "Don't worry about it, dear."

Leaning in toward Jude, Micah said, "She's the closest thing I have to a mom. She looks out for all of us. I'm hoping you'll enjoy getting to know each other."

Jude eyed him, but she didn't remark on his comment. Turning to Debbie, she said, "At least maybe you'll give me that recipe."

The kitchen was chaos, between the kids chattering, the dishes clanking on their way to the table, and the other adults introducing themselves to Jude. Micah was grateful when the doorbell rang again. He escaped into the front hallway to answer it.

When he opened the door, he nearly lost his breath. Chris stood there in jeans and a raspberry-colored polo shirt. His small silver earrings winked in the porch light, and his smile caused Micah's stomach to flip. He smelled nice, too—some light, woodsy scent. It took nearly half a minute before Micah could greet him.

"H-hey," he stammered. "Come on in."

Micah didn't miss the way Chris's gaze flicked over him, and heat crept up his neck. He swallowed his nervous energy, repeating his internal chant of *just friends*. It was all right to notice how good he looked, though, right? Friends could find each other attractive. It didn't have to be any more complicated than that. Nor any more complicated than how much Micah looked forward to spending time with him. That, too, was normal for friendship. He ignored the voice in his head that reminded him how well "just friends" had worked out with Cat and exactly why that train of thought was highly inappropriate at best.

Dinner was a lively affair, with multiple conversations going all at once. Micah preferred to listen in, not having much to say himself unless asked directly. As predicted, Jude got along well with both Sienna and Debbie. Micah caught bits of chit-chat, including Sienna promising Jude to introduce her to her other friends and inviting her out with them for the following evening. A moment later, he congratulated himself again when he overheard Jude offer to come help Debbie with her yard. He decided that his one and only effort at setting anyone up would be his last; he could live with a one hundred percent success rate on creating friendships, even if nothing more developed.

In a side conversation, Chris spoke with LR and Jamal about his church job and his work at the community center. Once or twice, Micah heard his name, and Chris glanced at him with a hint of a smile. Eventually, Micah was drawn into a discussion with Jude about school and the new set of standards, but his attention kept wandering to Chris. He shook himself out of it in order to reply to something Sienna had asked about students with disabilities. Now, that was something about which Micah wasn't short on opinions.

After their meal, while the others pitched in to help, Micah stood at the sink washing dishes while Chris dried them. It was the first real chance they'd had to talk to each other, with both of them taken up in conversation with others. Micah had tried to keep things balanced, not wanting Chris to think the dinner was a thin disguise for inviting him over. Too much attention on him and it might've seemed that way. Too little and Chris might've wondered why he was there in the first place.

"You look like you're thinking hard," Chris remarked as he picked up a glass dish and ran the cloth around the inside.

"Oh...uh..." Micah searched for a topic, anything to cover his real thoughts. "I was wondering how to bring up something I'd wanted to talk to you about."

"Yeah?" Chris glanced at him and smiled.

"About..." He paused, and then it came to him. "...queer theology."

Chris raised his eyebrows. "It's a pretty broad topic. I don't think we'll cover it all while we do the dishes." Before Micah could say that was all right, Chris continued, "But I can give you a start, and maybe we can talk more later."

"Sure."

A tap on his shoulder made Micah turn his head. LR had Robbie in a just-rescued-from-something hold around his middle. "Hey, have you seen Maya?" she asked.

Micah frowned. "Last I knew she was looking at a picture book in the living room."

"She's not there."

Scanning the kitchen, Micah spotted Emily talking animatedly to Jude and miming playing the cello. Langston was seated across the kitchen table from Sienna, listening wide-eyed to whatever story she was telling him. Robbie was kicking in LR's arms. No Maya.

"I'll go look. She can't have gone far—the house isn't that big." He turned to Chris. "Sorry about this."

Chris waved him off. "I'll finish up. You go find your niece." He took over the soapy water.

Micah peeked in the living room and the dining room for good measure, then looked up the stairs. It was completely dark, and he was pretty sure Maya wouldn't be up there alone. He opened the doors to the bathroom and the office. As he was turning around, he saw light coming from Cat's old room. The door was ajar. Moving closer, he pushed it open gently.

There, in the middle of the bed, Maya lay curled on her side, fast asleep. Thomas, who had been pressed up against her back, raised his head. His green eyes met Micah's, and he let out a mighty yawn before settling back down. Micah stayed still, watching the two of them.

LR stepped up beside him and peered into the room. "I'm

sorry," she said. "Maya shouldn't be in here. I'll get her out." She made to go inside.

"Wait." Micah put a hand on her arm and turned to face her. He looked again at Maya, and the way she and Thomas were cuddled together was so natural. She belonged there, just as Thomas had. Micah said, "It's all right. Maya can stay. I think it's time someone did."

"But you don't let anyone—" LR stopped as she looked in again. "You've rearranged it."

Micah followed her gaze to the soft blankets he'd added, the pet bed by the closet, the scratching post, and the cat tree with its topmost perch at exactly the right height to look out the window. When Micah looked back at LR, he smiled.

She did too, for a second, and then her face crumpled. She leaned against Micah, and he folded his arms around her, stroking her hair as her tears wet his shirt. Behind her, the kitchen quieted. Micah watched Jamal pass Robbie to Sienna before coming toward them down the hall.

When Jamal put a hand on her back, LR straightened up and wiped her eyes. "I'm sorry," she said.

"I understand." Micah glanced over his shoulder at a tiny sound from within the room. "Looks like Maya's waking up."

Maya's eyelids fluttered and then opened. She blinked a couple of times and stretched. Thomas meowed softly and walked to the edge of the bed, where he leapt to the cat tree in the window. Maya sat up.

"Mommy?" she asked.

"Here, sweetie." LR hesitated, but then she stepped into the room. She sat on the bed beside Maya, who crawled into her lap.

"I found Uncle Mike's kitty."

"I see that." LR smoothed Maya's hair away from her face.

Maya looked up at LR and put her little hand on her mother's cheek. "Are you sad, Mommy?"

LR raised her face to meet Micah's gaze before returning her attention to Maya. "Yes," she said. "I miss your Uncle Cat."

"Oh," Maya said. She was quiet a moment. Then, "Is it okay if I miss him too? I didn't know him much."

"Aw, baby." LR held her close. "It is definitely okay."

"Will you tell me about him again?"

Micah spoke up. "Wait here. I have something for you."

He ducked into the office across the hall. After visiting with David's mother, he'd left the photo album she hadn't wanted in with Cat's letters and the other items from the attic. Now he retrieved it and brought it to Cat's old room. He handed it to Maya, who flipped through it.

"This belonged to your Uncle Cat. Those are pictures from a long time ago, even before I knew him. Your mommy can start with those."

"Who's the man in the pictures?" Maya asked.

LR ran a finger over one of them. "He's someone Uncle Cat loved before he met Uncle Mike."

Maya's eyes grew big. "People can do that?"

Micah chuckled. "Yes. It's a little like how your mommy and daddy and I all love you and your sister and your brothers, all at the same time."

"Not quite the same," LR said, but she smiled.

"No, not quite."

By this time, the others had gathered in the hallway to see what was going on. Micah looked up at them, and his eyes met Chris's. It was hard to read his expression, but Micah thought he saw both sadness and understanding. Micah nodded the smallest bit, and Chris acknowledged it with a tilt of his chin.

"We should go," Jamal said. "Robbie's not going to take much more."

LR stood up with Maya still in her arms. The others dispersed to let them by. One by one, everyone bid Micah goodnight until only Chris remained. Surprised to find him still there, Micah turned to him.

"Some evening," he tried to joke, but something in Chris's eyes stopped him.

There was a long silence before Chris said, "You asked me earlier about queer theology. If you really want to know, it'll be easier to show you. I can bring you the book tomorrow, or..." He paused again. "You could come over after class."

"Are you sure that's a good idea?" Micah asked, hoping he wasn't reading into it more than what was intended.

"No," Chris answered. He sighed. "But I'm not sure it's a bad idea, either."

"All right, then."

Chris gave a quick nod and turned to open the front door. "Good night, Micah. See you tomorrow."

"Good night."

Micah closed the door. He felt something move at his feet and looked down to see Thomas winding around his legs, tail lashing. Micah bent and stroked his back, making Thomas arch up into the touch. His rumbling purr vibrated up Micah's arm.

"C'mon, you," Micah said to him, straightening up. "Let me get your dinner."

He headed for the kitchen, Thomas swishing his rear end ahead of him. Once he'd fed the cat, Micah sank into a chair. He looked down the hallway to the back rooms, thinking about Maya asleep on Cat's old bed. He wasn't ready to go back to Cat's last days, not until he'd gone through the rest of the letters. He stayed seated for a few more minutes then slowly got up and made his way into the office.

CHAPTER FOURTEEN

YOU SHALL KNOW THEM BY THEIR FRUIT

CHRIS'S APARTMENT was cozy and tidy. To Micah's left was a closed door, and to the right was a closet with sliding doors. He shrugged out of his jacket, and Chris hung it in the closet with his own. They passed a second door, ajar far enough for Micah to see it was the bathroom, and entered the living room. For a moment, Micah was sure Chris's apartment was paradise. He had three floor-to-ceiling bookshelves plus an end table with shelves and a two-tiered coffee table. Every inch was taken up with books.

Beside him, Micah heard a quiet chuckle. He turned to Chris, his neck heating up. He must have been nearly drooling at the sight, and it obviously amused Chris. Micah shook off his embarrassment and laughed at himself.

"I'm sorry. I was awed by your collection," he said. "I've never seen so many."

"This is only a fraction of what we had when I was growing up." Chris smiled. "My parents are both readers, so I am too. I had more books than toys when I was a kid."

"I believe it," Micah replied. "We never had many, and they

were mostly religious or the kind of Christian fiction that was allowed. This was the eighties, so Frank Peretti, John Bibee, C.S. Lewis, that kind of stuff, plus the classics because they were 'clean.' I used to sneak all my books from the public library."

He stepped over to one of the shelves and began reading the titles. They weren't alphabetical, but they did seem to be arranged by type. One whole section was devoted to classic literature, and another had science fiction. Micah was pleased to see Chris had a substantial section of romance novels, all varieties. He spotted one of his favorites, a book Zayne had given him eons ago when she'd first challenged him to write. He hadn't realized at the time that he was already working through the complexities of a sexuality he hadn't been able to pin down.

"I love that one," Chris remarked. "You know, reading it was the first time I recognized I was identifying with the man and not the woman."

Micah nodded in understanding. "I get it." He huffed a laugh. "It was similar for me, feeling excited by a man and woman taking such pleasure together. Only I didn't know what to do with that information after years of identifying as gay, so I buried it. God, that book has one of the sexiest scenes I've ever read. I only wish I could write like the author." He kept it to himself how he and Cat used to read that part to each other in bed.

Chris interrupted his thoughts. "Would you like something to drink? Water, tea or coffee?"

"Water is fine."

In the kitchen, Chris poured them each a glass and carried them to the living room. He set them down and offered Micah a seat on the couch. Once he was settled, Micah looked at the stack of books on the table. There was a Bible and another book, open to the middle. Beside them was a tablet.

"Working on a sermon?" Micah asked.

"No, a study for some of the members. You know, we don't need to talk about my job if you'd rather not. I have the impression you don't have a lot of positive experiences with clergy."

"You understand why, right?" Micah wasn't sure where this was going, even though he'd been the one to bring up Chris's beliefs the night before. He was beginning to wonder why he'd agreed to go back to the apartment in the first place.

"I do, and I don't think you're wrong about how much damage has been done to humanity in the name of vicious, cruel deities. I hope you understand I'm not now, nor will I ever, try to convert you."

Micah studied him, searching for something that might indicate he wasn't being fully honest. Intellectually, he knew Chris was far from the only one who was able to reconcile his duties as a minister with his open-mindedness. Jeremiah had come a long way, even though he was only now coming to an understanding of his own identity. Micah didn't push, but he'd gently nudged Jeremiah to consider whether his career was the only reason he'd never married. They'd both had the disadvantages of their father's and Elijah's hateful beliefs. Chris, like Cat, had grown up with parents who loved and accepted him. The difference was, Chris's religious practice seemed more mainstream, like Jeremiah's, rather than Cat's radical faith.

"What's wrong?" Chris asked.

"I'm not sure," Micah replied. He ran his thumb over the rim of his glass. He tried to think of a way to phrase it without bringing up Cat. At last he said, "I don't understand how you hold the tension between your beliefs and what the church has traditionally taught."

"For starters, I've done enough study to see a lot of it as metaphor and other parts as poor translation. It's meant to be read and understood in community, not in isolation."

Micah frowned. "That's not what I mean." He didn't want every conversation they ever had to revolve around Cat, but he needed to grasp the difference between being tolerant and being actively welcoming. "Don't you have rules? Or a list of things you're supposed to avoid?"

Instead of answering immediately, Chris stood up and went to one of the bookshelves. He took down a thin volume and brought it back over to the couch. "This is where queer theology comes in," he said. "A singular interpretation for all people and all times is a modern concept, not an ancient Hebrew one."

"That sounds like something—" Micah shook his head as a

memory bubbled to the surface. "It sounds like something Cat used to say." He cleared his throat. "Sorry."

"It's all right. What was it?" Chris tilted his head, waiting.

Micah's cheeks warmed. "Uh," he replied.

"You don't have to tell me, but I'd love to hear it."

Chris's voice was gentle, and Micah relaxed. He replied, "Cat used to say—when we were having sex—that it was like being filled with the Holy Spirit." Micah chuckled in spite of himself. "He was being unironic."

Instead of laughing, as Micah had expected him to do, Chris nodded. "I'm sure for him it was that way. That's certainly one aspect of queer theology, yes."

"I suppose." Micah sighed. "He also used to say that fucking is holy. Uh...sorry. Again."

"You don't have to censor yourself for my sake," Chris said. He put out a hand, but he withdrew it quickly. "Neither your language nor about Cat."

Surprised, Micah replied, "All right. Well, that's how he said it, too—all matter-of-fact, like he was explaining how some scientific principle worked." Micah took on the tone he used with his students and imitated Cat's posture. "'Now remember, Micah, fucking is *holy*.'"

One side of Chris's mouth lifted in an almost-smile, but then he turned serious again. "He was right, in a way. We learn that our kind of sex is so shameful, so dirty, that it's hard to imagine God's approval. Yet Cat saw something in that, a kind of holy beauty. I have no doubt he felt deeply connected to both you and God when you were experiencing pleasure together." Chris smiled. "That makes people really uncomfortable. Church folks tend to talk about sex—married, heterosexual sex, of course—as being a *reflection* of God's relationship to the church. Sex itself as *worship* seems out of place, especially if the partners aren't church-sanctioned."

It made sense, sort of. Micah could relate to all of that. "I asked once what it felt like to him," Micah said, knowing he was turning red again. "What it felt like to come. I...always had trouble with that. I mean, I could come, and it felt good, but it was functional— just a release. I couldn't be present. Cat taught me how. It was one of the few things he experienced physically as pleasure because his body had been badly damaged. So I asked him to describe it."

"What did he say?"

They had moved closer, and Micah smelled Chris's woodsy scent. It comforted him, and he took a deep breath before continuing. "The way he described it sounded almost otherworldly. He said it began not in his dick or his balls or even his stomach but in his chest—a rush that spread out everywhere." Micah swallowed, his own nerves tingling. "He said it settled low in his belly and moved downward, narrowing and concentrating between his legs before racing through his balls and shooting out. Right after, he said he felt warm all over and deeply contented." Micah drew in a shaky breath. "He said he also felt a sense of peace and being loved. Not just by me—he said he felt the same way when he was alone. He said the pleasure of orgasm was proof of God's love because it's so pure, intended exclusively for joy."

If any of that shocked or upset Chris, he didn't show it. He closed his eyes, and Micah wondered what he was thinking. At last he returned to the moment and opened his eyes again.

"Beautiful. That does indeed sound spiritual."

Micah let out a breathy laugh. "Everything was like that with Cat. He saw holiness all around him. I think he liked sex best, though."

Chris laughed along with him, the sound almost musical. "I'll bet." He paused. "Is that how you feel, too?"

"No." Micah sighed. "When I was young and only beginning to admit who I was, the sex I wanted was considered of the devil, something to be gouged out like the eye that has offended. I tried, you know. I went to a place to be cured. And then I went the opposite way—as much sex with as many men as possible, simply because I could. It wasn't until Cat came along that I was able to feel properly again, and only after getting help. By himself, he wasn't enough to fix what was wrong."

"And now?" Chris's voice was low and quiet.

"I don't know," Micah admitted. "I don't see sex as holy, no." He angled a little toward Chris and realized how close they were sitting. "But I don't see it as sinful or something to be ashamed of, either." Wanting to get off the topic of sex before he did something foolish, he said, "Is that all there is to queer theology?"

Chris shifted away slightly and opened the book. He showed the table of contents to Micah. "As you can see, it's not. There are lots of different ways to read the text."

Micah peered at it. "Ah, so viewing some of the stories as same-sex love, right? Like reading David and Jonathan as gay?"

"Something like that." Chris put his finger on the title of the chapter about David and Jonathan. "I don't prefer to read them that way. If anything, David would've been bisexual. However, he was also a murdering rapist, if you read the stories literally. Not quite someone I want to emulate." He chuckled.

"Oh, god. Yeah, I remember thinking that some of it was disturbing."

"There are other good examples, but I'm more interested in other interpretations of the text as having queer themes." Chris closed the book and handed it to Micah. "You don't have to, but you're welcome to borrow this. I like the author's style, especially because it's mainly explanatory rather than proselytizing. It's also put in layman's terms rather than heavy-duty theological ones. Though I gather you'd be more than capable of reading the more dense stuff."

"I would, but I don't care to." Micah gazed at the book in his hand for a while before he said, "Maybe we can talk about it again some time."

"Sure," Chris replied. "I'd like that." He stood. "Want to stay for dinner?"

"All right." Micah grinned. "I promise not to burn anything helping you cook it."

He followed Chris into the kitchen, both of them still laughing as they pulled things out of the refrigerator.

When Micah arrived home, he set the book from Chris on the coffee table. Then he moved it to the mantel, decided it looked too much like he was displaying it in either place, and laid it face up on the bookshelf in front of the other titles. He went into the kitchen and poured a glass of water, which he set next to his laptop while he waited for it to boot up. His mind strayed back to the book, and he returned to the living room.

He picked up the book and examined the glossy cover. It made him tense just holding it. His mind raced from thought to thought, darting between memories of Cat, anxiety over the contents of the book, and nagging worries about what Chris expected him to find in the pages. He was on the verge of a genuine panic attack; he spotted all the warning signals. He closed his eyes and breathed slowly, letting his body relax enough to uncover what it was he needed to do to stop the train.

The first thing was to deal with the book. Intuitively, Micah knew Chris never would have sent it home with him if he'd known it would do Micah any harm. Micah allowed the rationally functioning part of his mind to see Chris as a friend and not an enemy. Instead of hurling the book at the nearest wall—which a small part of Micah felt would be highly satisfying—he set it back on the shelf. He had to find a spot for it where it wouldn't feel like it was aggressively staring him down.

Thomas's creaky meow interrupted his thoughts, and he looked down into the cat's unblinking eyes. Thomas came closer and brushed up against Micah's leg. The gesture comforted him, and he bent to run a hand along Thomas's fur.

"Thank you," he murmured. Thomas merely nudged Micah's face with his head.

Micah stood up again. There might come a time when he could read through the book but not tonight. Calmer now, he identified the source of his anxiety. It wasn't the book; Chris wouldn't be upset if Micah returned it and said he couldn't read it. It was the feeling of exposure after revealing something so deeply personal about his relationship with Cat. Even Zayne didn't know the details of what their intimacy meant, and she knew almost everything about Micah. He felt now as though he'd betrayed Cat's trust.

He sat on the couch and put his head in his hands. He could talk to anyone who would listen in general terms about how much he missed Cat. But he had no one in whom to confide missing the way their lovemaking reached a part of his soul he'd never entrusted to anyone else. Yet there he had been, in another man's apartment, wading in the shallow end of that pool. One day, he would have to confront the truth.

Thomas hopped up beside him and continued to meow, a rusty, chirping sound accompanied by shoving his head into Micah's arm until he moved it to stroke Thomas's fur. Once Thomas had his attention, he leaped down and walked away, curling his tail high over his back. He paused at the doorway and looked back with another meow. Micah stood to follow him.

Out in the kitchen, Thomas jumped onto the table. He proceeded to walk across the keyboard, earning an eye roll from Micah. At least he hadn't added a string of nonsense characters, as there wasn't anything open yet for him to leave a contribution. He meowed one final time, got down from the table, and sauntered off.

Micah sat at his laptop and pulled the next letter off the pile. He slit the envelope and drew it out.

Dearest Micah,

I was thinking about sex the other day. Oh, who am I kidding? When am I not thinking about sex? Yeah, all right. Some days are now so bad that it's the last thing on my mind. Other days, all I can think is that it's a damn shame nothing works anymore. I miss it, you know. God, we were like bunnies for years.

Did I ever tell you how much I loved it with you? I mean, yeah, it was hot. So hot. Scorching, even. Fuck...I'm getting distracted, and I can't even properly get hard. Okay, deep breath. It's not how good it felt—though that was fucking amazing. It was how good it was with you specifically. I mean, I've had some really, really good sex. Aside from the time I nearly died, I used to love fucking in the bathroom with my first real boyfriend. And of course it was good with David, figuring out how my body worked again. Does this bother you? I hope not.

It was different with you. Not some weird soul-mates thing, like I waited my entire life for the perfect man to come along or anything. It's how much you showed me you loved me. You were never upset about anything. Even then, sometimes I couldn't get my body to work right or I was too sick. You never complained or got angry. You used to lie in bed or on the couch with me while I infused. Lately, you still do, except you're usually helping me with it. After, you would touch me wherever I needed it. It always awed me how my scars and my mediport and my swollen joints and even my false teeth didn't faze you. But you didn't avoid them, either. You used to put that stuff Zayne gave you on my joints, and you would kiss my skin right above the mediport. Sometimes, you brought humor into it when I was worried about how you might see me. You included every part of me when we made love.

When I was healthy enough for sex, you trusted me with your body too. Remember the time we tried that whole blindfold trust thing? I thought then it was a bad idea, and it didn't work the first time. But we tried again, and every time you lasted longer before having to uncover your eyes. The time we both did it blindfolded was one of the hottest things I've ever done. That first time, though, was scary for us both. I hope you don't see it as a failure because it wasn't. It's one of the bravest things I've ever seen you do.

Micah finished reading the letter and set it aside. He remembered exactly what Cat had been describing. It had taken a long time before he was able to fully trust both Cat and himself, but the blindfold had ultimately eliminated the greatest part of his shame.

He couldn't write about it directly. It was too intimate, too personal, too deeply bound up in his spiritually damaged psyche. He thought about it for a while then made a few notes on the page. It would take some consideration to figure out how to write about it without delving into something too sensitive. He tapped his finger against his lips. If he could figure out how to communicate it differently, he might be able to help Chris understand too.

Slowly, Micah rose from the table. He closed everything out and shut down, then stretched and yawned. He would work on it more in the morning. Looking down, he saw Thomas, poised and ready to follow him upstairs. Micah smiled in spite of his serious mood, warmed by the kindness of his companion.

CHAPTER FIFTEEN

Put Your Hand into My Side

The dentist left them alone to discuss the situation while he collected contact information for the oral surgeon and made a note for the staff to begin the referral process. Cat flopped back in the chair and blew out his breath so his bangs stirred.

"Damn it!" he muttered. "I'm only thirty-three, and I'm losing all my teeth. This just sucks."

Quietly, Micah said, "I hear blow jobs are better when you have no teeth."

Cat angled to face him, mouth open. "Did you just—"

"I'm sorry! I'm sorry! God, I'm such an ass." Micah put his head in his hands. He looked up and said, "You're going through all this, and all I could think of was to make a sex joke."

For a minute, Micah thought Cat was going to say something angry. Instead, the silence hung over them for another few seconds, and then he laughed. His whole body shook, and it was a long time before he calmed down and wiped at his eyes.

"Oh, my god. I'm sitting here, about to get fucking dentures, and you're talking about how hot it's going to be when I blow you." Cat leaned in and kissed Micah soundly. "This, honey, is why I love you." His face turned serious. "You make me feel like I'm still your sexy chipmunk."

"You are, beautiful, you really are." Micah ran a finger down Cat's cheek. "No matter what, you still get me so hot."

~ ** ~

Micah woke with a smile on his face. He'd been dreaming a sort of skewed version of the second story Cat had shared in his letter, and now it returned to Micah in full color. Instead of a stabbing, painful reminder of what he'd lost, it was a warm memory of what he'd had. There were so many little ways they'd cared for each other over the years, ways in which they'd both had the right words or the right gestures. He burrowed deeper under the blankets to enjoy his last few minutes of semi-wakefulness before rising.

His smile turned to laughter as Thomas head-butted him with a frustrated meow. Micah scratched between his ears, and Thomas kneaded his chest. The tiny claws pricked his skin through the thin cotton of his t-shirt, and Micah flinched.

"Ow! All right, mister. I'm getting up."

As though he understood, Thomas backed up and hopped off the bed. Micah followed to dish up the cat's breakfast before grabbing himself something to eat. Coffee cup at his side, Micah set to work. He had papers to grade and lessons to plan, but he needed to get the next part of the story out before he forgot what he'd dreamed. He was sure he had a way to tell it without writing any more graphic sex. It wasn't a matter of being embarrassed; he'd written plenty of sex scenes over the years. They were typically hazy on the details, but he wasn't bothered by writing them. When it came to Cat, though, he drew a line at the most sacred parts of their union.

He began to type, the words flowing almost exactly as they had in his dream. In a different way, he was writing about the very thing Cat had mentioned in his letter: trust. He only hoped his students would like the direction he took.

~ ** ~

Micah was still dressed for work when they went upstairs. He'd kept the tie on, even while they had dinner. Cat kept looking at him, and it was obvious he liked what he saw, but he also seemed confused. It wasn't the sort of thing Micah wanted to discuss over their meal; he felt strange enough as it was.

It was early, but Micah didn't want to lie around watching television in his work clothes. He held out his hand and invited Cat to follow him up the stairs. He sat down on the edge of the bed, and Cat came to stand between his knees. Looking down at him, Cat drew his fingertips over Micah's cheek. The lust in his expression was gone, replaced by worry.

"Please, honey, talk to me," Cat said. His voice was low, and his lip trembled. "You still scare me sometimes when you get like this."

"I promise I'm safe," Micah assured him. "I'm just nervous." He gave a breathy chuckle. "I know I shouldn't be, but I am."

Cat bent forward and kissed him. "It's okay. I've got you. Can you talk about it?"

"It's…it's something my therapist suggested this afternoon when I went to see him." Micah swallowed several times, trying to shove down the anxiety. He promised himself he wouldn't throw up this time—at some point, he had to be able to talk without expelling bodily fluids first.

"All right."

Micah knew Cat would at least try to understand. "He thinks I should let you blindfold me."

Cat frowned. "I'm not really into bondage. I could get hurt, and I'm definitely not a Dom."

"Not bondage." Micah shook his head. "I can't…it would trigger me if we went too far with it, even accidentally, since neither of us is experienced. My therapist suggested the blindfold so I have to rely on my other senses to experience making love with you." He closed his eyes as they welled up, the tension building in him just thinking about what this meant. "We need a safe word, even though it's just a blindfold. If I get scared…" He opened his eyes and looked up at Cat.

Cat's eyes were crinkled around the edges, still confused and concerned. "Okay, honey. If this is what you need, then it's what we'll do."

"Tonight?"

"Are you sure?"

Micah nodded. "If we don't, I'll freak, and we won't be able to." He was already shaking.

Cat stepped back. "What about our safe word?"

"Dr. Alberti suggested using stoplight colors. It's pretty familiar and easy to remember."

The concerned expression was back. Cat said, "You know that 'no' and 'stop' are perfectly good words."

"We can use those?" Micah frowned.

Lips twitching, Cat replied, "Of course we can. We don't have an agreement to ignore them. Your 'no' is always and forever good, and I trust you to listen when I say it."

Micah relaxed, feeling a thousand times less anxious than he had before. The formality and the implication that Cat might not respect him had put him on edge. "I like that."

Without another word, Cat loosened Micah's tie. When it was off, he climbed onto the bed to kneel behind Micah, gently covering his eyes with it. He knotted it at the back, and Micah felt the bed shift. In a moment, Cat's hands were on him again from the front, unbuttoning his shirt. Micah breathed slowly in an effort to calm his rapid heartbeat. He whimpered, and Cat paused, but Micah kept his mouth shut. He wouldn't stop them unless he absolutely had to.

When his shirt was off, Cat tugged at the hem of his undershirt, and Micah lifted his arms so Cat could extract it. The cool air in the room raised goosebumps, but he remained still. Cat's warm breath tickled the skin of his bare shoulder, and Micah inhaled sharply. All over his neck, shoulders, and chest, Cat placed hot but gentle kisses. They awakened Micah, and he grew aroused, but the feeling was accompanied by heightened anxiety. When Cat brushed against him, Micah felt how hard he was inside his pajama pants, and it made him groan and shudder.

"You do this to me," Cat said softly. "Only you."

He continued his ministrations for a few more minutes then urged Micah to lie back. After unfastening Micah's belt and his fly, he tugged until Micah raised his hips so Cat could draw his pants and underwear off. Cat carefully peeled off each sock until at last Micah lay stretched before him, utterly naked and utterly at Cat's mercy. His chest rose and fell with the shaky rhythm of his breathing, and he wanted to tear off the tie. He wanted to curl up and hide from Cat's gaze, to shift so he was face down against his pillow where he could let loose the heavy emotions. Instead, he repeated the words, "I am safe" over and over until he felt steadier. There would be time later to cry, and Cat would let him—he would hold him like he did so many times when they gave each other pleasure.

Cat didn't ask what to do. He simply used his hands and his mouth on every part of Micah's body, from the shells of his ears all the way to the tips of his toes. Cat kissed, licked, and sucked his way down Micah, over his lightly stubbled jaw to the hollow of his neck to his nipples. He dipped his tongue in Micah's navel before kissing his way back up and making a path down Micah's arm. He took Micah's hand and sucked on each of his fingers, then repeated the process on the other arm. He ran his tongue along Micah's side to his hip, leaving a cooling trail in his wake. Bypassing Micah's cock, he made his way down his thighs, over his knees, and to his feet. He gave Micah's toes the same treatment he'd given his fingers. At last, he shifted so his mouth was level with Micah's erection, and his hot breath puffed against the sensitive skin there.

Micah gasped and clenched his muscles. He twitched, a combination of desperate lust and overpowering anxiety stirring in him. He panted, whether from fear or arousal even he didn't quite know. To combat the terror, he used his other senses. First, he inhaled deeply through his nose, trying to catch Cat's scent. He found it: a warm, delicate smell tinged with the clean fragrance of his shampoo and soap. It was comforting and familiar, and Micah relaxed. It was his own Cat who was touching him, and Cat felt no shame in their sensual play.

Next, Micah opened his ears. He listened to the faint sounds of Cat's mouth wherever it landed on his skin. A slight pop or a tiny slurp, almost a smack. Everything was quiet and gentle. He heard Cat's breath as it hitched whenever Micah squirmed under his touch, and every now and again he caught a small, pleasurable hum. Cat was both turned on and enjoying making Micah feel good. It made Micah's eyes sting, but he held himself in check.

Giving in, Micah lost himself in the sensations—the damp patches on his skin from where Cat's lips and tongue touched; the chill as the air hit the spots and dried them; the fluttering sensations all over his body where Cat ran his hands; the ache in his cock and the tension in his balls as his need grew. As he turned himself over to the sheer pleasure of it all, Micah almost didn't register the sounds he was making until Cat ceased touching him.

"All right?" Cat's voice was soft and low.

"Oh, god. Oh, god," Micah managed. "Yeah…fucking keep going…" A cry escaped his lips, so desperate was he to keep going.

For a moment, nothing happened. Then the tip of his penis was engulfed in heat, and he arched off the bed. The sudden rush of pleasure and fear hit him all at once, and he cried out—not in ecstasy but with the need to make it stop. He felt for Cat and pushed when he connected with what he thought was a shoulder.

"Micah?" Cat's voice broke.

"N-no," Micah mumbled. Then louder, "*No*. I need to stop."

Cat let go of him, and a moment later, the blindfold was off. As soon as he could see, Micah connected with Cat and then rolled onto his side. He curled up with his knees to his chest, feeling like a failure. He wouldn't allow himself to cry; that was a reward for letting Cat make him vulnerable. Instead, he tried to focus on breathing through the shame. Why couldn't he have let Cat continue?

Warm arms wrapped around him, and Cat's chest pressed against his back. Cat laid soft kisses all over his neck and shoulder, in between murmuring, "Shh. It's okay." Cat wasn't angry with him, but Micah felt the waves of pain and confusion rolling off him. It wasn't that Micah had hurt him, only that Cat's heart was aching for him. He, too, knew what it was like to be afraid of touch.

After some time, the storm calmed, and Micah turned over. "I'm so sorry."

"No, honey. I told you—it's okay." Cat was silent for a minute. "That was too much at once. What was the therapist thinking we should accomplish?"

The use of "we" made Micah relax. "I have so much trouble being present and giving over control. Letting you make me come…" He tensed. "I have to trust you completely. He thought it might be easier if I couldn't see you. Less embarrassing."

"Oh." Cat shifted so he was draped over Micah. "I think I have an idea, if you want to hear it."

"All right."

Cat pushed himself up so he was looking down at Micah. "We should masturbate together."

Micah raised an eyebrow. "We already do that."

"No." Cat shook his head. "I don't mean touching each other. I mean lying next to each other, touching ourselves. You keep control, but you have to be open enough to me to let me see you make yourself feel good without my hand or mouth on you. It's less threatening because I'll be kind of…busy."

Micah let the idea sink in. It sounded like something he could manage. "We could try." He ran his fingers through Cat's silky hair.

"Good."

Cat moved so he lay on Micah's left, and Micah put an arm underneath and around him. Shifting a little, Cat rested his head on Micah's shoulder and his right hand on Micah's leg. He would have to use his non-dominant hand, but he didn't seem to care. The pause had made both of them lose most of their arousal, but it wouldn't take much to bring it back. Micah reached his shaking hand down to rest it between his legs at the same time Cat imitated him with his own.

Micah closed his eyes and focused only on touching himself. It felt good, both the stroking and the sense of being fully in control of what happened. He could stop any time, but he found he didn't want to. Beside him, Cat was making small sounds of his enjoyment that excited Micah in multiple ways. He loved Cat's noisy indications of his need. Micah sped up his hand, listening to Cat's moans and the slick sounds of their hands on their cocks.

He looked over to see Cat's eyes on him, watching the motion of his hand and then slowly inching his gaze upward to Micah's face. Cat's expression was a mix of concern, awe, and desire. For a moment, Micah faltered, feeling exposed. He wanted to bury himself in pleasing Cat, to distract him from watching. The urge passed as pleasure peaked in its intensity, and Micah knew he was almost there. He groaned, incapable of holding back.

"Shit…shit…shit…I'm—" Micah cut himself off with a moan, thrusting upward.

Cat panted beside him, and Micah kept rubbing until he stiffened and arched his back, his toes scrunching and his fingers curling, his orgasm burning a fiery path through him and out of his cock in long, thick spurts. He held still through the first wave, then undulated his hips through the smaller aftershocks. At last he lowered his ass back to the bed and relaxed against the pillows, eyes still closed and ears open to the sound of Cat giving himself over to his own climax.

"Fucking fuck," Micah growled when he could speak.

Turning onto his side, Cat touched Micah's cheek. "You didn't stop us this time," he remarked.

Micah looked at him, startled. No, he hadn't stopped them. He was awed and almost proud of himself. He hung on that thought for a moment before he let himself go and rolled to sob into the pillow. Cat curled against him, his chest to Micah's back.

"Honey, I've got you. You're okay. I promise."

Eventually, Micah wiped his eyes and turned over. "I love you so much," he said, his voice small.

"I love you too." Cat kissed him firmly. "I'm so incredibly proud of you."

Micah was still for a few seconds then said, "I want to try again. With the blindfold. Not tonight, but I'd like to be able to do that with you."

Cat ran a finger down Micah's cheek. "Okay. If it's something you want, I'm willing." He dropped the serious tone and said, "We can always go back to what we did after, though. Damn, that felt good."

Micah chuckled. "I got that impression. You were really into it."

The pink flush on Cat's cheeks deepened. "I could probably make a hobby out of jerking off. I've always liked to, even when I had someone to fuck around with. I didn't want you to feel bad because I don't ask you for sex every time I need it, so I didn't say anything before." He bit his lip. "No, that's not it, really. I didn't want you to think I was doing it because you wouldn't put out or something."

"Oh," Micah replied softly. "I might have been worried about it, but I'm not now."

"Good." Cat kissed him again.

They settled down in each other's arms, and Micah leaned so his head rested on Cat's shoulder. He had no idea anyone could be so patient and loving, nor did he know what he did to deserve it. He only knew he was grateful to God, fate, or the Universe itself for giving him the person with whom he was now entwined. Sleep descended, and he let it overtake him.

~ ** ~

This week, when Micah finished reading his chapter to the class, the room was full of noisy excitement. He didn't stop them; they were chattering about the plot twist involving the threat to He'chatul's peaceful kingdom and the magical training he was undertaking with Benjamin. Chris was looking at Micah thoughtfully. He usually didn't speak up during class, and Micah held his breath, waiting for what he was going to say.

"Their training sessions," Chris began. "They're...intimate, almost sensual, but there's nothing physical except the magic between them in those scenes."

Hope nodded. "I felt that too. It's actually better than if you'd written pages and pages of them having sex."

Micah chuckled. "I didn't read those parts out loud to you."

The rest of the class laughed. Dyl said, "Why not?"

Arching an eyebrow at him, Micah replied, "Some things should remain a mystery, at least for now."

Dyl shrugged. "I kind of wanted to hear it."

"You can wait until it's published. I don't think it's appropriate for this setting." Before Dyl could argue more, Micah addressed the class as a whole. "Let's call it a night. Stop up here and pick up this week's list of writing prompts, and next week, you'll be able to share what you did with it. Anything is fair game, as long as you incorporate the prompt in some way. I'll leave it to you to be creative with that."

He set a stack of papers on the corner of the desk, and everyone picked one up as they filed past. When Jude grabbed hers, Micah stopped her before she could escape out the door.

"Hey," he said. "How'd it go helping Debbie out with her yard work?"

"Good." Jude looked at him pointedly. "I'm going over on Friday after work to help her rake and talk about living arrangements. Just how much did you have to do with that?"

He laughed. "Not much. I invited her over and introduced you. I told you, I'm not a matchmaker in any sense. Or not a very good one, anyway."

"No," Jude agreed. "You did pretty well, though. I thought you were setting me up with Sienna."

Micah winced. "Not exactly. I thought you might prefer to hang out with some people your own age rather than mine. Although..." He tilted his head.

"Nope. We're just friends," Jude said, but she grinned. "I did meet this super cute hairdresser she knows. She's totally my type, too." She leaned in conspiratorially. "I might ask her out next time we're all together."

"Sounds like you're settling in."

"I am. Hey, great class tonight. I really liked what you did with the story." Jude tossed the paper in her bag and slung it over her shoulder. "I'll see you Saturday."

"Speaking of that," Micah said. He cleared his throat. "I, uh, promised you could look at that cello I have. Did you want to stop by after you're done at Debbie's?"

"Yeah," Jude said. She studied Micah for a moment, making him feel as though she could see right inside him and read all the complex feelings he had about giving away another of Cat's possessions. "I would like that very much."

"All right. I'll see you then."

She walked out, turning in the doorway to give him another brief glance. He smiled and gave her a tiny wave, which she returned. Once she was gone, Micah distracted himself from the creeping guilt and sadness by tidying the room and gathering his things. By this time Saturday, he'd be able to tick off one more box on his list, and he couldn't decide how he felt about it.

CHAPTER SIXTEEN

THEY WILL LIVE, EVEN THOUGH THEY DIE

MICAH HAD his hands in bread dough when he heard the knock on his door. Thomas, who had been staring at him from on top of the refrigerator, expertly jumped from surface to surface until he hit the floor. Micah pulled his hands out and wiped them off.

"I wish you could answer the door," he muttered as he traipsed into the foyer. He let Jude in, apologizing for the state of the kitchen.

"No problem," she said. "It smells great, by the way. I finished up at Debbie's. She's on her way over. I hope you don't mind."

"Not at all. I told her to stop by so we could all have dinner after you two were through." Micah waved a hand at the living room. "Make yourself comfortable while I finish the dough. You want a drink?" he called on his way out of the room.

"Water's fine," Jude answered. "But it can wait until you're done."

He finished as quickly as he could and brought two glasses back in with him. Jude was standing by the bookshelf, looking over the titles. Micah didn't have anywhere near as many as Chris, but he had the one shelf. He preferred eBooks, and so had Cat, so they'd had an impressive collection between them. Micah had given away most of Cat's trashy romance novels, but he'd saved one which Cat had particularly liked. It had a hunky-but-cheesy pirate on the cover. That was the one Jude currently had her hand on, and she was obviously trying to suppress her laughter.

"Go ahead," Micah said. "You can make fun of the book. It's not even mine—it was Cat's."

She gave him an incredulous look. "He was into pirate bondage books?"

Micah snorted. "Not really. He was basically into anything with enough sex in it." Realizing he might have said too much, Micah flushed. "Sorry."

"It's fine." Jude grinned. "I can't decide what to make of that."

Frowning as something occurred to him, Micah said, "Wait...how did you know what the book was about?"

It was Jude's turn to blush. "I've read that one."

"But...you...what?" Micah burst out laughing.

"Don't tell me you never read any lesbian fiction," she said.

"Well, yeah, but I...never mind." He took the book from her hand and reshelved it. He eyed Jude sideways. "Unless you want to borrow it."

"No, thanks." Jude's gaze came to rest on the book Micah had borrowed from Chris but had yet to try reading. "Huh," she said. "This book changed my life."

"Yeah?" Micah stepped away from her and sat down in the recliner.

Jude put the book down and perched on the couch. "I'm not really sure what I believe anymore," she said. "For a while, I wanted to try to still be a good Christian and be a lesbian. Not change who I am or be celibate or anything, just still go to church and try to follow Jesus properly and stuff." She sighed.

"But?" Micah prompted.

"It's complicated." Jude was silent for a while. "Minister's daughter. And Dad's hard-line. Mom's a mouse, and she never defended me. I'm the second youngest of six, and I'm pretty sure my younger brother is queer. He never says it, but he's left clues for me specifically, like he wants to come out to me and can't. My older sister is married, and she confided in me last year that she's bi but mainly interested in men." Jude paused. "Is that weird? Three of us in the same family? Especially when our family is so messed up."

"No," Micah said. "Not weird." He thought about his mother's relationship with Debbie and about Jeremiah's awakening sense of himself, though Micah didn't dare pin a label on it until and unless Jeremiah did. His mind wandered to Pam and Cooper, then to his other friends and family. Many had queer relatives, and many did not; there didn't seem to be any predictability to it at all.

"Anyway," Jude said, freeing Micah from his thoughts, "I read that book, and it made me see I didn't have to choose my parents' way or my way. I'm not sure what I'd call myself now, but I don't care about the rules-bound crap my parents force-fed me."

"I suppose that makes sense. I'm not religious at all, and I don't care much about any of it. Chris let me borrow it because I asked him what it meant." Micah didn't want the conversation to turn heavy, so he stood and set his glass on the coffee table. "Come on. I'll show you the cello."

He led her into Cat's old room, where he'd set out the cello. Cat's handwritten sheet music, which Micah had brought down from the attic, lay on the bed. Jude crossed the room to the cello case and ran her hand down it.

"Go ahead," Micah urged. "Open it up. You'll want to have a look. It hasn't been played in years, and it probably needs...whatever instruments need, I guess. New strings, maybe?"

Jude popped the latches and looked inside at the beautiful instrument. "It's a hybrid," she said, glancing back at Micah for confirmation.

"Yes. It's specially made. The former owner of the shop in the village used to make them."

"I can't take this," Jude said. "It's too much. Do you know how expensive these are? At least let me get the money together to pay you."

Micah shook his head. "I'm not selling it. Cat left me instructions not to—how did he put it? Oh, yes—let him 'sit on my shelf collecting dust and sadness,' I think. He would've wanted me to give it to you."

Jude still looked conflicted, but she nodded. "Can I play it?"

"Sure. It's meant to be played either acoustically or amplified. I have everything you need."

She pulled a chair from the desk and sat down. With the cello resting against her shoulder, she tightened the bow and ran the rosin over the hair. She poised, ready to play, when her gaze drifted to the bed.

"What's that?"

"Some sheet music from the attic."

"Can I see?"

Micah handed her the book, and she thumbed through it. She selected something and set the book aside for the moment. First, she spent a long while tuning. Then she ran some scales. She urged a good sound out of the instrument, despite its years of disuse.

Looking up at Micah, she said, "It's got a nice tone. Definitely needs new strings, but that's easy."

She turned her attention to the book, which Micah propped for her on the music stand he dragged out of the closet. A moment later, the melody flowed around them, low and sweet then soaring to high and plaintive. Jude stumbled on a few measures, but her reading was good, and she made the cello sing. It took a bit before Micah recognized the song. It was one of the first ones he'd ever heard Cat play, something he'd written on the spur of the moment. By the time Jude reached the piece's climax, Micah had to sit down, unable to contain his overflowing emotions. Jude finished the piece and looked over at him.

"I'm sorry," she said. "I didn't mean—"

He held up his hand. "It's all right." He smiled at her, but he knew it was weak. "You couldn't have known."

"Known what?"

"He—Cat—wrote that piece. He wrote all the ones in the book."

Micah lost it, burying his head in his hands. He felt the bed dip, and Jude's arms were around him. He leaned on her, and he heard her sniffle. They were still like that when the sound of the front door startled them both. A moment later, Debbie appeared in the doorway.

"Did I interrupt something?" she asked as she took in the scene.

Jude wiped her eyes and sat up straighter. Micah reached for a tissue from the nightstand and handed one to Jude as well.

"It's fine," Micah said. "Jude was trying out Cat's old cello."

"Ah, my dears."

Debbie joined them on the bed at Micah's other side, putting an arm around him and squeezing. She gripped Jude's hand with her free one. No one said anything for a long time.

Eventually, Micah shifted, and the women let go of him. "I think it's been long enough I can put the dough in the oven. I should have dinner ready shortly."

He stood, and the others followed suit. They made their way into the kitchen, and Micah put the finishing touches on the loaves while he preheated the oven. He had dinner in the slow-cooker, and Debbie peered through the glass lid at it.

"You've made enough for several families," she remarked.

"It's a big recipe." Micah sighed. "Tomorrow, I'm taking some next door, and then I'll bring the leftovers around for Jones and Alonzo."

Debbie nodded. "How are they?"

Micah shook his head, and she acknowledged what he wasn't saying. Winter was coming, and there was no doubt in Micah's mind that one or both of them would have a rough time getting through it. Debbie gripped his arm lightly, and he kissed her cheek.

"You're a good man, Micah," she said as she turned to help Jude set the table.

~ ** ~

Micah stretched out in bed next to Cat. It had been a long day, and he was worried. Cat had barely spoken at dinner, which was unlike him. Micah was used to having Cat be the one to carry the conversation. He would talk animatedly about something-or-other or wax enthusiastic about a new book or share something new he'd learned. It had been less and less lately. The winter had been hard on him, leaving him exhausted, and he hadn't regained his full strength even though the weather had been warm and sunny for some time.

Cat lay on his side, facing away from Micah. When Micah placed a hand on his shoulder, he shrugged it off. Micah withdrew, worried that Cat was in pain again. His shoulder had been bothering him on and off. Letting his hand hover, Micah debated touching him somewhere else. He refrained, dropping his hand to the bed between them.

"Talk to me," he said softly.

There was a long silence, and after a while, Cat's back shook. He took tiny, shuddering breaths, barely audible. Alarmed, Micah propped himself up. It wasn't like Cat to sob like that; he wasn't much of a crier—that was normally Micah's territory.

"Cat, please," Micah begged. "Tell me what happened."

He heard Cat's sniffles as he brought himself back under control. At last Cat rolled over, his face wet and his eyes red and swollen. Micah reached out and brushed Cat's red-gold hair away from his forehead, keeping his touch light.

"I went to see Dr. Stern," Cat said.

Dr. Stern was his hematologist. He was semi-retired, but he'd kept Cat as one of his few patients. Micah had been urging Cat to see him when his symptoms didn't improve after the weather changed. Glad Cat had heeded his advice, Micah nodded.

"What did he say?"

Cat didn't answer immediately. When he finally did, it took everything Micah had not to react. "It's...bad." Cat shuddered. "I'm dying, honey."

At first, Micah panicked. He'd known it was coming, and he wasn't ready. A moment later, he had the urge to laugh. Cat had been dying, more or less, for the entire nine years they'd known each other. "What's Dr. Stern's plan?" he asked, keeping his voice calm.

Cat's mouth dropped open, and then he snapped it shut. He frowned. "I don't think you understand."

Micah scoffed. "We've been through this several times. What's changed?"

"Don't," Cat snapped. "Don't do this. It's hard enough as it is."

Micah recoiled. Something more was going on, and antagonizing Cat wouldn't get it out of him. "Just tell me, then."

"My heart, my kidneys, my liver…I have multiple organ systems failing. That's why I'm always in pain and short of breath."

Swallowing, Micah tried to control his fear. "What's Dr. Stern's plan?" he repeated, hoping for something to hang onto.

"Nothing," Cat said, shrugging.

"What do you mean, nothing?"

"Exactly that. The plan is to make me comfortable." Cat sighed. "I'm hardly a candidate for transplants, and definitely not more than one. I'm tired of fighting. My body is tired. I hung on as long as I could, but it's time to let go." He choked.

"Baby? What is it?" Micah reached out for him again, and this time, Cat settled against him.

"I'm so selfish," Cat mumbled through his tears. "I'm sorry."

Micah brushed at Cat's cheeks, collecting the drops. "No, sweetheart. You've been nothing but generous. How could you say that?"

"I always told you I was okay with this," Cat said. "Even now, I said I have to let go. But…" He trailed off, drawing his lip between his teeth. "I don't want to. I want to stay with you forever. I'm not ready for it to be over—to say goodbye to you."

~ ** ~

Micah woke the next morning with a heavy heart, fragments of another dream about Cat clinging to him. Slowly, he packed the leftover food into containers. Once he was ready to go, he bagged up the food and headed first to LR's house. She opened the door and let him in to witness the usual Saturday morning chaos. Emily was playing—loudly—with Robbie on the kitchen floor. Langston was descending the stairs in a princess gown and a pair of LR's good shoes, singing the big song from the latest Disney movie. Maya was nowhere to be found. She had Micah's sympathies; he would've hidden too.

LR must have sensed Micah wasn't in the mood for their antics. She took the bag from him, delivered a quick hug and a thanks in return, and let him go. He returned to his car and drove into town. Jones and Alonzo had moved into a small senior neighborhood where they wouldn't have to worry about taking care of a house and yard. Alonzo hadn't been doing well, and Micah figured they had more use for the leftovers than he did.

He pulled into their short driveway and got out of the car. One of their neighbors was out walking her tiny poodle, and she waved to Micah. He waved back as he rang the doorbell. Jones answered, and his face broke into a tired grin.

"Micah! What's all this?" he asked, gesturing to the bag.

"I made dinner for about four times as many people as I had in my house last night. Thought I'd bring you some so you don't have to cook for a couple of days."

Jones let him in, and Micah brought the bag into the kitchen. He unloaded the containers into the fridge while Jones put on the coffee pot. Micah sat down at the kitchen table, and a few minutes later, Jones brought their coffee and joined him.

"How are you doing these days?" Jones asked. "Heard you're working hard at the community center."

"Mm-hm," Micah said. "Teaching a class. You should take it next term."

Jones chuckled. "No, thanks. I do get down there occasionally for retirees basketball, but that's about it." His smile faltered. "I don't like to be away for too long."

Micah nodded. "How is he?"

"Good days and bad days. You know how it is."

"I do." Micah reached out to grip his hand.

Jones looked away, out the window at something in the tiny back yard. When he returned his gaze to Micah, he looked as lost as Micah had felt from the moment Cat told him he was dying for real, not in an abstract sense.

"I miss him," Jones said, and Micah knew he wasn't talking about Cat. "Already. Those days when he can't remember who I am...damn it." Jones put a hand to his forehead and slumped over. "He was my rock. Who do I lean on now?"

"I know," Micah said. "Believe me, I know."

While they sat sipping their coffee in silence, Alonzo shuffled in. He was still in his striped pajama pants and a worn sweatshirt. Micah looked to Jones, not sure what kind of day Alonzo was having. Jones lifted one shoulder a little, enough to let Micah know he wasn't sure either. They watched Alonzo pour himself a cup of orange juice and carry it over to the table. He looked at Jones and then at Micah.

"Morning, love. Hello, Micah." A better day, then. "What are you doing here so early?"

Micah relaxed. "I'm in town for a class at the community center. I'm not sure if I mentioned I'm learning to cook."

Alonzo laughed. "You? Well, all right then."

"Hey, I'm not so bad anymore. I made too much food last night, so I brought you guys some of the leftovers."

"Good, good." Alonzo was quiet for a moment then looked back and forth between the others. "What's the plan for the day? You sticking around, Micah?"

Micah glanced at Jones again. "Uh...no. I'm going to my cooking class. But I'll hang out for a while before I leave. That okay?"

"Sure, sure." Alonzo looked down at himself. "Maybe I should go get dressed."

Just as Micah was about to say it was all right, Jones said, "I put some clothes out on the chair for you."

"Thanks, love." Alonzo gripped Jones's shoulder briefly as he passed, shuffling back to the bedroom and leaving his orange juice untouched on the table. Jones gazed after him.

Once the bedroom door was closed, Jones said in a low voice, "Today's not so bad."

Micah's only response was to take Jones's hand again as he watched him struggle to hold it together.

CHAPTER SEVENTEEN

THIS SON OF MINE WAS DEAD

WHEN MICAH woke, he was stiff from sleeping with the cat at his back. Thomas was still behind him, but he stretched and hopped off the bed as soon as Micah moved. He disappeared out of the room. Micah arose, still a little sleep-foggy. He had a slight headache and an unsettled feeling he couldn't place. Rubbing his tired eyes, he picked up his phone from the nightstand and cringed when he saw the date. That explained his unease.

How had it slipped his mind that Cat's death-iversary was approaching? Had he been that busy? Yet here it was, the day. He sat back down on the recliner and rubbed his aching forehead. It was Saturday, which meant his therapist wasn't in the office. He was available for video chat, but Micah didn't think it would help for some reason. They had a standing agreement that Micah was welcome to talk on Death Day, and yet he'd never taken the offer. Monday, and his regular appointment, was soon enough.

Micah didn't want to be alone, though. Later, he would have dinner with LR and her family as they did every year. She would spend the earlier part of the day with her parents while Jamal took the kids to do something fun. The previous two years, Micah had made the drive up to Rochester to see Zayne, but he hadn't made plans with her this time. He had class at the community center, and he hadn't done anything to rearrange his schedule.

He scrolled his contacts and paused on Jude's number. She knew about Cat, and there was no pressure with her. He called her. "Hey," he said when she picked up. "What are you up to this morning?"

"Going to get my first tattoo!" she said, sounding both excited and nervous.

"Ah, okay." Disappointed that she had plans, Micah thought to change the subject and save himself the embarrassment of explaining why he'd called.

"Are you busy? You want to come with me?"

"Uh...sure."

"Great! I was going to call around to see who was free, but you've now saved me the trouble." She laughed.

"You don't want it to be one of your other friends?" Micah considered himself an odd choice, as the most he'd ever done was get his ears pierced.

"Nah," Jude replied. "Always good to have family with you. Uh...even if they're just coworkers. Right?"

Confused by what she'd just said, Micah replied, "I suppose."

"Good. Now that's settled, why did you call?"

"Um." Micah took a few seconds to collect himself. "It'll sound weird."

"Creepy-weird or normal-weird?"

"You tell me." Micah chuckled, losing some of his tension. "It's the anniversary of Cat's death, and I don't want to be alone. I was going to call around to see who was free."

"Ah, I see. Works out for both of us, then. Meet me in town? We can grab something to eat at that cute little cafe, too."

"Sweet Beans? Sure. See you soon."

They ended the call, and Micah hurried to feed the cat and get ready to go. Thomas polished off his breakfast, but he didn't follow Micah around. He returned to his room, and Micah left him staring out the window into the yard, probably imagining himself chasing all the birds.

After breakfast at Sweet Beans—without Audrey, who had taken the day off, but with her co-owner and her nosy questions—they headed for the tattoo and piercing place. Regal Ink, like many local shops, had been a family-owned business since long before Micah moved to Concordia. Micah and Jude stepped inside, and Micah was drawn right away to the jewelry case.

They always had a lot of religious items. The owner's family was Catholic, and he handmade rosaries. He'd made Cat's pot leaf and magnetic earrings as well as the jade ones they'd worn for their wedding. Although Micah hadn't spent much time in there, it brought up a lot of memories of his life with Cat. Today, they felt easier to bear as he half-listened to Jude going over what she wanted done.

There was a pair of earrings he liked, right at the front. They were round tiger's eye studs, wire-wrapped with sterling silver. Micah tried to picture them on himself, and it almost made him laugh. Then he imagined what they'd look like on Chris, who nearly always had earrings in. They would look good on him, a nice complement to his caramel-colored eyes.

Jude interrupted his thoughts. "Time to go in," she said.

It was the younger of the owner's daughters, Evvie, who did the actual inking. Micah stood by, letting Jude grip his arm while the young woman worked. Once or twice, he was sure Jude would leave a permanent mark on him. The whole process took a lot less time than he'd been expecting, and before he knew it, Jude was done.

"What'd you get?" Micah asked. Her wrist was covered with a bandage, so he couldn't see it.

"Here," Jude said. She held out the card she'd brought to show the artist. "It's similar, but not identical. Mine doesn't have color."

It was a dandelion with the seeds blowing off. As they floated away, they turned first into butterflies and then a bird. It was nice, and Micah thought it suited Jude perfectly.

"I like it. You know, that's the first time I've ever seen anyone get a tattoo." He still couldn't fathom why Jude wanted him there in the first place.

"Yeah?" She grinned. "Does that mean it's your turn next? I'll come with you."

"Hell, no!" Micah exclaimed. "To the tattoo, not to your coming with me."

She shrugged. "Anything else before we go?"

"Actually..." Micah stepped up to the counter. "I'd like those tiger's eye earrings," he told Evvie.

"Oh, those are my favorite," she said as she pulled them out of the case. "Dad did a nice job with them."

Jude eyed Micah. "You have pierced ears?"

"Yes." He didn't want to tell her he was considering them for someone else.

The thought made him suddenly and overwhelmingly sad. Watching Jude get her tattoo had distracted him from dwelling on the reason he'd wanted company, and he felt wrong for buying a possible gift for a man he wasn't dating on the anniversary of his spouse's death. He stood frozen to the spot, no longer able to move even to make his purchase. He was aware of both women's eyes on him, but he couldn't unlock his body.

"Micah?" Jude asked softly.

That did it. His muscles unclenched, and immobility was replaced with surging pulse, nausea, and a desperate need for oxygen. "I have to get out of here."

He slapped money on the counter, not caring that it was too much for the earrings, and took off without the box. He needed air and some distance between himself and the shop. Wandering away a short distance, he leaned against the corner of the building to collect himself.

Maybe he should have called his therapist after all. He'd been distracted while Evvie worked on Jude, but now he was back where he would've been had he stayed home alone. He fought it, not wanting to entirely lose his shit in the middle of the sidewalk on a busy Saturday morning. The hand on his arm startled him, and he looked up to see not Jude but Chris. Micah shuddered, but he was determined not to vomit all over the person who had been on his mind when the anxiety began.

"Micah? You don't look so good. Can I help?"

A moment later, Jude appeared from inside the shop. "You left this," Jude said, holding up a bag which must've contained the jewelry box. "You okay?"

He shook his head, and within seconds, the two of them were on either side of him. They led him back inside the shop, and Evvie pulled up a chair. She stepped away to get some water. She handed the bottle to Micah, but he didn't take it. Chris accepted it and set it on the floor when he knelt down. He put his hand on Micah's arm, and Jude rubbed soothing circles on his shoulder. Micah took slow, deep breaths until he finally calmed down.

To her credit, Evvie didn't try to intervene. She moved around them, letting Chris and Jude take care of Micah. Chris picked up the water, and Micah took it this time.

"What happened?" Jude asked.

"P-panic attack," Micah managed. "I get them from time to time, but it's been months since the last one." He closed his eyes, embarrassed but reminding himself these were his friends. "I'm sorry."

"Any idea what brought it on?" Chris asked.

"Yes, but I don't want to discuss it here." He couldn't tell Chris it was the earrings; that would lead to an entirely different kind of discomfort.

"That's fair." Chris stood.

"What are you doing here?" Jude asked Chris. "That was...completely random, actually."

Chris cringed. "I was meeting with a congregant and their wedding planner. The ceremony isn't for months, but apparently it's complicated. We'd just finished, and I happened by." He turned to Micah. "Are you feeling any better?"

"Much, thanks."

"Do you need to go home?" Jude asked.

"No. I—" He looked between them then addressed Jude. "I'm still planning to go to class. I could use the distraction."

"Understandable," she said.

Chris frowned slightly, but he nodded. "I'm on my way there. See you in a bit." He touched Micah's shoulder, and his hand lingered before he gave a squeeze and released his grip.

"Come on," Jude said. "I'll walk with you to our cars." She

handed him the bag. "Don't forget this. Your change is in there."

Micah looked at it, hesitating before reaching out and taking the bag. He was sure he could find someone who might like the earrings after all. Bidding Evvie goodbye, he followed Jude out of the shop.

Micah's performance in class was less than stellar. The recipe tasted all right, but it didn't look great. He'd been too distracted and missed a step, having to correct it later. By the time class ended, he was annoyed as well as still being on edge from the morning. He packed up his things and tried to figure out what he was going to do with the rest of his day.

He might have gone to see Debbie, but Jude had checked on him and was already on her way over there. Micah didn't want to intrude, and he also didn't feel like having both of them all over him. Almost everyone was busy. He regretted not planning ahead to see Zayne, and he wondered what had made him think he could manage on his own.

Shouldering his bag, he stepped out of the room and nearly collided with Chris. "Sorry," he said. It came out more snippy than he'd intended, and he backtracked. "That was rude of me. I apologize."

"It's all right. I came to see how you were doing."

Something in his tone and words irritated Micah, as though Chris was playing pastor with him. He kept a lid on his frustration long enough to say, "You didn't have to do that."

Chris's frown was more sad and confused than angry. "I know I didn't. You haven't seemed like yourself today, and I thought maybe you'd like to...I don't know. Go somewhere quieter. To talk?"

"You don't have to counsel me. I'm not one of your congregants." Micah tried to step around him.

Catching his arm, Chris said, "Is that what you thought?"

"Yeah, I guess so."

"First of all, I don't offer therapy. Second, I'm doing this as your friend, not as your minister."

Micah let out a sigh and leaned against the wall. "I'm sorry. Again."

"No need." Chris paused. "Can you tell me what's going on?"

"It's the anniversary. Cat died exactly three years ago today."

"Ah, I'm so sorry." Chris's hand on Micah's arm was warm and comforting. "And you're here instead of at home."

"I didn't want to be alone today." Micah sniffled, but he held it together for the most part. "You know what I usually do? I go visit my friend Zayne and sit on her couch, eating ice cream and talking about him."

Chris stepped back. "You could come over. I probably have some cookie dough ice cream, and my couch is pretty comfy."

Micah stared at him for several seconds before he completely lost it. He sank down onto the floor and drew his knees up, covering his face as he bawled. He could almost feel the shock coming off Chris as he sat down too, pulling Micah closer.

"Sh," he murmured. "I've got you."

"I-it was his favorite," Micah blubbered. "C-cookie dough. He couldn't have the real stuff. Lactose intolerant. Made him really sick. Oh my god, I miss him."

Micah sobbed in Chris's arms for a long time. No one but family—which included Pam and Zayne—had seen him like this. Woven in with his grief was shame and the fear he was placing too much of a burden on Chris by asking him to stay. He took several gulping breaths and tried to stem his tears. At last he had enough control that he could sit upright. Chris kept an arm around him and reached into his jacket with his free hand. He passed Micah a packet of tissues.

"God. I'm sorry, for the third time. You don't need me going on like this." Micah wiped his face.

"It's really all right. Why don't you ever talk about him?"

Micah shrugged. "I'm never sure when is the right time or how much is too much. I'm not even always sure when I need to. Grief is...weird."

"It can be," Chris agreed. "Do you want to go somewhere? This is an important day. If you need to talk about Cat, I'm here."

"I'd like that." Micah pushed himself off the floor and picked up his bag. "Meet you in town?"

"You got it."

Chris was waiting for him by his car when Micah arrived. They walked up Main Street, looking for a place. Micah didn't want to go in Sweet Beans, even though it was the most convenient. There were too many reasons why he couldn't take it at the moment.

On the way, a group of teenage girls passed. Only one of them said hello to Chris. The rest all waved and called a cheerful, "Hi, Mr. Forbes!" to Micah. A woman hanging a string of lights in one of the shop windows called out a greeting, and two nearly-grown young men gave him fist bumps on their way down the street. Chris chuckled, and Micah turned to look at him, amused by Chris's reaction.

"What?" he asked.

Chris grinned. "You accused me of knowing everyone, and yet all these people said hello to you and not me."

Micah shrugged, but he smiled. "I've taught almost everyone in this town between the ages of eleven and twenty-three."

"Small towns certainly have their own charm, eh?"

"They do."

Micah and Chris entered a small waterfront grill. While they waited for their order, it was Micah's turn to tease Chris when a family stopped to say hello to him. He looked at Micah sheepishly, and after the family left, they stifled their laughter behind their fists.

"What was that about small towns?" Micah asked.

"I'll never get used to this," Chris replied.

"You will. I grew up in a big suburb, and it took me a few years to get the hang of everyone knowing my business."

Chris gave a dramatic sigh. "I'm from the city. I have no idea how any of this works."

There was music playing in the background, and a mellow version of an older song came on. Chris glanced up. "Wow. It makes me feel old hearing this played elevator-style. It was popular when I was in high school thirty years ago."

"I remember this one too, though I think I was in college at the time. I seem to recall a very, very good make-out session to this soundtrack."

"Oh, yes. Although...I was kind of weird. My first real girlfriend and I—" His face went tomato-red. "We had sex in the dorm room with her Newsboys mix tape in."

Micah's mouth dropped open. He hooted. "Okay, you may have me beat. My first time was with my best friend, who I thought was a boy at the time. We were listening to Amy Grant."

"Her voice is damn sexy," Chris blurted then blushed again.

"There's a reason she always had a loyal following of queer folks." Micah pondered what Chris had said. "Newsboys, eh? I think I had you down as slightly more nineties hipster than that."

"Oh, I was," Chris assured him. "I was a pretty awkward teen. I mean, we all were, but I kept trying to be sort of a soft butch. I couldn't figure out why I still felt out of place, even among girls who dressed or acted that way. I thought I was crushing on my flannel-and-jeans-clad male youth leaders, like any good church girl. I mean, I probably was, but it took years before I figured out I wanted to be them, not be with them. Even after I realized I was a man, I still thought I had to relate to certain 'guy things.' It was a long time until I felt okay about wearing jewelry or polishing my nails again." He rubbed his head and smiled. "Not growing my hair out, though. I never had a lot to begin with, but going bald was a little surprising."

"It looks nice on you," Micah said. It was his turn to flush. "I don't know what that feels like, discovering your gender. It's nothing I ever had to consider. It was different, being with Cat. He was so comfortable in who he was. He never liked words for his gender. He used to sometimes say he was a genderfuck, but I'm pretty sure it's because he liked the word 'fuck.'"

Chris snickered. "That sounds like him, from what you've told me and the little bit I remember of him." He put his hand on top of Micah's, and his expression turned serious. "It really is all right to talk about him. I'm listening. That's why we're here."

Their food arrived, and as they ate, Micah talked. Somehow, in recounting stories of their time together, Micah felt less lonely and sorrowful. He wasn't limited to Cat's years of worsening health or rehashing his last moments. Micah was free to share the small things that shaped their life together. Chris listened, occasionally throwing in a comment or two but mostly letting Micah get it all out. When he'd said as much as he felt he could, he felt different. Lighter, as though he'd been carrying around the entire weight of another person on his shoulders and now the burden was gone.

It took all the way until they'd paid their bill and walked to their cars for Micah to realize Chris had never once let go of his hand during their meal.

They were inside a car. Not Micah's car nor Cat's truck. It was unfamiliar, and Micah could smell the new material of the seats. There were people in the front seat, arguing about something that didn't make any sense to Micah. The woman turned around, and Micah stared at his mother. The man in the driver's seat kept his face turned away, staring at the road. They weren't moving, but everyone seemed to be acting as though they were.

Cat put his hand on Micah's face and turned his head so they were looking at each other. He held out his free hand, in which there was a gold box. He put it into Micah's hands and closed his fingers around it.

"This is for you," he said.

"What is it?"

"Sh," Cat whispered. "It's a secret."

"I can't take it," Micah told him, all of a sudden feeling it to be true.

"Yes, you can." Cat kissed him. "You'll know what you need to do when the time comes, honey."

"When what time comes?" Micah demanded, but the dream was already fading.

Micah woke with a start, a damp nose pressed up against his. Thomas chirruped, and Micah groaned. He looked at the clock on the nightstand. It read three-thirty-one. He flung an arm over his eyes and muttered, "G'way" at the cat.

Fragments of the dream remained at the forefront, and Micah tried to make sense of it. He had been dreaming of Cat, but not anything related to the letters or his real memories of their life together. *You'll know what you need to do when the time comes.* What had Cat meant by it? Except it was only a dream; he hadn't meant anything by it because he hadn't really said it. Micah turned over and tried to go back to sleep.

Thomas was persistent, though, so after several minutes of

resisting, Micah emerged from under the covers. He shivered and threw on a sweatshirt and thick socks. Thomas led him out of the bedroom and down the stairs, where he sat facing the door. Unsurprised, Micah opened the door. Usually, Micah let him out in the morning and evening, leaving him stocked with food, water, and fresh litter in the box before he left for school. Lately, Thomas had been demanding to be let out more often.

It was a clear, chilly night. Thomas prowled around the shrubs for a while before going and sitting in the driveway, facing out into the darkened street. Micah looked up at the sky, wrapping his arms around himself. The moon had dipped low, hiding behind the trees across the road, and only a few wispy clouds drifted past to obscure the sparkling stars. Micah's breath was visible in smoky puffs. He curled his toes, the cold seeping into his socks from the concrete stoop.

After a few minutes, he called to Thomas softly. The cat looked back at him, eyes gleaming in the dark driveway, but he didn't move. With a sigh, Micah retreated into the house. Thomas would scratch at the door when he wanted to come back in, and Micah didn't want to stand there freezing his ass off while he waited.

He thought about getting some more writing done, but his eyes were dry and tired from lack of sleep. Anything he put down would only need to be edited out later for its incoherence. Instead, he lay on the couch. He debated turning on some relaxing music, but his thoughts kept returning to the dream, turning it over and over in his mind.

The next thing he was aware of was the light scratching at the door. He blinked and sat up, rubbing his eyes. The scratching became more insistent, and Micah went to the door to let Thomas back in. The cat stalked past him, bringing a draft of cold air into the house. Hurriedly, Micah shut the door. Thomas hopped up on the recliner, indicating he wasn't going back upstairs any time soon. He stood there, unblinking. Waiting.

Micah looked at the clock in the kitchen, surprised to see it was nearly five-thirty. "Oh, all right," he said to Thomas. "I guess we can sleep down here."

He retrieved his phone and set it on the table beside him before settling into the recliner with Thomas purring away on his chest. As he drifted off again, Cat's words floated to the surface. *You'll know what you need to do when the time comes.* If only he knew what that was.

CHAPTER EIGHTEEN

I GIVE ETERNAL LIFE TO THEM

THE SECRETARY left a message for Micah to call Jeremiah, his oldest brother, during his planning period. Despite having grades to enter into the system, a stack of quizzes for review, and adjustments he needed to make to the next day's lessons, he picked up his phone. Jeremiah knew he would be working and wouldn't have called if it weren't important.

Jeremiah's voice was flat, no hint of sadness. "Elijah's dead."

It figured Elijah would die on the anniversary of Cat's funeral. It was even the same day of the week Cat died. It was almost anticlimactic. Micah had expected that one day, he would hear the news and feel something. Not grief, but at least a sense of relief or closure. Instead, he felt as though Jeremiah had told him nothing more than that it might rain on Friday.

"All right."

"That's it?" Jeremiah sounded incredulous. "You're not even going to ask what happened?"

"Would you like it better if I pretend I care?" Micah snapped. He wished he could take it back. His brothers hadn't been close in years, but they were only two years apart, much closer in age than either of them was to Micah. They'd grown up as each other's first friend. Elijah's death would have hit some kind of nerve with Jeremiah, and even if Micah no longer had any interest, Jeremiah likely did. If nothing else, he would have been saddened over Elijah's failure to show love or kindness.

"Yes, I might prefer it over your immaturity here," Jeremiah replied. "I understand you weren't fond of each other. You could show some compassion for his family, at least."

"I don't even know them, remember? I met his wife a handful of times, and even when I was trying to be the perfect son and cure my sinful lusts, they didn't like their kids being around me. I never met a single one of my nieces and nephews. Excuse me while I don't bother."

There was no mistaking Jeremiah's exasperation. "Fine, then. There's a funeral on Saturday, which they've informed me is my job. Are you coming?"

"No," Micah said. He didn't care whether or not he sounded like a stubborn brat by that point.

"Not even for me?" Jeremiah asked.

Micah counted to ten in his head so he wouldn't blow up. He kept his voice as calm as he could. "I didn't attend Pop's funeral, and I am absolutely not attending Elijah's."

Jeremiah's sigh was loud in Micah's ear. "I think that's a mistake. Didn't you wish you'd gone after Pop died? Just to make sure he was really dead?"

"Hell, no. I had all the closure I needed the day I walked out of church and yakked into his precious rose bushes."

There was a low growl on the other end of the phone. "Fine. But this is different. Now that he's gone, you can meet the nieces and nephews he refused to introduce you to."

"Even more fuck no for that one," Micah snarled. "You don't really think they're all the loving, tolerant type, do you? Surely at least one of them turned out to be as much of a raging bigot as their father. Besides, what the hell am I supposed to do, just waltz back into their lives? I think they might wonder why I've never sent so much as a birthday card."

He swallowed the building fury as he recalled all the years Elijah had sent him their family Christmas photos, always with Bible verses on the back begging him to turn from his sinful ways so he could have contact with their family. They weren't written lovingly with hope for Micah's eternal soul. The sentiments were ugly, hateful words designed to break him—which they nearly did. Years of self-torment culminated once in a long hospitalization. If Cat had always brought out the best in Micah, Elijah brought out the worst.

"You know what, Micah? I've tried. I've been damn patient with you over the years with this. I agree with you, I really do—Elijah was a master of being an asshole. He turned it into an art form. But he's dead, and you've been free of his kind of hate for years now. You show up at his funeral, and you can send the message that you are all out of fucks to give over his unholy mess of a life."

Micah paused. He'd occasionally heard Jeremiah swear, but this was the most he'd ever thrown into a single breath probably in his entire life. Micah was indeed out of fucks to give regarding Elijah, but Jeremiah was wrong about one thing.

"I will never be free from the hell Pop put me through and Elijah encouraged from the time I was old enough to comprehend the word faggot," he said quietly.

"Micah, I'm sorry. Please, just listen to me."

"No. You listen to me. I will consider what you've said, but I am not promising to show up ready to mourn our loss. I hated him. And when I say hated, I really don't care what your Bible says about that and whether or not I murdered him in my heart with my wicked, wicked thoughts. He repeatedly shit on me while I was growing up, and his brand of religion has literally killed people like me. I can't go there and pretend to be sad he's gone, and I'm not sure I want to watch his widow and children grieve for a man who has been responsible for putting countless people through hell on earth."

There was silence on the other end of the line. At last Jeremiah said, "Do what you need to, then." He ended the call.

Micah sat staring at the phone in his hand. Elijah was gone, and he didn't want to feel any sorrow over it. In a sense, he didn't. He hadn't seen Elijah in a dozen years. Yet a small part of him did feel, if not grief, then regret. Not because they hadn't seen each other but because Elijah's life was a wasted one. He'd spent all of it being angry, and Micah had never been able to discern why. All his rage had been concentrated on Micah and anyone like him. Micah had the impression Elijah blamed him somehow for their mother's suicide, but the hatred he'd harbored went far beyond that.

He set his phone away in his desk and tried to concentrate on the tasks he still had to finish. It was impossible. On the one hand, he didn't want to know any more details. On the other hand, he wished he'd asked after all. Had Elijah succumbed to the combined strain of his professional ministry and his anger, the way their father had? Did he suffer some long-term illness, his body wasting away? Or was it something his congregation would find lurid, like a hidden urge carried out in self-destructive ways? Micah supposed if he went to the funeral, Jeremiah would tell him.

While he stared at the stack of papers in front of him, waiting to be entered electronically, the full force of his disappointment hit. He'd never been given closure with Elijah, neither a chance to see if he'd changed at all nor the opportunity to tell him once and for all the damage his beliefs had caused. Micah still had the scars from the first time he'd attempted suicide, when Zayne almost hadn't been able to stop him.

Everything boiled over. He crossed his arms on his desk and laid his head on them, sobbing. That was where Jude found him less than five minutes later. He heard the knock on his door and looked up as she opened it. He didn't have time to make himself presentable before she entered.

"Are you all right?" She grimaced. "Sorry. It's obvious you're not. What happened?"

Micah wiped his face with a tissue. "A family member died unexpectedly." It was all he could say to her without breaking down again.

"Oh, no. I'm sorry. Were you close?"

A bitter laugh escaped Micah's throat. "Hardly. My brother was...not a nice person. We hadn't spoken in more than twelve years—not since I took sides with our stepmother to shut down one of his vile church ministries."

"Your brother?" Jude looked stricken. "Which—I mean, oh, my god. I'm, uh, sorry." Her face was ashen.

Micah rubbed his temples. "I'm all right. It was more the frustration of having unfinished business and never seeing him move past the hate and anger he harbored."

"I was going to ask if you were taking a lunch break, but under the circumstances...well...I'll leave you to it. I should go...do...stuff." She ducked hastily out the door, and Micah heard her footfalls increase in speed as she went.

Frowning, Micah stared at the place she'd vacated. Her reaction was strange, but it was possible she didn't have a lot of experience with death or grief. Or maybe it was close to something she had experienced. Jude had said she grew up in a strict evangelical home, so Elijah's behavior might have been too familiar to deal with. Micah would have responded similarly at her age; her life and his had more parallels than he'd thought. Or...

His thoughts whirled. All those parallels made a bit too much sense to be mere coincidence. He stared at the stack of papers in front of him, trying to add it all up. Unable to fully connect the dots to confirm his suspicions, he stood up and stretched as he crossed the room to his sink to wash his face. He needed to put this aside for the time being and concentrate on work. At the end of the day, he could call Chris and discuss it before making a decision on the funeral. A small pang hit him at the realization he wanted to talk to Chris and hear his sound advice. As much as Micah had loved Cat, sometimes Cat fed into his grief and anger. Chris had the objectivity of not having known Micah during the worst of his recovery, and he wasn't likely to use sex as a communication tool, given the fact that they weren't so much as dating.

Micah flushed. It still made his stomach flip. Thinking about Chris brought a smile to his lips despite the serious situation. He sat back down at his desk to grade, feeling calmer than he had ten minutes before.

Back at home, the day caught up with Micah. He couldn't muster the energy to do more than heat something out of a can. Everything gnawed at him, and he had no answers for any of it.

Thomas sensed his restless confusion and hung around, following him everywhere he went.

After half eating his pathetic dinner, Micah climbed up to the attic again. He was sure he still had all the horrible Christmas cards Elijah had sent over the years, even though he'd been tempted more than once to shred the lot. If Cat's secret had been the beauty of his relationship with David, Micah's had been the ugliness of his relationship with Elijah. Cat had never known more than half because some things were too much to make his lover bear. There was no need for Cat to see every hateful word Elijah had written. It was enough for him to have seen the permanent etching on his wrists.

After some time of digging, Micah at last unearthed the small book in which he'd kept the holiday photos. He pulled them out one by one, refusing to turn them over and remind himself of Elijah's viciousness. The photos stopped when Elijah's youngest was around five. By that point, it was clear they weren't having any more, so he'd stopped sending cards. Micah studied their faces, hoping to find something to confirm what he already knew in his heart was the truth.

He sighed deeply when he found it. He would need to say something, but he couldn't fathom what. She should have told him, or he should have guessed sooner. He didn't know whether or not to be angry with her for not telling him. After all, it was Elijah who had created the mess in the first place.

Micah placed the pictures back in their book and left it in the bin where he'd found it. Unlike Cat's things, he had no sentimental attachment to it. He also had no desire to give it away, as he couldn't think of anyone who wanted a handful of family photos emblazoned on the back with the equivalent of "God hates fags." He gave the bin a solid kick for good measure and went downstairs again.

The tension and his indecision about whether he was going to attend Elijah's funeral made him jumpy. He needed something, but he couldn't figure out what. Maybe to talk to someone. He eyed his coat, but there was nowhere he wanted to go. When he sat back down on the couch, he felt his phone shift in his pocket. Of course.

He needed to call Zayne.

She answered on the first ring. "Hey, baby. Everything all right?"

"No," he said curtly.

"I need to sit down for this, don't I?" she asked. There was a slight pause. "All right. What's going on?"

"Elijah's dead." He said it more or less the same way Jeremiah had.

"Well, shit."

"My feelings exactly." Micah flopped back against the couch cushions. "Jer called me this afternoon. He asked me to go to the damn funeral."

"Are you going to?"

"I don't know. I'd rather not."

She was quiet on the other end for a bit. Eventually she said, "Are you safe?"

"I am." He ran his hand through his hair, catching his fingers in the curls and tugging. "I thought I would feel...something. Relief or anger or even sadness. I've got nothing, just this vast emptiness. I don't even care that he's gone. I sat here thinking about what would make me feel less restless and apathetic, you know? But I didn't want anything at all—not a drink or to gouge my skin or...or...to die. Nothing." He smiled then, even though she couldn't see him. "Except to call you."

Zayne's laughter was soft. "Oh, baby. You know I'm always here for you. Did you need us to come down? I can take some time away."

"No. Your boutique and salon need you." He thought better of it. "Maybe you could come with me to the funeral this weekend. I don't want to do it alone."

"Of course I will. If you need me to, I'll go back to your place with you afterward."

"Pam too?"

"I'll ask. I love you, baby." Zayne made a kissing noise into the phone.

"You too. Thanks."

He ended the call and set the phone on the coffee table. Dragging himself from the couch, he went upstairs to get ready for bed. He lay curled on his side with Thomas tucked up at his back, but sleep wouldn't come. His mind went back over the details of the day until all he could focus on was that Elijah was gone, suddenly and without ceremony. It seemed far less dramatic than it should have been.

Unwelcome, Micah's thoughts strayed to Cat's last hours. He, too, left with barely a whisper, even though Micah had watched him slip away for months. He had left a legacy of his letters and belongings. Now Micah wondered what final words Elijah might have for him. He turned his face into the pillow, but instead of tears, he let out a muffled yell of rage. Slowly, his breathing returned to normal and he settled down, left only with his muddled thoughts and the confused blending of his grief and anger.

~ ** ~

Main Street in town provided a much-needed respite for Micah. He didn't intend to stay long, but he had to have a break. The visiting nurse was in, and she would keep an eye on Cat just fine without Micah's interference.

It was strange being there at noontime on a weekday, and stranger still being away from his classroom. In an ordinary year, one in which he hadn't taken a leave of absence to care for his dying spouse, he would be managing a classroom full of sleepy students who had stayed out late and eaten too much Halloween candy. He would be making up for the homework he hadn't assigned, knowing it wouldn't be done even if he'd given it to them.

A number of shops already had Christmas displays. They hadn't even waited until all the bins of leftover plastic pumpkins and artificial spider webs had been cleared out before stocking tinsel and candy canes. Micah paused to look in one window, and he had to swallow around a lump in his throat. Like everything else, Cat loved Christmas and delighted in the sparkles and lights and jingle bells.

Every year since they'd been together, they attended the town tree lighting. Even Micah had to admit the display was gorgeous, a celebration of the town's diversity rather than something dedicated to the specific holiday. Cat liked to drag Micah to all the festivities and then come home to cozy up on the couch with hot tea and the first Christmas cookies. Micah flushed at the memory of their other Christmas tradition, though he knew no one else nearby could have read his thoughts. He figured in this town, probably very few people thought that trading blow jobs to a soundtrack of Amy Grant Christmas songs was strange in the least.

Micah tore himself away from the small display of Christmas chocolate in the window front. It was both too early and too late to be dreaming of holiday magic. Cat wasn't going to make it to Thanksgiving, and even if some miracle saw him through until December, they wouldn't be keeping up their usual plans.

He shoved his hands in his pockets and headed toward the bakery for a loaf of bread. LR had offered to make dinner, and he wanted to have something to go with it. Not because they needed anything but because he needed time away and something to do with the fidgety energy he had. Watching over your spouse to see if they were still breathing lost its appeal in the first two minutes.

Half an hour later, Micah returned home with the bread in one hand and the hand-dipped chocolates in the other; he'd bought them after all, even though Cat couldn't eat them and he didn't want them. LR's kids might enjoy them, if she let them have the candy. He set the bags on the kitchen table, shed his windbreaker over the back of the nearest chair, and retreated to the back of the house to see how the nurse had gotten along while he was gone.

Cat was propped up a bit, which was out of the ordinary. He wasn't lucid most days, and he'd mostly stopped speaking. Micah didn't know whether Cat recognized him anymore, but it didn't stop him from lavishing affection anyway. He stepped over to the bed and bent down to kiss Cat's forehead and stroke his thin hair. Illness had turned it almost white-blond, and his freckles had faded as well.

"Hey, beautiful," Micah said.

For a moment, Cat turned his gray-green eyes toward Micah. He blinked, and then his whole body seized up. Micah backed away and called out for the nurse. She hurried into the room and moved to the opposite side of the bed, assessing. While Micah stood helplessly by, wondering what was going on, Cat grabbed his hand.

"Please," he begged, the first words he'd said to Micah in three days. "Don't leave me."

Micah knelt by the bed, keeping hold of Cat's hand. The nurse worked around Micah, but he wasn't paying any attention to what she was doing. Cat took a gasping breath, and then his rhythm settled into something with an almost otherworldly quality to it. The sound was almost painful, but Micah stayed put. He fumbled in his pocket for his phone, needing to call LR and tell her what was going on.

Later, when the dust settled, Micah could not have described a single thing about the rest of Cat's last few minutes. He could recall the nurse speaking to Cat, her voice low and calm. He remembered her telling him things too, but the words didn't sink in. Micah thought there were other people he should call, but he didn't want to do anything except sit at Cat's side.

He couldn't have said how long it took. Minutes, probably, but it felt closer to hours. Watching Cat's breaths become more shallow. The nurse had given him something, for pain or sleep or both. The actual moment of his passing was uneventful. Micah supposed he thought the universe would shift in some dramatic way, but all that happened was Cat slowly stopped breathing and his heart stopped beating.

The nurse asked if Micah wanted to be alone with him for a few minutes, and Micah looked up at her in confusion. Was that a thing some people did? He didn't know whether he should or not or what he needed in the moment. He'd expected to feel something right away, some sense of loss or change. All he felt was relief that the uncertainty was over.

He stood up and looked down at Cat's body, empty now of the person who had occupied it for thirty-six years. Micah had a strange sense of duality, as though the real Cat might come through the bedroom door at any moment and ask what Micah was doing. Yet there he was, lying on the bed as though sleeping while in reality he grew cold and stiff. Micah wandered dazed into the other room and sat on the couch to wait for LR to arrive.

When she came in, he hadn't moved from his spot on the couch. He turned toward her without really seeing her. "I guess we need to start planning. There were so many things he wanted. I have a list somewhere…" He was rambling, but he couldn't stop talking. And he was cold; why was it so cold in the house? He shivered violently.

"Micah." LR came and sat by him on the couch, stopping the runaway train his mouth had become.

He angled toward her, and her presence finally clicked. "I'm sorry. I'm so sorry."

LR didn't answer. She curled up against him, and he put his arms around her. LR sobbed, but Micah—usually the first one to cry—was so caught up in his racing thoughts he couldn't express the magnitude of his sorrow. For a long while, it was the two of them against the hurricane-force winds of their grief, clinging to each other for safety.

CHAPTER NINETEEN

LEAVE THE OTHER NINETY-NINE

IT WAS still pitch black when Micah woke, unable to sleep. He rose from the bed, and Thomas stretched but didn't follow him out of the room. Micah descended the stairs and flipped on the light in the kitchen, blinking in the sudden brightness. He started the coffee pot, knowing he wouldn't be going back to bed before he had to be up for work.

He sat at the table and began to write without looking at the next letter on the pile. It wasn't important. He had to release the tension into the story, regardless of what else Cat had to say to him. It was an almost frantic desire to vomit the words onto the page. For the next two hours, he let it happen, funneling it all into a more manageable format. At last he closed his laptop and pushed it away.

In his agitated state, he'd forgotten about the coffee. Now he poured a mug and stood at the sink, staring out into the dim yard. The sun was coming up, tinting the lake an eerie, hazy purple, but the other side of the house was still in darkness. For a long time, he didn't move.

Thomas's soft meow caused him to look down. The cat brushed

against him, unusually subdued. Micah sighed and dumped the last of his coffee down the drain. He slid down until he was seated on the floor, his hand stroking Thomas's back. Everything hurt, and he was foggy from his restless night. It was going to be a long day. Thomas head-butted him gently, and Micah gazed down into his bright eyes.

"You do always seem to know what I need," he said with affection. "Don't know how I'd have gotten through this without you." Thomas merely mewed in agreement, causing Micah to chuckle.

His laughter turned into tears, and he drew his knees up to rest his elbows on them. Burying his face in his hands, he let everything out. More than ever, he wished Cat were there to take care of him. He would've known exactly what to do in such a moment. Micah could almost hear what he'd have said about Elijah being gone. He'd have made some remark about Elijah being all too happy to make everything about himself. Then he'd have urged Micah to go, if for no other reason than that Elijah wouldn't have wanted him there.

That was it, then. He was going, like he'd told Zayne. Later, he could call Jeremiah and let him know. He thought about Jude and what he was going to say to her. Whatever it was could wait. Her day wasn't likely going to be any better than his, and confronting her—whether to offer his sympathy or to demand an explanation—could wait until they weren't at school.

Micah got to his feet and looked down at Thomas. "Might as well get started," he said, and Thomas acknowledged him with a swish of his tail.

Micah was barely focused in class at the community center. He hadn't paid much attention in the one he attended, and now he was zoning out on the one he was supposed to be teaching. He hadn't taken any time off, though he probably should have. There was nothing he had to do to be ready for Elijah's funeral, and he figured he could take a few days afterward. He'd scheduled an appointment with his therapist, but he was out of the office for the week, so that would need to wait as well.

The class was restless, as though they were aware of how off Micah was despite his best efforts to cover it. He let them talk amongst themselves about the previous week's prompts, sharing snippets and offering advice. It took several seconds before he was aware they'd finished and were waiting for him to tell them what was next.

"Oh. Uh..." Micah blinked and looked around. "That was excellent." He glanced at the clock. "I think we should end a bit early. I have a busy weekend coming up, and I may be out next week." He began packing his things away.

"Wait," Dyl said. "You haven't read us this week's chapter."

Micah paused with his hand on his laptop. "I don't think it's a good idea. It's really rough. I didn't have a chance to look it over at all before coming in."

Dyl gave him a pointed look. "I thought that's what we were supposed to be doing. Come on. You always say it's rough, and then you read it to us and it's fine."

Around the room, heads nodded in agreement. Micah relented. He opened his laptop and pulled up the file. He stared at the chapter, fully aware of what had been in his heart and mind when he wrote it. Once more, he tried to escape it.

"It's not going to make you happy," he tried.

"Just read it," Carlie urged.

Micah closed his eyes, wishing he had a god to pray to for strength. He opened his eyes, took a deep breath, and began to read. The room fell silent, and he didn't dare look anywhere but at the page in front of him. He didn't want to see his students' reactions. Despite the ache in his chest, he read on, keeping his voice as steady as he could. When at last he was through, he sat back and finally glanced up at the class.

He instantly wished he hadn't. All eyes were on him, and the shock and confusion around the room was tangible. Maricela and Carlie were both fighting tears. Hope's mouth hung open. Even Jude and Chris looked shocked, and Dyl was outright angry. Guilt stole over Micah; he'd ensnared his entire class in his web of grief and loss. He tensed, clenching and releasing his fist while silently pleading for someone—anyone—to speak.

"How could you?" Carlie asked through her sniffle.

"I can't believe you let He'chatul die like that," Dyl said. His face was red, and his eyes were narrowed. "After everything you put them through, you didn't even let them get their fucking happy ending?"

"I—" Micah started.

"No!" Dyl yelled. "I was hoping. I mean, I saw it coming, but I thought you were better than that. You let him die! You had a choice, and you didn't even try to save him!" He was shaking with fury.

Micah stared at him. He had a feeling this wasn't about a fictional character anymore. Slowly, he rose from the desk and went around to the other side. "I'm sorry," he said quietly.

Dyl peered up at him from beneath his bangs. He let out a sound, something stuck between rage and anguish, before breaking down and sobbing. He crossed his arms on his desk and dropped his head to them, his back quivering. Carlie and Maricela moved to either side of him, putting their hands on him. When Dyl's cries petered out, he raised his head and wiped his face. Hope handed him a tissue.

Micah inhaled deeply, steadying himself before he spoke. "He was my spouse. The details are obviously different, but He'chatul was the person I was with for nine years. I watched him die slowly over several months." He swallowed. "I always thought I should have done more or convinced him he didn't have to die. He chose not to treat anything because it was complicated, expensive, and only prolonging the inevitable. As much as I understood it was what he wanted, I've always been a little angry with him for it, and angry with myself for not arguing."

Hope nodded. "My husband had cancer. I was pissed off with him that he didn't get it checked out sooner. I don't think it would have mattered, but it's hard not to wonder sometimes."

"My dad died when I was really little," Carlie said. "I don't even remember him. I wish I did, but I feel bad because my stepdad is so amazing and I love him too."

Nods of agreement, murmurs of acknowledgment. Micah sagged against the desk in relief. He'd finally spoken his thoughts, the things he hadn't told anyone because to do so felt selfish. Here, no one was judging him.

"My boyfriend," Dyl whispered. "Last summer when he came down here to visit me. It was a freak boating accident, and it was my fault. We shouldn't have been out there." Fresh tears ran down his cheeks. "I wasn't allowed to say goodbye. His family didn't know about me. Didn't even know he was gay."

"Damn it," Micah muttered. He knelt in front of Dyl. "I'm sorry," he said again. "It wasn't your fault, and I'm sorry you were alone."

Dyl suddenly reached out and grabbed Micah's forearm. "Don't leave it this way," he pleaded. "Give at least Benjamin his happy ending, okay? Make it count."

"I will," Micah promised.

The class was subdued as they packed up and left. Micah slid his laptop away, waiting until most of them were out of the room before calling to Jude. She turned around, and by the look on her face, Micah knew she was aware of what he had to say to her. She looked like a child who'd been caught stealing cookies, and if it weren't for the serious nature of the current circumstances, he might have laughed.

She approached his desk slowly. "Yes?"

"You don't need to act like you're in trouble. I'm not even really angry. I just want to know why you didn't tell me who you are."

"When did you figure it out?" she asked.

"After Jeremiah called me. He didn't mention you either, but maybe he thought I knew."

Jude sighed. "I moved here to find you and see if what my father said was true. If I'd told you right away, would you have talked to me?"

Micah frowned. "Of course I would. What makes you think otherwise?"

"He told us you hated us and that's why you never called or visited or sent us things."

She fiddled with the zipper on her coat then shrugged out of it and sat back down at one of the desks. Micah came around the teacher's desk and sat beside her.

"That's what he said?" Micah snorted. "I'm surprised he didn't use me as an example of a life gone horribly, sinfully wrong."

"Oh, he did," Jude said. "He told us you were lost to God, and that's why you hated us. When I finally decided I needed to come out, I went to Uncle Jeremiah first. He told me the truth and where to find you, but I wasn't sure."

"I guess I can understand that. Why didn't you say anything once you knew I was all right?"

Jude shrugged. "The same reason I changed my name. I figured that was my old life, and I didn't need to care about it anymore. I could live here as a new person, and you would never see me as his daughter. Then, when I was able, I'd bring Ike—that's my brother—here too, where he'd be safe."

"Except then your father up and died, leaving us where we are now."

"Yes," Jude said. "At least now you know the truth."

Micah put a hand on hers. "'You shall know the truth, and the truth shall set you free.'" It was one of the few Bible verses he could still quote.

"John eight, verse thirty-two," Jude said. "Are we ever really free?"

"Yes," Micah assured her. He squeezed her hand and let go. "Are you going to the funeral?"

"I'm expected to, and I don't want to leave Ike without any support. I'm worried about him." She bit her lip. "He's so, so much like you. He even looks like you."

"I'm looking forward to meeting him." Micah offered her what he hoped was a reassuring smile.

Jude stood up and put her coat back on. She slung her bag over her shoulder, paused, then offered Micah a one-armed hug. She waved over her shoulder as she walked out. He supposed it would be awkward for a little while, but they had plenty of time to get to know each other without such a consuming secret between them.

He finished gathering his belongings and was about to leave when there was a light rap on the door. Glancing up, he saw Chris leaning against the wall just inside the classroom. A mix of longing, relief, and nerves sloshed in his gut.

"Hey," Chris said. "Thought I'd see if you're all right. It was rough in here tonight." He looked behind him at the hallway where Jude had disappeared.

"I'm fine. It's been a hell of a week, though."

"Yeah?"

"I shouldn't have read that chapter tonight. I wrote it while I was trying to deal with one too many things. My brother died a couple of days ago. The one who spent my childhood calling me names and threatening me for being queer."

"That must have brought up a lot of unpleasant memories." Chris came farther into the room.

"Not so much of him. It made me think of Cat." Micah sighed. "I'm sorry I keep bringing him up like this."

Chris didn't respond right away, and the air between them was tense. He said, "I shouldn't have pushed you like that. The truth is, I wasn't sure if I was ready to live in his shadow. I'm still not."

Micah wanted to reach for him, but he held back. "It isn't like that. I'm never sure how much I'm allowed to say and whether people will get sick of hearing about him."

"I'm willing to listen," Chris said. "It's all right for you to talk. I told you before, you don't need to censor yourself. I assumed you were holding back because you were trying to split your time between us. I see now that's not the case."

"It's not."

"Did you want to come somewhere with me on Friday night?"

"What did you have in mind?"

"A group of us who were part of the community center project are having a bonfire down at the beach. We're having one last night before it's really too cold." Chris put his hand on Micah's arm, and the touch sent a warm wave through him.

"I'd love to," Micah said. "What time, and where on the beach?"

"Six-thirty, the opposite end from the boat docks. It's probably getting too cool for many boats, but we don't want the traffic. We've rented the fire pit there."

"Excellent. I'll meet you there." Micah picked up his bag and slung it over his shoulder.

"Good." Chris flashed him a smile before letting go of Micah.

They walked out together, and when Chris waved goodbye, Micah wanted to keep him there longer, talking like they had on the other days after class. He stood with his car door open, watching Chris pull out of the parking lot. He wasn't sure what to do with the thoughts trying to break free in his head, so he climbed into his car and took off for home.

Friday evening, after changing into warmer clothes, Micah parked in one of the grassy side areas near the beach. He grabbed his chair and his contribution to the communal food table. It wasn't anything special, just some sausages he'd picked up at Wegmans on the way over. He was sure Cat would have had something to say about it, both a jab at the lack of creativity and a suggestive comment about the meat. He'd always been the one to make what they needed for this sort of thing, if for no other reason than to assure he had something he could eat. Micah scolded himself internally for fussing over what he'd brought, knowing no one else would object.

He brought the meat to the couple of people who seemed to be in charge of the grills and then wandered down by the water. Some of the braver teens had rolled up their pants and were splashing ankle-deep in the cold lake. It was a fine, clear evening, a curtain of deep purple-blue descending in front of Micah where he stood facing the water. The winking stars had popped out, dotting the sky. Several people were already working on the bonfire, and a healthy blaze had started.

After a few minutes, a hand on his shoulder made him jump. He turned around and grinned at Chris, whose eyes lit up. The soft smile on his lips and the casual way he'd left his hand on Micah's arm made Micah's stomach flip. Not for the first time, he noticed how attractive Chris was. Micah took a step back, wanting to distance himself from those thoughts until they were more clear on where things stood between them.

"Hungry?" Chris asked.

"What? Oh, the food. Sure, I could eat."

They made their way to the food tables along with the rest of the crew. Once everyone had something, people settled around the fire in small groups, talking and laughing. Micah hung back, not familiar with most of the people there.

"Come on," Chris said. "I'll introduce you to my gang. These are the people from the church, but don't let that scare you off."

Micah followed Chris over to one of the fire pits. Chris introduced him to everyone, but Micah wasn't able to keep all their names straight. He had no problem remembering seventy-five students' names, but it was different in a social setting.

They added their chairs to the group, and Micah listened to their conversation, only joining in when asked something directly. Chris stole glances at him periodically, but Micah only smiled back and returned his attention to the discussion. Mainly they were talking about their families and what everyone was up to. One of the men had a daughter in Micah's class, so there was at least one part of the conversation to which he could contribute.

At some point, a young man pulled out his guitar and began playing. It wasn't a tune Micah knew, but it had a familiarity to it which took him back to his adolescence. He stood up and wandered away down the beach, the voices of the others floating after him as they joined the song.

Micah sat on a flat expanse of rocks, and he realized after a moment it was the same one where he'd first met Chris a dozen years before. He murmured softly to himself, "'Man looks at the outward appearance, but the Lord looks at the heart.'"

A soft chuckle beside him caused him to look up. Chris walked around and sat beside Micah on the rocks.

"Didn't exactly picture you as the type to quote the Bible," he said, nudging Micah with his shoulder.

"I'm not." Micah bumped him back. "You said it to me years ago, right on this very rock. I used to know the Bible pretty well when I was a teenager, but I've forgotten where that one came from."

"First Samuel sixteen, verse seven. I said that?" Chris tilted his head. "Huh."

"You were talking about Cat and how I should look beneath the surface for both of us." Micah glanced over. "Your advice was pretty solid, by the way."

"I gathered." Chris grinned. "Anyway, I came to see if you were all right. Seemed like tonight was a bit more than you're used to."

"It is. I spend a lot of time alone or with a few people. I'm not much on parties." He laughed softly. "And that guitar reminded me of my years in church youth group."

"Oh, man. I can see why. I was a Young Life kid myself. Used to go up every summer to Saranac Lake. A lot of memories."

"Those weren't good years for me." Micah looked out over the water, listening for a few minutes to the faint strumming. He thought about Elijah and his wasted life.

Chris interrupted his musing. "I know what you mean."

"Do you?" Micah angled toward him. "The song they're singing is different, but it has a similar feel. It might surprise you that there was one song I really liked back then, about always being on the run but coming back home again or something." He sighed heavily. "That was me, for a long time. But when I stopped, it was because I found Cat. Not a god who hated who I am." He lay back, one arm under his head.

Chris followed suit. "I may be a pastor, but I do understand the ways in which my religion has been used to violate and condemn people."

Micah didn't answer directly. He understood Chris had his own history, and they'd only touched on some of what he'd been through. But he had the support of at least some family. Micah didn't know how to explain his envy.

"I'm supposed to attend my brother's funeral tomorrow. Our oldest brother is taking care of everything, so I know I won't have to hear a hateful sermon. He's pretty progressive these days. Still, part of me would rather not."

"I can understand why."

They were quiet for a bit, then Micah said, "I used to hope heaven and hell were real. Sometimes I still do. Maybe it would mean my father and my brother got what they deserved in the end."

"I have those wishes too," Chris said.

Surprised, Micah met Chris's eyes. Chris hadn't chastised him for his bitterness or tried to convince him he was wrong. Micah hesitated then moved his free hand closer to Chris's. He craved the warmth of contact and the security of knowing someone else was in it with him, someone who understood at least a little of his heartache. Chris's fingers brushed against Micah's, and Micah linked them. The rush of nerves and pleasure took him by surprise, and he inhaled sharply as he turned his head.

Chris was so close, the heat of his body a heady contrast with the cool stone beneath them. Micah didn't have time for a careful risk-benefit analysis before Chris had leaned close enough there was only a fraction of an inch between their lips. It wasn't clear who moved first, but in the next second, they were kissing. Nothing heavy, only a soft, questioning press of their closed mouths. Micah closed his eyes, his head spinning from the sensation. It had been far too long since he'd enjoyed such sweet intimacy.

They parted a moment later, and Chris looked apologetic. "That was...inappropriate of me. I'm sorry."

"What?" Micah said. His thoughts were still a little jumbled. "No, it was fine."

"I've been wanting to do that for a while, but it didn't seem right."

"It was tonight." Micah gave his hand a little squeeze.

Chris smiled. "Are we supposed to talk about what this means?"

Micah chuckled. "I don't know. My experience is pretty limited. I was never one for big conversations." *Except with Cat.* He didn't say it out loud, though.

"Want to head back over? I think the singing is done."

They rose from the rock, laughing at themselves when they were both a bit stiff in the joints. Micah shoved his hands in his pockets, not quite ready to hold hands on the way back over. Chris understood. He copied Micah's posture, but he walked close enough their arms bumped a few times. It was a promise but not a demand, and it warmed Micah more than the fires along the shore.

CHAPTER TWENTY

The Exalted Shall Be Humbled

In the morning, Micah rolled groggily out of bed. He'd stayed up far too late, talking to Chris after the bonfire. They'd gone to Sweet Beans, and when that closed they'd made their way to the Neanderthal. Now he had a long drive ahead, up to Rochester for the funeral.

He was running late as it was, and he rushed around to find something appropriate to wear. Pam and Zayne had said they would meet him outside the church. His father's church. Elijah's church. He'd only lasted a few months before their father's wife had exposed some of the morally ambiguous ways he was bringing in money. Jeremiah himself had only stayed on another year, and Elijah had been welcomed back with open arms by the half of the congregation who hadn't followed Jeremiah out the door. Micah wondered who it would belong to now. Perhaps Elijah's oldest son had become a minister and would be given the job.

Hastily, Micah fed Thomas and made sure he had what he needed for the day. Micah would be back after the funeral. He had no intention of staying for any kind of reception and enduring more awkward tension. Even so, it was longer hours than Micah was usually away, and he wanted to be sure Thomas had his creature comforts while he was gone.

In the car, Micah turned on the radio for company, but it was intolerable noise. He shut it off and drove the entire way in silence, his mind running over every possible scenario. In between, he remembered what Cat had said of his own funeral, wondering if Elijah had left such detailed instructions. The memories weren't as sharp, whether because they were muted by Micah's current anxiety or because it had been long enough he could think about them without distress. One day, he might be able to share them with someone other than LR.

~ ** ~

Cat was seated at the kitchen table, swinging his sock-covered feet a little and scribbling on a piece of lined notebook paper. Micah dried the last few dishes and glanced over his shoulder, smiling at the way Cat put the eraser of his pencil between his teeth. It was a nice moment, one he wanted to capture. His smile faded as he remembered what that meant—he wanted to hold onto it after Cat was gone. He turned back to the sink so Cat wouldn't see his eyes mist over again.

"No cheesy songs," Cat said.

"What?" Micah ran his thumb under his eyes and set the cloth on the counter. He faced Cat, who looked up.

"Hm? Oh, just thinking out loud. I don't want any sappy songs at my funeral. When David died, some dickhead high school friend of his thought it would be the awesomest if he sang 'Candle in the Wind' for him. It utterly pissed me off, but there was nothing I could do about it. David's mom had already said he could."

Knowing even what little Cat had shared about David and his various medical conditions, Micah cringed. Whoever had thought turning him into a cliché was a good idea clearly hadn't been particularly clued in. Nothing like that would happen at Cat's funeral. Micah swallowed, realizing what he'd just thought. He covered his pre-season grief with anger.

"You can't plan your own funeral," he snapped.

Cat raised his eyebrows. "The hell I can't."

"Funerals are for the living. As awful as David's friend was, he was grieving in his own way. You need to let us do the same." Micah crossed his arms.

"I'm not making plans for me." Cat swallowed visibly. "This is for you."

The rage boiled over, and Micah wanted to tell Cat to go fuck himself. Instead, he said, "Yeah? And what if you don't die next week or next month or next year? What if what you think I want changes?" He didn't care particularly that he wasn't making any sense. He whirled around and gripped the edge of the sink, breathing shallowly.

"Micah." Cat's voice was soft, controlled. "Don't do this."

"Fuck you."

"You can't keep saying that to me," Cat snipped. "I've had nine years of it, and honestly, hon? It doesn't make me like you better."

"Maybe you need to stop doing things meant to piss me off." This wasn't going anywhere fun, but the train was already out of the station.

"Turn around and look at me," Cat demanded.

"No."

Micah heard the scrape of Cat's chair as he stood. He wanted to tell him to stop—Cat had a hard time staying on his feet these days, and it wasn't fair to him to make him try. Micah was too lost in his own heart and head to do anything, though. It seemed like an eternity later when Cat's gentle hand was on his back.

"Honey, look at me. Please?"

Unable to resist the soft plea, Micah turned to face Cat. He couldn't prevent the tears sliding down his cheeks. Cat reached up and brushed them away with his fingers.

"Micah, I'm going to die. Not in some unspecified number of years but soon—days or weeks, maybe, but not months. Not many, anyway." Cat sighed. "We've known all along. I can't keep my body going. I'm tired, honey. I need rest."

Micah nodded. "But—" He choked then cleared his throat. "You said yourself you don't want to."

"I know what I said. It doesn't change reality."

Cat swayed, and Micah caught him around the waist. "Here, let me help."

Together they made their way to the living room, and Micah helped Cat get comfortable on the couch. He left him for a moment to retrieve the pen and paper from the other room. When he held them out, Cat took them, but he didn't resume his plans right away. He looked up at Micah, remaining silent for a long time.

"I meant it when I said this was for you. We can do this together. It'll be awful, but it can be one last thing we choose. I don't want you to have to do this when you're busy trying to figure out what to do with everything else. If anyone asks, you can tell them it was my idea."

"Okay." Micah sighed. Part of him knew Cat was right; he wouldn't be able to focus, and someone else would have their say in his place. The rest of him wanted to go on denying the necessity of planning. On good days, he could still pretend they had all the time in the world.

"No cheesy music," Cat repeated. "You can choose hymns if you like, but absolutely not pop songs about dead people." He shuddered.

For a while, they sat together on the couch, Cat making notes of their ideas in his messy script. Each new note they made led Cat to another story about some aspect of his life in the time before he knew Micah. He talked as though he had too much to hold in any longer, wanting it all to spill out before he was gone and couldn't tell Micah everything he needed to say.

"I want you to find my pink hat," he said.

Micah frowned. "What pink hat?"

"It's this old knit thing I've had since I was thirteen. My friend Blaze gave it to me before he moved." Cat laughed softly. "When we were eleven, he cut his own hair. Snipped his long braid right off his head, and it made all his hair stick up. He wore the hat to cover it until he'd saved enough to get a real boys' haircut. His mom was angry at first, but she eventually calmed down." Cat slumped a little. "That was why they ended up moving. Once Blaze hit puberty and started getting his period and stuff, his parents figured out they couldn't really do anything but find a way to support him. He was a mess that whole spring, but once they came around, he was on the road to being okay. He gave me the hat the day they left. Afterward, we wrote letters for about a year before we lost touch."

"I'm sorry you didn't stay in contact," Micah said.

"It's all right. We had each other when we needed to." His sunny smile returned. "That was the year I came out to my family."

"Oh?" Micah replied. "I'm not sure if you ever told me that story." He had, but Micah wanted to hear it again.

"Didn't I?" Cat looked thoughtful. "Well, it shouldn't surprise you that no one was shocked. I gathered them all in the living room and stood up in front of them. I told everyone I was tired of pretending to be 'all boy,' and then I blurted out that I was gay. LR said to me, 'You have the fundraiser calendar of the Cornell swim team on your wall. Did you think we didn't know?'"

Micah laughed. "She was sharp for an eleven-year-old."

"She was a pain in the ass, is what she was. Still is, in fact." Cat grinned.

Sadness washed over Micah. He wasn't the only one losing his beloved. He frowned and plucked the pencil from Cat's hand. "Enough of this. Let's call LR and take the kids out somewhere. We've got your wheelchair, the weather hasn't turned cold yet, and I think we could both use some time outdoors."

"Fair enough." Cat nodded then brightened. "The zoo?"

Micah laughed. "If that's what you want, beautiful, that's what we'll do."

~ ** ~

Cat had become so childlike in moments at the end, wanting to do things he hadn't thought about or had interest in since he was little. Some of it was probably the renal failure dementia, but some of it was pure nostalgia. Micah had liked learning about some of Cat's favorite places. He saw the same thing sometimes with Alonzo and the way Jones cared for him, and it made his heart ache for them. Alonzo would likely live for a long time yet, perhaps even years. Micah didn't quite count himself lucky, but he wondered if a few months was easier to bear than a few years.

Thinking of Cat's pink hat brought a smile to Micah's face. He had indeed located Blaze, who had long since decided to go by the name Henry. Micah suspected Cat would have loved knowing he was at least partly responsible for connecting Henry with Elle. It would have delighted him to know Elle still griped about being the only non-queer in her entire family, which included her partner.

Micah pulled into the parking lot and got out of the car. As he approached the church, he saw more than the two familiar faces he'd been expecting. Pam and Zayne were there, of course, but Micah was shocked to see that Cooper and Lucy had come as well as Elle and Henry. He stopped walking a few yards from them, and Zayne left the group.

"Hey, baby." She kissed his cheek. "We all thought you deserved as much support as we could give you today."

He pulled her into a fierce hug, and she rubbed his back. By the time he let go, the others had joined them. He embraced each of them in turn before they made their way into the church. As heavy as his heart was, Micah suppressed a chuckle at the rose bushes out front.

Micah slid into a row toward the back of the church, wedged between Zayne and Elle. The church had been updated, though it had always been a modern structure. They'd gone with rows of padded chairs instead of pews, and the room looked nothing like a traditional sanctuary. It was more like an auditorium. There were none of the markings of religious ritual or worship. That was only partly Elijah's doing once he took over as the administrative pastor.

He was entitled to sit near the front, but he was avoiding a confrontation with Elijah's children. He knew there were five others besides Jude, four brothers and another sister. Micah had met the oldest two when they were first born, but as a shy, awkward teenager, he hadn't known what to do with babies. Before the second one was a year old, he'd burned most of his bridges, and Elijah and his wife wouldn't allow Micah to see them. Even after his attempt at curing his "sins of the flesh," Elijah had maintained Micah was potentially a pedophile. Fortunately, Elijah hadn't followed through with his threats to use his beliefs to have Micah fired from his teaching job.

They were the new breed of fundamentalists. Micah hadn't grown up with rules governing his mode of dress, nor had he been homeschooled or sheltered to the degree some of his peers had. It didn't stop his father from raising them to view the world as being hostile to their values. As Micah looked around, he remembered all the ways his family had fed into the fears of parents who didn't want their children to fall prey to the sins of the world. A pang of regret for Elijah's children hit him, and he wondered if among the six how many had turned out like Elijah. He couldn't imagine growing up under Elijah's roof.

Next to him, Zayne squeezed his hand. "You all right?"

"Yeah," he said.

On his other side, Elle was reading the program for the service. Micah glanced at his briefly then watched the people filtering in, slouching and trying to remain in the shadow of the others so he wouldn't be recognized. He was confident he wouldn't be. It had been almost thirty years since he'd walked out for good, and he figured he looked a lot different at pushing fifty than he had at twenty-two. A woman passed him who looked to be roughly his age, and he tried to figure out if he knew her. Their eyes met, and she seemed like she was having the same struggle. She shook her head and moved on. The man behind her and the teenagers in between them didn't even glance his way.

When the stream of people slowed and stopped, Jeremiah stepped out onto the stage to a podium. Micah looked around, shocked to see how packed the room was. It appeared that the whole church had turned out. It made Micah's skin crawl to think this many people had loved whatever Elijah ranted about from the stage. Micah swallowed hard, dread rising in his gut. He knew he wasn't at immediate risk, but he didn't know how many people shared Elijah's views about people like Micah or his friends. He breathed slowly to quell the unease and turned back to the front.

Jeremiah made a motion, and Elijah's family entered. His wife strode in first, on the arm of a man Micah assumed was her oldest son. He looked exactly as Elijah had at his age. Behind him trailed his family, followed by the rest of Elijah's children and grandchildren. Micah noticed the younger ones didn't have families with them, and he wondered about it. He spotted Rachel, his stepmother, last in the line. Her hand was on the shoulder of the young man in front of her, almost guiding him. She paused and looked at Micah, a slight smile passing across her lips.

Jude had been right about her younger brother. His resemblance to Micah was uncanny, and he had an almost identical way of carrying himself—a kind of apology to the world. One of Elijah's other children glanced back over their shoulder. Micah's eyes met Jude's, and his mouth dropped open. She looked nothing like the person he knew from work. Instead of her smart trousers and collared shirt, she had on a long dress. Her hair was combed almost flat rather than being spiked, and she was wearing enough makeup Micah could tell she had it on. She looked uncomfortable, to say the least.

At last the family were all seated, and Jeremiah began the memorial service. Micah only half paid attention, his mind still on Elijah's family. Once or twice, he caught Jude turning around to peek at him, and at one point, she nudged her brother Ike, who also glanced back. Later, Micah would catch up with them.

He turned back and faced the front, trying to keep his body and face neutral. The service opened with one of the members of Elijah's congregation singing something Micah didn't recognize. It reminded him of the type of music Cat had expressly forbidden at his own funeral. Micah restrained himself from rolling his eyes.

After she finished, Jeremiah said a brief prayer and invited anyone who wanted to come say a few words about the deceased. Micah's eyebrows rose steadily as the line lengthened. He hadn't realized so many people wanted to speak about Elijah. A small, mean part of him hoped they were queuing up to confirm Micah's opinion about his brother.

He was out of luck. Most only had a sentence or two, but they were largely positive messages about his skill as a preacher or his leadership. It was nauseating, and Micah's anxiety rose as he listened. Was no one aware of the things he did? Perhaps he had kept it all secret from them, but Micah couldn't see how. He trembled, now questioning his memories of his life before he cut Elijah out entirely.

Beside him, Zayne put a hand on his arm. He shook her off and stood up, brushing past the knees of the others in his row. He headed up the side aisle toward the doors. Glancing back briefly, he saw Jeremiah looking over at him. Micah ignored him and kept going. He made it as far as the small lounge outside the auditorium before he felt a hand on his shoulder. He turned around and then jerked out of Jude's grasp.

"What do you want?" he snapped.

"I—I came to see if you were all right."

"Do I look all right?" When she shrank back, he relented. "I'm sorry. I couldn't sit in there and listen to the bullshit those people were saying. I know he was your father, but he was an asshole."

"You don't have to tell me that. I'm aware," she said, gesturing to her clothes. "You gave me an excuse not to listen."

Jeremiah came around the corner. "Micah, please come back in."

"Why should I? Why should I sit there and listen to all those people who are either lying or clueless? I'm here because you asked me. You said I should have closure. This is about as far from 'closure' as I could possibly get."

"They're almost done. I haven't spoken yet, and I think you need to hear what I have to say."

Micah clenched his fists, tensing and releasing while he tried to regain control. "Why? So you can try to save me, just like Pop and Elijah did?"

"No. Absolutely not. I've never met anyone less in need of 'saving' than you." Jeremiah put his hand on Micah's shoulder, and this time Micah didn't try to free himself. "You, and everyone sitting there, need to know the truth. Please?"

For a long, tense moment, Micah stared at Jeremiah. He thought about all the ways Elijah had tormented him and all the times Jeremiah, as the oldest, could and should have stopped it. Yet something in Jeremiah's pleading expression and the words "the truth" compelled Micah.

"All right."

Jeremiah turned and walked back toward the auditorium. Micah and Jude followed. Before they went in, Jude whispered, "We'll talk later, and I'll introduce you to Ike." She escaped up the aisle to join her family again. Micah slipped back in between Zayne and Elle.

The last few people had their say about Elijah, and then Jeremiah was back up at the podium on the low stage. Around the room, people shuffled a bit during the transition as they found their way back to their seats and got comfortable. Jeremiah took out a few sheets of paper and placed them on the podium. He stared at them for a minute before he spoke.

"My brother was not a good person," he said. Instantly, the whole room went silent. Jeremiah looked out at them then resumed his speech. "Elijah was a troubled man who believed not so much in God but in the rules he attributed to God. He didn't have a healthy relationship with the world, and he tried to relieve his pain in the only way he knew how. His drug of choice was the Bible.

"He spent countless hours reading and re-reading anything he could find to support his views. When we were boys, he denied himself any form of pleasure, believing he could make himself more like God through his do-not list. Any time he messed up, and any time he found a new rule, he would go that much farther to prove he was righteous. He was certain that being perfectly holy was the key to success. Our father had taught us being righteous and being better than others at following God would lead to happiness.

"When it didn't, Elijah became angry. First he took it out on our youngest brother, believing he must have allowed 'sin' into his life at a young age. Later, he blamed our stepmother for not recognizing him as superior to our father. Over and over, he took out his frustration on others at his lack of joy. He repeatedly cheated on his wife, antagonized our brother, and spiritually abused and confused his own children.

"I'm glad he's gone." At the collective gasp, Jeremiah held up his hand. "Not because I hated him. No, I'm glad because at last he's at peace. He is no longer tormented by his unhappiness in this life. I won't call his sudden death from an aneurysm a 'blessing.' However, God, in his infinite wisdom and mercy, chose to take him quickly, that he would not suffer any more.

"As imperfect as I was at it, I loved my brother. I tried to help him find the joy and peace he craved. In so doing, I failed our youngest brother and my nieces and nephews." Jeremiah looked up, and even from that distance, Micah saw his eyes shimmering. "I didn't protect them as I should have, and for that, I'm sorry.

"If we can learn anything from Elijah's life and his pain, it's that he isn't the one we should emulate. Of the three of us, our youngest brother is the one who has most exemplified the teachings of our Lord. You'd be hard-pressed to find a more generous soul or one who cares more deeply about the people society has forgotten." Jeremiah kept his eyes on Micah as he said, "Hear these words from Micah chapter six. 'With what shall I come before the LORD, and bow myself before God on high? Shall I come before him with burnt offerings, with calves a year old? Will the LORD be pleased with thousands of rams, with ten thousands of rivers of oil? Shall I give my firstborn for my transgression, the fruit of my body for the sin of my soul? He has told you, O mortal, what is good, and what does the LORD require of you but to do justice, and to love kindness, and to walk humbly with your God?'

"Do not be like Elijah, looking for fulfillment by avoiding a list of sinful thoughts and behaviors, looking to please God through your self-sacrifice. Instead be like Micah—either of them, the biblical prophet or my brother—by seeking justice and kindness. To do this is, indeed, to walk humbly with your God. Amen."

Jeremiah stepped down from the low stage. For a second, the pianist looked like she had no idea what to do, since he'd given no lead-in to the last part of the service. He turned around and motioned to her then continued up the aisle. Micah watched him as the pianist started playing. Jeremiah's steps were weary, as though speaking had taken his last ounce of strength.

Zayne nudged Micah, and they stood along with the rest of the assembled guests. Jeremiah's words echoed in Micah's mind as the service concluded. He followed the others out of the sanctuary for the brief greeting of the family. Since they weren't staying for the reception, Micah made his way to Jude to pay his respects.

She smiled briefly when she saw him. "I have something for you. Let me get the others, and we'll walk you to your car." She grimaced. "It'll be a good excuse to escape for a bit, since I'm stuck here all day." She turned to speak to the quiet young man beside her, and they both stepped away. Motioning to her sister, the three of them moved farther from the crowd.

Micah said to Zayne, "I'm going to go talk to them for a few minutes."

She kissed his cheek. "We're going to get our things, and we'll meet you at your place later."

They parted ways, and Micah followed Jude and Ike out to the parking lot. Jude led Micah to her car, where she withdrew a box from the trunk. She handed it to him.

"First, this is my brother Ike and my sister, Joy. Guys, this is our Uncle Micah."

Joy gave him a warm hug, but Ike hung back, reserved. Micah had respect for him; he would've done the same. Micah extended a hand, and Ike shook it.

"It's good to meet you," Micah told them.

"I'm sorry the others weren't willing," Jude said. "My oldest brother shares some of our father's beliefs, though he isn't as cruel. The others...well, give them time."

"What's in the box?"

"A gift." Jude smiled. "From the three of us, courtesy of our father. Wait until you get home to open it. You'll need some time."

"Are you coming back to Concordia later?" Micah asked.

Jude shook her head. "I'll be out for a few more days, but I'll be back in time for class at the community center next week."

"Good." Micah embraced her again, and she and her siblings returned to the church.

He put the box in his trunk and climbed back into his car. Jeremiah would be busy for the foreseeable future, but Micah would call him after the dust settled. They needed time together, just the two of them, whether or not they talked about Elijah. For now, it was time to go home.

CHAPTER TWENTY-ONE

MY BROTHER AND SISTER AND MOTHER

WHEN MICAH returned home, Thomas was nowhere to be found in the house. Micah had no idea where he could be; in theory, he shouldn't have been able to escape. He didn't seem to be hiding anywhere that he might have gotten stuck, although it was still a possibility. Micah searched for him, worrying over what might have happened in his absence. Guilt ate at him for leaving Thomas, even though it wasn't much different from leaving him while he was at work.

He stepped out onto the porch to have a look around. A flash of orange caught his attention as it streaked past him from the house. A moment later, Thomas's face came into view through the shrubs. Relieved, Micah stepped off the porch toward him, intending to beckon him. He considered returning to the house for a bowl of food to entice the cat back. Before he could move, Thomas blinked at him then took off into the bushes.

Micah almost followed, but he knew it wouldn't do any good. Thomas had made his decision. He'd been getting antsy, and the last few times Micah had let him out, he'd gone a little farther each time and been increasingly slow to come in. Micah had known from the beginning that he wouldn't be able to keep Thomas. After all, such a sleek, well-fed animal was surely someone's pet. Thomas had taken what he needed from Micah, and perhaps given as much in return as he was able. Now it was time for him to go back where he'd come from.

That didn't mean it hurt any less. Micah had gotten used to having a warm body near him when he slept. He'd become accustomed to their early morning conversations—one-sided though they were. Thomas had filled something in him he hadn't realized he needed. It felt now as though that had all been ripped away, and he might never find it again. It was all his fault for letting himself be talked into going to the funeral. As irrational as Micah knew it was, he decided Thomas had somehow determined he was no longer wanted. Micah stood on the porch, immobile, with his arms wrapped around his middle.

God only knew how long it was until LR found him that way, still as stone and staring into the shrubs. He barely noticed her arrival until she was almost on top of him. She tapped his shoulder, and he jumped.

"Micah?" She frowned. "What are you doing?"

"He's gone," Micah mumbled.

LR turned to face the same direction. "Who? Elijah? That's where you were, right? I was going to call to find out when you were returning from the funeral, but Emily took apart my phone again. I saw your car and figured I'd stop by to see if you needed anything."

"No, not Elijah." His brain didn't seem to want to unstick itself from Thomas. "I was going to feed him before Pam and Zayne came. They're visiting to help me go through Elijah's box."

"Okay," LR said. There was still confusion in her tone. She didn't seem to understand the importance of the situation. Frowning, she finally caught on. "Oh, your cat."

"Yeah."

"Come on inside," LR said, her voice softening. She put a hand on his elbow, guiding him back into the house.

"He's going to be all alone." Micah shook his head. He let LR lead him to the couch, where he plopped down.

"I'll get you some water." LR disappeared into the kitchen.

While she was in there, Pam and Zayne showed up as promised. They'd brought Elle, too, but it didn't quite make an impression. Micah was as lost in his own twisted thoughts sitting on his couch as he had been when standing on the porch. The three of them came in and dropped their bags in the entryway, but Micah only glanced up at them without saying a word.

LR came back out to find the three of them peering into the living room. She set the glass down and returned to the entryway, taking their coats and hanging them on the hooks on the wall. She ushered them in, and the four of them stood in front of Micah. He looked up at them, but he couldn't formulate words.

"Cooper, Henry, and Lucy are on their way," Zayne said. At Micah's lack of response, she turned to LR. "What's wrong with him this time?"

LR shrugged. "He lost his cat."

Micah scowled at her. "Not lost! Ran away. There's a difference."

"Of course there is, baby." Zayne sat down next to him on the couch, and Pam joined them on Micah's other side. "Tell us about it."

"He's gone!" Micah said. His knee bounced, and he gripped it to stop the shaking. "He left me, and he isn't ever coming back." Micah choked out a half-sob. "I miss him so much, and I don't know what to do." Everything caught up to him at once: guilt and anger and sadness, all of it blowing up, the wire tripped by Thomas's escape.

Zayne pulled him close, and he wept in her arms. "Oh, baby. Sh. It's okay."

Pam rubbed his back with long, gentle strokes. Elle settled down on the floor, resting her head on his knee, and LR knelt beside him and took his hand. They held him while he spilled his grief onto their sympathetic shoulders.

The door opened again, and Micah pulled himself together. He wiped his eyes on his sleeve so he could see. Cooper was in the doorway to the living room, flanked by Henry and Lucy. Elle got up from the floor to stand by Henry. She slid her hand into his, and they exchanged a glance.

"What's going on?" Cooper asked.

"Micah's cat," LR said.

"He left," Pam added. She squeezed Micah sideways.

Micah turned his head toward her. Pam understood some things better than the others. She would never be able to give Micah a satisfying answer on why her life was spared and Cat's was not, but she didn't try. He leaned against her and closed his eyes.

"I'm not sure I can keep going without him," Micah said.

"I know," Pam murmured into his hair. "It's all right."

LR still clung to his hand. "Me neither. But we do, don't we? Every day we do, a little bit at a time."

"You have us," Lucy piped up. "Whenever you need us."

"Of course you do, baby." Zayne put her hand on his cheek.

Nodding, Micah reopened his eyes. Cooper looked like he might say something, but he changed his mind. Instead, he craned his neck to peer into the kitchen.

"What's that box?"

"Hm?" Micah sat up and straightened his shoulders. "Oh, that. Elijah's kids gave it to me, but I haven't looked inside yet."

"Do you feel up to it?" Zayne asked. "Because I'm desperate to know what that menace left you and if it's anywhere near as ridiculous as what your father did."

Micah snorted, and it turned into a laugh. "Nothing would surprise me at this point. Hey, Pam, you want to put on some coffee and hot water? You all can stay and satisfy your curiosity."

They dispersed, and in short order everyone had a hot drink in hand and had settled back down in the living room. Micah carried the box from the kitchen and set it on the coffee table. It wasn't big; an average-sized packing carton labeled in black permanent marker *For Micah*. Jude had said it was a gift, and he half expected it to be full of Elijah's personal things. Micah couldn't imagine why his brother would have wanted him to have any of it or why his wife would've allowed her children to deliver it. He was nervous about opening it, fearing it might be the same sort of jab his father had made by leaving him a dilapidated house. This was obviously on a much smaller scale, but Elijah's nastiness had far-reaching consequences. Whatever was in the box might be even worse than fixing up a run-down lakefront property.

For a moment, Micah choked again. What his father had intended for ill had given Micah nine years of something far better than any of them could have imagined. Micah frowned at his own thoughts. No, it hadn't been only nine years. What he'd had with Cat was deeper than only the length of time they'd spent together. Micah sat up straighter. Whatever Elijah had left in the box would never be bad enough to erase his life with Cat, and that was all the courage Micah needed to look inside.

He ran a pair of scissors over the tape, and the box flaps popped open. Micah folded them back and lifted out the first item, an envelope. He tore into it and pulled out the single sheet of paper. From the first line, his jaw dropped, and he looked up at the others.

"What's it say?" Elle asked.

Micah read it aloud.

Dear Uncle Micah,

We knew Dad wouldn't have left you anything. He spent a lifetime taking instead of giving. A few of us got together and decided to put together this box. We've missed out on knowing you all these years, but we hope you'll give us a chance to make it right.

Love,

Jude, with help from Joy and Ike

Micah looked up again. "It's Elijah's two youngest and his older daughter. I got the impression the oldest agreed with Elijah's views, and the other two boys aren't sure. These are all the ones who saw what he'd done over the years for what it was."

"The ones you were speaking with at the funeral?" Pam asked.

"Yes."

Micah set the letter aside and reached into the box. Inside were three scrapbooks. He flipped through, with the others looking over his shoulders. There were pictures of all his nieces and nephews, but this one was mostly Joy. Photos of her as an infant all the way through her college graduation, wedding, and the birth of her own children. Alongside each photo was a description and a note about what else was going on in her life at the time.

Laying it on the coffee table, Micah picked up the next album and the next. Each one had a slightly different style, but they were all constructed in a similar fashion to the first. He thumbed through Ike's next. His heart lurched at the first photo, the family Christmas picture from the year Ike was a baby. Micah remembered that time, and not fondly. He exchanged a significant glance with Zayne. She, too, must have recalled Micah's self-destructive behavior when Elijah sent the photo, complete with his hate-spew written on the back. Micah suspected Ike's photo didn't include a homophobic rant, but he didn't take the picture out to look. He flipped the page quickly.

Through the magic of genetics, Ike's resemblance to Micah was uncanny. Scanning the photos was like a trip back to his own childhood; only the surroundings were different. Micah grinned when he saw Ike's achievements included work on the school paper, the yearbook, and the annual poetry contest. He mentally crossed his fingers that Jude would be able to bring him safely to them once he was out from beneath their family's control.

Zayne must have picked up on his thoughts because she said, "It'll be different for him, baby. I may not know him, but I know you. Even if you wanted to, you couldn't leave him without help." She reached out and squeezed his hand.

"We won't leave him without family," Pam agreed.

Nodding, Micah set the book aside and picked up Jude's. Her childhood photos were mostly of someone who looked distinctly uncomfortable pretending to be the model of demure femininity. If he hadn't known why she'd tried so hard, it might have been almost comical how out of place she appeared. Micah did smile when the familiar woman she'd become emerged in the pictures of her at college. There was pride and fierce joy in her during those years. At the end, he saw she'd enclosed a personal note for him, tucked inside the back cover.

I'm sorry for not telling you the truth sooner. I hope you'll forgive me. You're family, and I want us to have a relationship beyond what we've had at work and as friends.

Of course he would forgive her. Maybe she was right that he wouldn't have trusted her if he'd known from the start. When they were both back at school, he would find her and make sure she knew and that he wanted the same with any of Elijah's other children who were willing. Talking to her would be easier than facing Jeremiah and figuring out how to finally move beyond the years of hate and emotional violence inflicted on them both.

Micah stacked the albums on the coffee table. "I don't know what to say."

"Are you going to see them again?" Pam asked.

He nodded. "I'll at least still see Jude at work, and it'll be better now that we both know."

"And the rest?" LR asked.

"I think so. They want to see me, and they don't agree with what Elijah did to me. Or to them, for that matter. He kept us apart because he didn't want my influence on them. And yet, even without my presence, he managed to raise three queer kids." Micah exhaled. "If he hadn't been so much of an asshole, this would be funny. As bad as it was for me growing up, I can't even imagine what it must have been like to have Elijah for a father."

He stood up and took the photo albums to the shelf, where he added them to the other books. His eye caught the queer theology book Chris had loaned him, and he sighed. He would need to deal with it at some point, knowing he would never be able to get through it no matter how much he'd wanted to try. This wasn't the time. For now, he needed to be with his family.

Turning around he said, "Is anyone hungry? I could make us something." At Zayne's arched eyebrow, he laughed. "Seven weeks of cooking classes have paid off. I promise, I won't poison you all."

"I can vouch for him," Cooper said.

The others laughed, and they picked up the coffee cups to bring to the kitchen. LR pulled Micah aside and gave him a quick hug.

"I should go. I told Jamal I wouldn't be long when I stopped by. We'll talk again soon, though." She smiled. "We'll be all right."

She stepped around him, and he watched her go before heading back into the kitchen with the others.

CHAPTER TWENTY-TWO

I AM WITH YOU ALWAYS

THE HOUSE was quiet. Everyone else had long since gone. Elle and Henry had been up with the sun to drive back to New York. Cooper and Lucy had hung around for lunch, after which they'd gone to Watkins Glen to look at a few houses. Pam and Zayne had stayed until late afternoon, but even they had to return home to their responsibilities.

Restless, Micah moved from room to room, searching for something to occupy his mind and body. In the office, he paused. The box with Cat's letters was on the desk, and there was one more he hadn't yet opened. There was something too final about it, and he hadn't been ready before Elijah's funeral. Now, he stood in the doorway and debated whether he still needed time or if he was only stalling.

He looked down, half expecting Thomas to give him a nudge before memory caught up to him and he realized the cat wasn't there. He was on his own this time, both in making the decision and in carrying it out. Before he could change his mind and put it off again, he retrieved the letter. This time, he didn't bring his laptop. The moment felt too precious to use it right away in finishing the story. He returned to the living room and sat down on the couch, setting the letter on the coffee table.

The envelope lay in front of him. He stared at it until his hands itched to hold it, and he was overwhelmed with a need to find out what Cat's last words to him had been. He lifted it slowly and turned it over in his hands. Only his name was written on the outside in Cat's tight, neat printing. Micah slid his finger under the flap, unsealing it. Hands shaking, he withdrew the single piece of lined notebook paper. He unfolded it and smoothed it out on the table.

Dearest Micah,

This is my last letter to you. That sounds horribly clichéd. Let me try again.

I'm too sick to have many good days left when I still make sense. I can feel it, and I'm sure you can see it too. Tomorrow, I'll talk to you about it. We need to make some plans so you don't get stuck taking care of the funeral when you'll need all your energy to keep going. You're going to argue with me and probably tell me to fuck off, and if I'm feeling good enough, I'll say it right back.

Micah chuckled. He had, of course. Their last fight—one of many "lasts" they'd shared, in much the same way as they'd shared "firsts."

If I'm lucky, you'll have read all these letters instead of leaving them on your shelf until long after you're gone too. I know you. Maybe you're ready to move on, though, and that's why you're reading. I'm sorry they haven't been as good as your writing. You know I'm shit at that kind of stuff. Remember when I tried to help you with your novel and mostly just made a mess? Yeah.

I told you before, and again in my first letter, that you shouldn't hold on to me. You should get rid of my things and try not to think about me too much. That was stupid, okay? I shouldn't have said it. Why didn't you remind me about how I kept some of David's shit in my room? I hope you found a use for it, by the way. Were you able to save the pictures? Not that I care, I guess, but if you did, he still has family who might want them.

Unless you already did that, in which case just ignore me. Ugh, I'm rambling.

Anyway, that's not what I wanted to tell you. I wanted to tell you it's okay for you to still think about me, to still love me, but maybe have room in your life for other people. I don't mean you have to marry someone else or anything. Just don't shut out all our friends and family, okay? Don't get so caught up in memories of me that you forget how many other people love you and need you.

There's this Bible verse (yeah, I know you hate that crap, but by the time you read this, I'll be dead, so I don't care). It says, "where your treasure is, there your heart will be also." It's supposed to mean caring less about having stuff and being powerful and more about loving God and others. But I think it works for you here. I'm not the only good thing there ever was in your life. Maybe I wasn't even the best thing. Maybe it has yet to happen. Whatever. But we were good together, and I think that's worth remembering. What I mean is, don't fool yourself into thinking you'll find me in my belongings. Hold on to what helps you remember the best in us, and let go of what will hold you back from all the wonderful things still to come for you.

Put your treasure in the people who love you and are still alive to tell you so. Take care of LR. Spend time with our friends. Write our story. And if one day, you meet someone new, it's all right. I promise not to be jealous. Love them with everything you have. Take all the awesome, amazing years we had together and bring all that love into your new relationship. The more people you love, the more room your heart has to expand (look at me and my fancy-ass words). When you make love with your new person, be present. Be joyful. Remember, fucking is holy!

I am always with you, in one way or another. Don't drown, honey. Live.

All my love,

Cat

Micah closed his eyes, letting silent tears stream down his

cheeks. Sitting there with the letter in his hands, he tried to make sense of it all. If anyone knew what it meant to have a life full of love, it was Cat. He'd found room in his heart for Micah, even though he'd loved and lost David. Almost nothing surpassed Cat's deep affection for everyone he met. Why couldn't Micah let go and be more like him, trusting that nothing would diminish the love they'd had for each other?

He thought about his past lovers: Zayne, his first close friend and teenage crush who had turned out to be a girl, but he'd quietly loved her even so. Matt, the college roommate who had changed his world. Gerry, the affair which had led to a lifetime of friendship with Gerry's ex-wife, Pam. Shel, his first lover after he'd gotten sober. Reid, who had forgiven him for being an ass for most of a summer, and his partners. Lola, the lilac-haired woman from his grief group whose activism helped them both begin to heal. And then there was Cat, the love of his life and the one he'd wanted to be his forever-love except he never could be. None of them had stolen part of his soul; instead, they had taken the fractured pieces and woven their own lives into the spaces to knit him together.

Micah's mind wandered to others, not lovers but those who had been part of the mending—to Jeremiah, who had needed healing himself, and Jude, who had escaped to shout her convictions to the world. Zayne again, who had been more than he could ever hope for in a best friend. Pam, Cooper and Elle, and their families. LR and Jamal and their pack of wild kittens, his nieces and nephews. Jones and Alonzo. Debbie, his second mother. His class at the community center. All the friends and neighbors and coworkers who had stayed part of his life for so many years and through so many changes.

Only then did he understand. He knew why Reid said he felt whole loving and being loved by three men and why Cat's spirit was so generous and free with his love that everyone in town knew his name. It was possible to love more than one person, whether all at once or over a lifetime, as lovers, friends, neighbors. Overcome, Micah wiped at his eyes as the last revelation descended—he had never been afraid of loving someone new at all.

What he'd been afraid of was sharing Cat with them, of doing what Cat had said and bringing with him all the joys and heartaches of their life together. It felt like a betrayal of trust, as though Cat would be an unwelcome guest. Over the last several weeks, he'd tried to purge Cat from his heart and mind through his novel. In the writing, it had become clear he would never be able to leave those years behind him. Now Cat was giving him a new commandment.

Put your treasure in the people who love you and are still alive to tell you so. Micah's whole being thrummed with possibility. Laughter bubbled out of him, and he sat on his couch, wiping his eyes and rocking with the pure joy of it all. When he was spent from the outpouring of emotion, he sat back. He knew what he had to do. Before he could talk himself out of it, he rose from the couch and went to the bookshelf. Taking the queer theology book, he grabbed his coat and keys and headed out the door.

Micah fidgeted, his phone in hand and a bouquet of flowers and the book on the passenger seat of his car. He couldn't recall ever being so nervous. In his entire life, he'd never gone to a man's house with a dozen roses and a prepared statement. After three long, tense minutes of internal debate, he finally called.

"Hello?" Chris's voice was warm and a little sleepy.

"Hey, it's Micah."

There was a little rustling in the background. "I'm glad you called. I was thinking about you."

"Oh, yeah?"

"Mm-hm. Wondering how you were doing. The funeral was yesterday, right?"

"It was. I'm sorry I didn't call you sooner." Micah paused. "Can—can I come up? I'm sitting in your parking lot."

Chris laughed. "Uh...okay," he said. "I'll be down in a sec."

They ended the call, and Micah got out of the car with the flowers and the book. He waited at the door until he heard footsteps. A moment later, the door swung open to reveal Chris in sweatpants and an old t-shirt. He looked like he'd been about to head to bed, even though it wasn't even eight.

Micah pulled his hand from behind his back and extended the flowers. "These are for you, if you want them." *If you want me,* he wished he could add.

Chris smiled as he took them. "They're beautiful." He touched the petals then put his nose to them. "Come on in."

Micah followed him inside, closing the door. Chris put the flowers in a vase and then turned to face Micah. "I get the sense you have something on your mind."

Extending the book, Micah replied, "I'm really sorry. I can't read this. It's not because I don't want to. It's not the religious stuff. I have trouble sitting in church, and I don't believe in any of it anymore. But that's not the problem. I listened to Cat talk about his faith for years because I loved him and I cared about what it meant to him." He took a deep breath and let it out slowly. "I don't want to read a book because I'd rather hear it directly from you instead. I care about what this means to you. I—I care about you."

"I'm all right with that, and I care about you too." He eyed Micah. "But why did you need to show up unannounced at my door on a Sunday night—with flowers, no less—to tell me?"

"I found another letter," Micah said, "from Cat."

"I don't quite understand."

Micah laughed softly. "He knew me so well. He knew I would try to hold onto him, even after he died. The last time he was able to talk, he told me to purge my life of him. In this letter, he said he was wrong."

Chris nodded. "Go on."

"So, he said what he really wanted was for me to live. To love." Micah reached for Chris's hand, encouraged when Chris didn't withdraw. "Not to feel guilty if I found someone else to share my life with, and not to feel ashamed of bringing my love for Cat with me."

A hesitant smile formed on Chris's lips. "All right."

"When I met you, I wasn't looking. I had the idea to take my mind off Cat by working at the community center. Only teaching that class ended up giving me the freedom to really think about him for the first time since he died. You all kept wanting me to tell our story, even if it was only in fairy tale form. It brought up all these memories, things I hadn't allowed myself to tell anyone else." Micah shook his head at his own stubbornness. "I kept them locked away, hoarding them like a dragon's treasure."

Chris chuckled. "And we unlocked the chest for you."

"Yes," Micah agreed. "Especially you. You let me tell you, but not in a way that left me feeling sad or angry. You listened in a way no one else has, either because they're too close or not close enough. I needed a friend, and you were there." He squeezed Chris's hand and took his own back. "But somewhere in there, I met you, too, and I liked you very much."

"Just liked?"

"At first, yes." Micah opened his arms wide. "Now? It's so much more. Not because you listened to me go on about my dead spouse but because you're someone I care about for yourself. I'm not ready to let go of Cat—I'm ready for him to let me go."

The words were soft, barely there, but Micah heard them. Chris's eyes never left him. "And where exactly is he letting you go to?"

"Anywhere we want."

Micah reached for Chris, who stepped into his embrace. Micah didn't kiss him right away. He needed to look at him, to see in his eyes that this was right and something they both wanted. A smile slowly spread across Chris's face.

Then Micah kissed him. Soft and sweet, like the night on the beach. He cupped Chris's cheek, liking the way his beard scratched his palm just a little. Chris's arm went around Micah's waist, and his other hand caressed Micah's neck. They let it go on longer than it had the other night, and Micah wished he didn't have to stop them. He pulled back, closing his eyes and resting their foreheads together. With a regretful sigh, he let Chris go.

Chris stepped away. "I get the feeling there's more you wanted to say."

"Three days," Micah said.

"What?" Chris frowned in confusion.

"I need three days to do everything. Cat says I'm supposed to 'store up treasure' in the right places. I suppose you probably know better than I do what he means. If I'm going to really live, like he asked me to, I need to do this. Then I'm all yours."

"Okay," Chris said. "I won't say I'm not confused, but take all the time you need."

"Three days," Micah repeated.

He turned to go, thought better of it, and stepped closer for one last, hurried kiss before retreating from Chris's apartment. He had some planning to do.

CHAPTER TWENTY-THREE

INTO YOUR HANDS

FIRST THING in the morning, Micah dropped off a folder with all his lesson plans for the substitute teacher. While he waited for his order at Sweet Beans, he made the first two of several phone calls, crossing his fingers that it wasn't too early. A hasty cup of coffee later and he was on his way. He ducked into the used queer bookstore on Main Street to pick up the book he'd asked the clerk to hold. She handed it to him with a smile. Once he'd paid, he was on the road up to Rochester.

Micah stood on Jeremiah's doorstep with the book in hand. He didn't hesitate before knocking. Jeremiah answered and ushered him into the kitchen, where he'd already put out a light breakfast. Micah sat down at the table, and Jeremiah brought over two steaming mugs—tea for himself, coffee for Micah. He sat across from Micah, and they were quiet for several minutes while they served themselves.

"So," Jeremiah said eventually. "How is everything? How's work?"

He was trying. Micah replied, "Not bad. Keeping busy with the students and some volunteering at the community center. You?"

Jeremiah put his spoon next to his cup, but he didn't take a drink. "Been thinking about finally retiring."

Micah snorted. "Not sure how you've lasted this long, but why now?"

"I've been in ministry for almost forty years, in one way or another. Maybe it's time to move on."

"Does that feel like the right thing to do?" Micah was genuinely curious. He'd never asked if Jeremiah enjoyed his work, and it now occurred to him that four decades was a long time to spend doing something he didn't like.

"Not necessarily, but lately..." He trailed off. The silence that followed was tense. Jeremiah kept his eyes on his plate, and his hand shook. At last he looked up. "Are we going to talk about him?"

With a sigh, Micah said, "I suppose we should, although I don't know what's left to say."

"Aside from how he was equally hateful as our father? I hope he was at least kinder to his children."

"He was, and he wasn't." Micah played with his spoon, rolling it over in his fingers. "Why didn't you tell me about Jude? She said you told her where to find me. A little warning might have been nice."

"She asked me not to. She'd changed her name and was ready to leave town without a backwards glance. I assumed she would fill you in."

"Did you see his kids much?"

Jeremiah shook his head. "When they were younger, yes. After you blew things up at Elijah's church, he stopped talking to me." He rubbed his forehead. "I was a sympathizer, so I became his enemy."

"Good god, that man had enough hate in him for several lifetimes."

"I miss him anyway. Maybe I shouldn't, but I do."

Micah's throat constricted. "I miss what he should've been."

They ate without speaking further. There was a quiet emptiness between them, and Micah wondered if something had been lost in Elijah's passing. Jeremiah had been on the verge of burning out a dozen years before when Elijah had proved himself to be incapable of managing the church. Yet he'd stuck it out, and when the time came, he'd left. Micah glanced at the book on the table next to him. Maybe he needed an infusion of something new.

Jeremiah's gaze followed, and he raised his eyebrows. "What's that?"

"A book, obviously."

"I can see that. Queer theology?"

Micah's thoughts went straight to Chris. "A...friend...gave it to me, but I didn't have a lot of interest in reading it, so I gave it back. I bought you a copy of your own."

"A 'friend,' eh?" Jeremiah chuckled. He picked up the book. "You want me to read this?"

"Only if you want to." Micah shrugged. While Jeremiah turned the book over to read the back cover, Micah said, "Why didn't you ever get married? Was it just seeing how Pop was?"

"Not really. I suppose I never wanted to." He gave Micah a pointed look. "I certainly didn't want anyone picking out my girlfriend for me."

"Because you weren't interested in girls?" Micah pressed.

"I wasn't interested in anyone." Jeremiah frowned. "I'm not like you, if that's what you're implying. I'm not attracted to men. Just never found the right person, I guess. It certainly made my life easier every time the next big thing with Pop or Elijah came up."

Micah gripped his wrist. "I marked the relevant sections in the book, Jer. There's a sticky note with a web site on it that I think you might like to read. You deserve to retire if you want, but I think people still need you. Especially if they're getting the real, whole you." He stood. "I should go. I only have three days and a lot of ground to cover."

"Three days?"

"That's all I took off from work." Micah wasn't ready to talk to his brother about Chris yet.

Jeremiah got to his feet. He clasped Micah's hands. "I am sorry," he said. "For everything."

"It's over now." Micah nodded to the book. "Read it. I'm here if you want to talk."

They embraced, and Jeremiah held onto Micah for a long time before releasing him. "Next time, I'll come see you."

"I'd like that."

Micah walked out into the damp, chilly air. One down, but it was the easiest. His next visits would be infinitely harder.

Micah stopped by his house to pick up the few things he needed on his way into town. He was meeting Reid for a late lunch, and he needed to get the box he'd set aside the night before. He hoped Reid didn't think he'd completely lost it when he saw what was inside. He had specifically asked not to meet at Sweet Beans. The odds of Audrey overhearing their conversation or seeing what was in the box were too high. Instead, they were having lunch at a nice seafood place by the water.

The day was gloomy and overcast, and every so often a few drops fell as a larger rainstorm threatened. Inside the restaurant, the hostess seated Micah by the large window overlooking the choppy lake. He set the box at his feet. Reid showed up a few minutes later.

"Did you change your mind about coming over?" he asked by way of greeting, grinning his perfect, polished smile.

Micah laughed. "No, which is why we're meeting here."

"Ah, damn." Reid laughed along with him.

"I'm sure you'll get over it." They placed their orders, and Micah turned serious. "I'm not sure if anyone filled you in, but my brother died."

"Which one? The evil overlord or the decent guy?" Reid cringed. "That's a horrible thing to say, even if he was vicious. I'm sorry."

"The evil overlord." Micah shook his head, but he gave Reid a wry smile.

"Do I offer condolences? I didn't get the impression you were close, but he was still family."

"I'm not sure," Micah answered. He still hadn't decided what his feelings were on the matter, and he couldn't expect anyone else to keep up. "It brought up a lot of memories of the last time I did this."

"I can imagine." Reid frowned. "You're going somewhere with

this, aren't you?" He leaned back. "Are you leaving us?"

"No! Nothing like that. It's complicated."

"Complicated, eh?" Reid said. "Well, now you've got my attention."

Micah didn't quite have the kind of relationship with Reid where he felt comfortable revealing his deepest thoughts. He'd have been more like a drinking buddy, if Micah still did that. Even so, Micah had to tell him something to explain the box under the table.

"Cat left me some shit," he said. "Told me to invest in my friends and family."

"Didn't you already take care of it years ago?"

"Mostly, but these were items of a more personal nature." Micah leaned forward and looked around as though to indicate he was letting Reid in on a secret. "Very personal."

Reid's eyebrows nearly hit his hairline. "You don't say."

"There's a box at my feet. Have a look."

Reid narrowed his eyes, but he ducked under the table. Micah held still, listening to the scrape of the flap opening. Reid reappeared so fast he nearly smacked his head on the underside of the table. He emerged with a what-in-holy-hell expression.

Leaning forward, he whisper-yelled, "Where in the fucking fuck did you get all those?"

"Where do you think?" Micah retorted. "We bought them. I have no use for them, and I thought you might have some idea."

"For an entire box full of sex toys?" Reid flopped back in his seat and stared at Micah. "Yeah, all right. I probably do."

"Good. For the record, I do not want to know what those are. You take care of them in whatever manner you see fit." He gave Reid a wicked smirk. "Including keeping them."

"Micah! For god's sake. That's...it's..." He opened and closed his mouth several times. "Maybe it's not such a terrible idea."

Their food arrived, effectively halting the discussion on the toys. Micah allowed himself exactly thirty seconds of contemplating what Reid might have in mind before he picked up his spoon and dipped it into the lobster bisque.

"So, on a different subject, how's the housing market in Watkins Glen? My godson and his wife are looking."

By the time they finished lunch, the rain had started. Large, cold drops pelted Micah's head as he dashed for his car. Shivering, he turned up the heat as he drove to the retirees' town houses. He left the car running while he pulled a small box with a gold lid from the glove compartment. Reluctantly, he turned the car off and climbed out to splash through the icy puddles.

Jones let him in, and Micah toed off his shoes so he wouldn't soak the carpet. He shrugged out of his jacket and hung it on a wall hook. The house was messier than it had been the last time, with more clutter in the living room. The curtains were closed, keeping out what little daylight there was. Micah followed Jones into the kitchen, glancing briefly at Alonzo, sprawled on the couch. Jones offered Micah a hot drink, which he declined. He sat at the table and rubbed his feet together, annoyed that his socks were damp.

Sliding into the chair next to him, Jones said, "I'm sorry I didn't clean up before you came over." He fiddled with the placemat. "It's been a bad few days."

"I'm sorry."

Jones slumped down in his seat. "I'm just so damn tired."

Micah glanced around him, at the dishes in the sink and the groceries Jones hadn't put in the pantry and the basket of clean but unfolded laundry in the hallway to the bedrooms. He stood and began putting the food away. Jones looked up at him.

"You don't have to do that."

"It's all right." Micah stacked some canned fruit. "When does the nurse come in?"

"Tomorrow, and we have an aide here for two hours every morning and evening."

Micah paused in his unloading. "It's not enough, is it?"

"No."

"What about respite care? You need a break."

"I can't," Jones said, his tone flat.

Micah returned to the table and sat back down. He put a hand on Jones' arm. "Do you need money? I could—"

"No, no." Jones put his hand on top of Micah's. "It's nothing like that. I have the money."

All too well, Micah thought he understood what held Jones back. "You don't need to feel guilty."

Jones sighed deeply. "I don't feel guilty, either."

"Then what is it?"

"I'm afraid that when I come back for him, he'll have forgotten who I am. At least this way, I can keep reminding him."

He hunched over the table, and his shoulders shook. Micah slid his chair closer, laying his arm across Jones's back. After a moment, Jones returned to himself. Micah released him, and together they went about cleaning up the rest of the kitchen.

"I know you didn't come over to do this," Jones said, waving his hand at the pile of now-clean dishes in the drainer. "So, why are you here?"

"Cat," Micah said.

"You'll need to do better than that."

Micah patted his pocket where he'd stored the box. "He left a few things for me, including a whole stack of letters. There was a lock box, too. I spent the last couple of months going through it all. He'd said he wanted me to get rid of all his things."

"Damn fool," Jones grunted. "Not that simple, is it?"

"Nope," Micah agreed. "He said as much in the last letter. He also asked me to look after all of you—LR, Debbie, you and Alonzo. I think Mark and Angie can handle themselves."

Jones chuckled. "I'm sure they can."

"I have something for you from him, if you want it."

"Well, let's have it, then."

Micah pulled the box from his pocket and handed it to Jones. He opened the lid and lifted the tissue paper to reveal Cat's pot earring and its mate. His mouth fell open, and he looked up at Micah.

"I can't—"

"Yes, you can. You should have them. I think they'd mean more to you than to me anyway, and I know Cat would've loved them on you."

Jones set the box on the counter and removed the earrings he had in. He slid in the dangling leaves in their place, setting his other earrings in the box. "How do they look?"

"Perfect." Micah grinned, but then he turned serious. "You asked me before who you lean on now."

"Yeah."

"Me," Micah said. "You lean on me and all our other friends." He pulled Jones into a hug.

They let go of each other, and without having to say another word, they carried the laundry basket into the bedroom and began folding the clothes.

The following day, Micah spent his time working on his manuscript most of the morning. After lunch, he braved yet another rain shower to dash down the street to Debbie's house. He was glad he'd put the box for her into a bag first so it wouldn't be drenched. He beat a cheerful pattern on her door. She opened it, and Micah saw past her to the boxes stacked in her living room. He shot her a look, but she only tutted.

"What in the world?" he asked.

"Jude's moving in this weekend. She brought some of her things by last week. I gather she's spending a few days with her family."

"Yeah," Micah said. "She called me Sunday morning. She's not happy there."

"Understandable."

Micah surveyed the piles. "You want some help taking these things to another room?"

"That would be fantastic, dear. I'll go put on some coffee. Yes?"

"Sounds good. Which room?"

Once Debbie had showed him where to put everything, Micah took several trips to carry it upstairs. Except for some furniture, the entire place had been cleaned out. Jude would have the top floor to herself, now that Debbie was only using the lower level. Selfishly, Micah looked forward to having Jude close by.

He returned to the kitchen in time to get out mugs. Smiling, he accepted the plate of muffins. Before he sat at the table, he remembered the box he'd left in the foyer. He retrieved it and set it on one of the empty chairs.

Debbie looked back and forth between Micah and the box. "No room upstairs?"

"It's not one of Jude's." He stirred sugar into his coffee.

"Either you're working up to it or you're teasing me with some big surprise. Out with it, you." She pointed a scolding finger at him.

"I'll get to it." He took a bite of a muffin and collected his thoughts. When he was ready, he said, "Do you remember when you gave me all those letters my mother sent you?"

"Of course. Thank you for returning them."

Micah nodded. "I brought you all the ones you wrote to her. They're in the box."

"You didn't have to do that."

"I know, but I wanted to. There's something else in there as well. Go ahead and look."

She stood and went around to the opposite side of the table. Carefully, she opened the flaps on the box. First, she withdrew the packet of letters she'd written to Micah's mother. He'd found them hidden away in the attic the summer he moved in. Now they were back with their rightful owner. Micah had no doubt Debbie would one day return them to him, but for now, she deserved the chance to read them again.

Setting them aside, she reached in again and removed a second set of letters. Her eyes widened, and she glanced back at Micah with shock written all over her face. He acknowledged her, and she turned back to the letters in her hand. For a moment, she stood there, and Micah thought she might put them away without seeing what was in them. She didn't; instead, she carried them back to her place at the table and sat down, placing the letters in front of her.

Micah took her hand. "All those years ago, you trusted me with your heart. Now I'm trusting you with mine."

Debbie ran her fingers over the lettering on the top envelope. She looked up at Micah. "His letters to you?"

"Yes." Micah swallowed thickly. "From those last few months when he knew he was dying."

"I can't—" she started.

"Yes, you can. I want you to have them for now. He asked me to burn them, but I can't do it. So, instead, I'm turning them over to you for safekeeping. One day, when it won't embarrass them anymore, my nieces and nephews can have them. Until then, they're in your hands."

She reached for him, and they hugged awkwardly around the table. When she let go, she wiped at her eyes. She glanced at Micah sideways. "What, exactly, is in these letters?"

Micah had the good sense to flush. "Our lives together. Even the not-safe-for-work parts."

"Hm," was all Debbie said.

"Payback is fair," Micah told her. "I suffered through your poetic descriptions of—"

She put up a hand. "All right. You've made your point."

Micah only hid a smile behind his coffee cup.

Micah arrived home in time to see that LR was back from picking the kids up. They lived too far from the village to make it worthwhile for them to take the bus, so she arranged her schedule around theirs. Micah waited until the babysitter, who had been caring for the younger two, had left. Once she was gone, he gathered what he needed and headed next door.

Langston answered his knock. Today he had on a shimmering purple shirt and stretchy black pants. He grinned up at Micah then called over his shoulder, "Mo-om! Uncle Mike is here!"

LR came into the foyer. She was still dressed for work, and she had Robbie in her arms. He was yelling his head off, but he didn't seem mad—it was more like volumized baby babble. From the kitchen, the sounds of Emily and Maya's light bickering filtered in. Micah held out his arms and accepted Robbie from a grateful LR, who returned to the kitchen to deal with whatever squabble the girls were having.

Micah set the bag he'd been carrying by the door and carried Robbie into the living room. They kept each other busy while Langston stood guard between the two rooms. Every so often, he would lean around to eavesdrop on LR's conversation with Emily and Maya. Bored with that drama, he turned to Micah.

"What'd you bring?" he asked.

"Some things for you and your sisters and brother," Micah answered. "But we'll wait until your dad gets home, I think."

"Aw, man." Langston's frustrated pout amused Micah.

"It's not that exciting," he said, laughing. Robbie looked up at him and giggled then handed Micah his well-worn stuffed bunny. "Why, thank you, sir." Micah accepted it and tickled Robbie under his chin with the ears.

"If you brought it, it's gotta be good," Langston said. "Ooh, Emily's in trouble."

"Lang," Micah warned.

"Okay, okay. Hey, can you help me with my homework?"

"Soon as your mom can take Robbie. I doubt you want him chewing on your school papers. What is it?"

"I hafta write three questions my book made me think of. I can only do one."

"If you get the book, we can talk about it until your mom is done."

Obediently, Langston went to his backpack—purple, his favorite color of the moment—and retrieved the book. He handed it to Micah, who hoisted Robbie into his lap and accepted the book with his free hand. He flipped the book over to read the synopsis.

"What chapter are you on?"

"Five."

Langston plopped down on the couch, and he and Micah talked while they waited. When Robbie grew bored and fussy, Micah reflected what a challenge it must be for LR to do this on a daily basis. It wouldn't be too hard for him to stop by a bit more often.

LR led the girls out of the kitchen, having resolved whatever it was. Robbie crawled off Micah's lap and headed toward his mother. Emily saw Micah at the same time and ran straight for him, throwing herself into his lap and nearly knocking him backwards, even though he was already on the floor. Maya half hid behind LR, clinging to her fingers.

"Good to see you too," Micah said, giving Emily a hug. He lifted his eyes to LR. "Hey."

Her smile was tired, but aside from that she appeared all right. "Hey, yourself," she said as she scooped Robbie into her arms.

"I brought a few things for the kids. When will Jamal be home?"

"Soon. You want to stay for dinner?"

"I can't," Micah said. "I have some work to do. I was just helping Lang with his homework for now."

"Okay. I'll leave you to it."

The girls went upstairs, and LR brought Robbie into the kitchen with her. Micah got up and sat on the couch next to Langston, and they resumed their conversation about the book. By the time Jamal walked through the front door, Langston had finished writing and was putting his schoolwork back in his bag.

The girls, having heard Jamal come in, came rushing down the stairs. Langston was at the age where he hung back a bit, but all three kids effectively swarmed Jamal the moment he'd set his bag down. Laughing, he greeted them one by one. A moment later, LR came in and gave him a light kiss. He took an enthusiastic Robbie from her. Micah watched from the living room, struck by how different life was for them than it had been for himself or even for Cat.

Jamal finally noticed him. "Hey, Micah. You staying for dinner?"

Micah shook his head. "Can't. But I wanted to wait for you before I give some things to the kids."

"Oh, yeah!" Langston piped up. "Uncle Mike brought us presents." He gave Micah a pleading look. "Can we see them now?"

"Of course."

Micah brought the bag into the living room and set it on the coffee table. The three older children knelt in front of him, wide-eyed. Jamal rocked Robbie, and LR sat down next to Micah.

First, he withdrew a box similar to the one he'd given to Jones. He handed it to Langston. "Careful when you open it. They're small."

Langston took the top off and peeled back the tissue paper. Inside, Cat's hoop earrings lay nestled. Langston peered up at Micah. "What are they?"

"Here. Come closer."

Langston shuffled to the couch, still on his knees. Micah took each earring out and put them gently around the shell of Langston's ear until he had a row of the magnetic hoops. Langston tried to peek out of the corner of his eye, and Micah chuckled.

"How about you go look at them in the bathroom mirror?"

"Wait." LR ducked out and returned a minute later with a handheld mirror. She gave it to Langston.

He looked at himself, turning his head side to side. "These are so cool! Where did you get them?"

"They belonged to—" Micah looked up at LR, who was now leaning against the door frame. "—your Uncle Cat. He couldn't have his ears pierced, so he wore magnetic ones. I figured you could have them until you're old enough to decide if you want real piercings."

"Thanks, Uncle Mike." Langston popped up and gave Micah a hug.

"Emily next," Micah said. He handed her an oddly-shaped package.

She tore into the wrapping to reveal the old-fashioned metronome. Turning it over in her hands, she said, "What's this?"

"It's a metronome. That's a thing you use to count beats for you when you play music. Watch." He took it and wound it with the key in the back then set it on the table. He pried the arm away from its locked position, and it moved back and forth, making a click each time. Emily watched, mesmerized.

"She might take it apart," LR warned.

"I figured she might, and I really think Cat would've approved. You know how he was."

LR laughed. "I suspect you're right."

Maya had been quietly watching the others, and Micah turned his attention to her. "This is for you, sweetheart." He took out a velvet bag and gave it to her.

Maya tugged it open and dumped the contents out on the table. It was a rosary, with rose-colored stones and a pewter crucifix. Maya touched the beads carefully with one finger.

"Pretty," she said.

"It is," Micah agreed. "When you're a bit older, I'll show you how to use it. Uncle Cat taught me."

He stood and pulled the last item out of the bag. He hadn't wrapped it, figuring Robbie probably didn't need him to. Instead of handing it to the baby, he brought it to LR. He looped the chain over her head, and she put a hand to her chest where the pendants lay.

"His MedicAlert tags," Micah said. "They're for Robbie. I know he can't use them—they have Cat's name and information on them. But he can have them, and we can all make sure he knows Cat even though they never met."

Micah looked back at the four children, Robbie in his father's arms and the other three still admiring their gifts. They were all very different. Langston was book-smart like his mother. Emily had a wicked temper, which suited her well when standing up for herself. Maya already showed skill with a paintbrush. Robbie was prone to the kind of mischief that could get him in real trouble. Yet in some sense, Cat lived on in all of them—in Langston's sense of style and Emily's handy curiosity and Maya's gentle insight and Robbie's boundless energy.

When Micah returned his gaze to LR, she had tears streaming down her cheeks. Micah reached for her, and they held each other. He let go of his reserve and wept openly while he clung to her. He didn't stop when he felt small arms go around his waist. It was a long time before his tears ebbed and he released LR. Jamal handed them both a tissue.

"Thank you," LR said, swiping under her eyes with the tissue. "For everything."

"It's what he wanted," Micah said. "He said I should 'store up my treasure' in you and the kids and our friends. So that's what I did. I gave his things to the people to whom they would mean the most." He looked down at the children and rested his hand briefly on each one's head. "He loved you all very much, and so do I."

LR pulled him into another quick, tight hug. As she let go, she said, "I love you, Micah. I'm glad you were the one he married."

"I love you too." He touched her cheek.

Micah delivered hugs to each of the kids and to Jamal. He kissed Robbie's forehead and gave his tummy a tickle. The resulting giggle made everyone else laugh, too. Micah took the bag from the coffee table, and with a wave, he walked out.

Back at his house, Micah paused on the doorstep and took a deep breath. He had one more day to finish everything. With renewed conviction and a lighter heart, he opened his door and stepped inside.

CHAPTER TWENTY-FOUR

MY PEACE I LEAVE YOU

LONG INTO the night, Micah wrote. He had to finish the story to bring for the last class of the session. By the time he was done, his wrists and fingers ached. He flexed them as he sat back, going over what he'd just written with a nod.

The story wasn't his usual, and he was fairly sure his publisher wouldn't take it. The question now was what to do with it. He stared at the screen so long the words stopped making sense before an idea occurred to him. He looked up at the clock and was startled to find it was the middle of the night. He rose from the table and contemplated going upstairs, but the thought was daunting in his exhausted state. Instead, he went down the hall and pushed open the door to Cat's old room.

He lay on the bed and pulled a blanket over himself, thoughts of his story and what he had in mind still swirling in his head. He was sure he would never get to sleep, nervous excitement coursing through him. But the room was dark and quiet, and the next thing he was aware of was the sound of voices and a car's engine.

They were in the car again. Micah recognized it this time, and he had the odd sensation that comes with knowing one is dreaming but being unable to wake from it. It was different from the last time. There was no arguing, for one thing, and the man who had been in the driver's seat was gone. It took a moment for Micah to realize he was the one sitting there. The other voices belonged to Cat and his mother, and Micah couldn't understand what they were talking about.

"I told you," Cat said, and that was the first thing that made any sense.

"Told me what?" Micah asked, but Cat didn't seem to see him.

Micah's mother nodded. "Yes."

Growing frustrated, Micah was about to grab one of them to get their attention when Cat turned toward him. "You did the right thing, honey."

He woke slowly, the room still mostly dark. Climbing out of bed, he went to the window and peeked through the curtains. The sun was coming up over the lake, gloriously pink and orange and gold, reflecting on the water. Micah let the curtain fall back into place and returned to bed. He lay there until he was sure it was late enough to make a few phone calls.

Cooper was first on the list. Micah hit the numbers, and Cooper's sleepy voice answered. "Hello?" he croaked.

"I'm sorry I woke you. I thought it was late enough." Micah glanced at the clock. "Wait...aren't you working?"

"I have a crappy head cold, and I don't want to make my patients sick. What's up?" He sounded a bit clearer.

"Is Lucy still doing some freelance work?"

"Yeah. Did you need something?"

"A manuscript," Micah replied. He smiled. "It needs some editing before I publish it."

"Oh, now that's—" Micah heard Cooper's forceful sneeze and winced. "—interesting." Cooper sniffled.

"Should I call her myself? Or are you up to talking to her?"

"I can do it. What's the story? And why not go with your publisher's editor?"

"My publisher won't want this," Micah explained. "It's not a romance, and it's a fantasy—she publishes broad-spectrum contemporary romance only."

"Okay. I'll have Luce call you when she gets home later. For now, send me the details so I can share them with her. Good luck, Uncle Mike."

They ended the call and Micah made a note to send the information to Cooper. Next, he put in a call to Elle.

"Hey, Uncle Mike," she greeted him. "How's everything?"

"Good. Better than good. I was going through your web site this morning."

"Oh?" Elle laughed. "My portfolio, you mean?"

"No, the one of your just-for-fun images. I need something kind of specific." He cleared his throat. "Cover art."

"Okay." She sounded confused.

"It's for my novel. The one I'm not giving to my publisher."

"Ah, now it makes sense. I'll send you the spreadsheet, and you can fill in the questions. I assume you want Henry to do something with it."

"If he can. Look, just so you know, I don't want any favors. I'll pay you whatever you're asking. You're the only one I trust with this."

There was a pause. "Uncle Mike, what's this book?"

He thought about what to tell her. He could keep it light, the way he had with Cooper. He hadn't wanted to influence Lucy's editing at all by knowing the truth. With Elle, he suspected it was important information.

"It's about Cat," he said. "And about life and death and...what comes next."

He could almost hear Elle grinning through the phone. "Oh, my god. That's awesome. I'll get back to you as soon as I can. I think I already have the perfect picture to use, and I can tell you now Henry will do it." She squealed with excitement. "I can't wait!"

"Thanks, Elle." He hung up.

If Micah wanted to be ready for class, he had a lot of work to do. He looked around Cat's old room. Going to the closet, Micah pulled out three pairs of Cat's shoes: the calf-high lace-up boots, Cat's favorite hot pink Converse, and the jade green pair he'd worn for their wedding. He carried them out of the room.

From the study, Micah retrieved the lock box. The only thing left inside was the lacy red-orange panties. Micah brought the box, along with the shoes, up to his bedroom. There, he added the wedding bands, the two pairs of jade earrings, and Cat's final letter to the box. He took the key, the lock box, and the shoes up to the attic and tucked them away in one of the bins full of photo albums. In exchange, he brought down Cat's old journals to return to his in-laws and Cat's musical composition books.

He left both of those bins by the door. He could deliver the journals to Audrey any time, and he would give Jude the sheet music at school. She would surely object, but Micah had his argument prepared. He and Cat had never had children, and Jude was family. She was as entitled to Cat's things as anyone, and she would get the most out of playing his songs.

Next, he returned to Cat's old room. He pulled Cat's prayer book from the bedside drawer and brought it into the study. On the desk sat the bag with the jewelry box in it. Micah set the prayer book inside with the box and left it with his laptop case.

Out in the kitchen, Micah stretched and opened the curtains above the sink. The sun was shining over the lake, and only a few wispy clouds drifted past in the brilliant blue sky. It was going to be a good day.

It was the last class of the term, and Micah had come prepared not only with his laptop but with several bins. He wouldn't allow Chris or Jude to look inside when they helped him carry them from the car. Once class began, all eyes in the room were on Micah, and the atmosphere was tense. He couldn't blame them after the way the previous class had gone. He handed around the evaluation forms from the continuing education program.

"You can fill those out while we talk. I'm offering this class again for the next session, and in January, I'm running an intermediate level class." He smiled at them. "I've enjoyed our time together, so I hope you'll consider catching up in a couple of months." Carlie returned the unused papers to him, and he continued. "Tonight, you'll get together in smaller groups and talk about what you feel you need to work on more—or whether you want to continue to pursue writing, professionally or not."

"And after?" Dyl asked.

"I can continue to read my novel. It's finished, and I'm hoping you'll like the end."

There was a strained silence before Dyl replied, "I would like to hear it." He looked around the room, and others nodded in agreement.

"It's settled, then. Find a group and get some discussion going."

While they talked and filled out the forms, Micah opened the file on his laptop. He scrolled through the last part of the story, and his heart was in his throat. He wanted his students to like it, of course, especially after he'd left them heartbroken the last time he'd read from it. More than that, he wanted them to connect to it, to understand the message in it.

Distracted, he almost missed when the class settled back down in their own seats, facing forward like obedient school children. Micah almost laughed; they were so much like his sixth graders for a moment. He surveyed them and cleared his throat.

"Is there anything you want to say before I read this?" At their collective no, he focused his gaze on the screen. "'In the days following the battle, the war-torn city...'"

He read for a long time. He was almost to the end when he saw their time was almost up. He paused, but Maricela whispered, "Go on. We'll stay." And so he did. He took them through Benjamin's stand to return He'chatul's kingdom to its peaceful, harmonious state and his bestowing of gifts on the people. Finally, he brought them into a time when Benjamin was ready to love and be loved in return. As he spoke the final words, he looked up at the class. There wasn't a dry eye in the room.

"Thank you," Dyl said. It seemed to be all he could manage.

"You gave He'chatul's life—and his death—meaning," Hope said.

Amid murmurs of assent, Micah rounded the desk and sat on it, facing the class. "Can I be personal here?" There were nods of agreement, so he went on. "You all challenged me. I don't know that I'd have seen meaning in the loss of people I cared about if you hadn't asked me to look. Thank you for holding me to a high standard."

"What are you going to do with the story?" Carlie asked.

"Publish it. Under my real name this time," Micah replied.

"We're long past the end of class. I hope I see all of you again in January, although I can't promise we'll have quite such an emotional ride next time." A wave of giggles went around the room, and Micah put his hand up. "One more thing. In keeping with the theme, I have a request of you."

He opened the bins he'd brought and invited the class to come look inside at Cat's shoes. He smiled at their confused expressions and then went on to explain.

"These belonged to my spouse. He spent about twenty years collecting them. When I met him, he had sixteen pairs, and now there are twenty-two. Here's what I'm asking you all to do. Take one. Or take a few. Give them away to someone who needs a pair. I couldn't bring myself to simply take the whole bin to Goodwill, and I don't think that's what Cat would've wanted. I think he'd have liked to know that they were given away in his memory. They need good homes, and I'm trusting you all to find them."

"Maricela and I can take a bunch back to school with us," Carlie said. "There are lots of people there who would love them."

Hope pulled out an electric blue pair. "Can I take these for Raven? They'll need to grow into the shoes, but I know they would love them."

"Of course," Micah told her.

"I'm sure there are folks at the church who could use some." Chris pulled a few pairs.

Dyl reached in and brought out the sunset orange ones, and Micah was hit with a wave of sadness. He'd loved that pair. Dyl held them up, and his eyes were bright with tears.

"Ca-can I have these?" he asked. He sniffled. "My boyfriend had a pair just like them."

Micah stepped closer and pulled Dyl into a hug. "Of course you can keep them," he murmured. "I think Cat would've liked that."

Every last pair of shoes got a new home or a promise of one. Everyone returned to their seats and packed their things away. One by one, they stood and came to say goodbye to Micah. Carlie and Maricela gave him simultaneous bubbly hugs. Hope held onto him for a long time. Jude gave him a squeeze and told him she'd see him at work. Even Dyl gave him a fist bump and a cheeky smirk, which made Micah laugh.

When they'd all left, Micah put away his laptop and stacked the bins. He was aware Chris was still in the room, but he wanted to be sure they were truly alone before he spoke to him. The last of the footsteps in the hall died away, and Micah picked up the two items he'd tucked into his laptop case. He left his things to walk over to where Chris lingered by the door.

"So," Chris said. "Last class."

"And now it's just the two of us." Micah stepped closer. "It's been three days, you know."

"Mm-hm. And were you able to do everything you needed?"

"I was." Micah was in Chris's personal space now.

"Good to know."

"I have something for you." Micah held out the prayer book first. "I think you'll enjoy this more than I would."

"I—" Chris said. He looked down at it. "It was Cat's?"

"Yes. I can tell you for sure he'd be glad for you to keep it."

"Thank you." Chris cupped Micah's cheek.

"And this." Micah produced the jewelry box. "It's from me."

Chris opened it to see the tiger's eye earrings. "You were buying these the other day when I saw you at Regal Ink. So that's what was in the bag."

"Yes. I imagined what they'd look like on you, and that's why I flipped out. My heart was out of control, grieving for Cat but already falling for you. If the prayer book is Cat's way of blessing us, then the earrings are my own."

Before Micah could react, Chris had shut the classroom door and pinned Micah against the wall next to it. Micah laughed as his back landed right between the door frame and the book shelf. Then he winced, discovering he didn't quite have the bounce-back of his younger years.

"Ungh," Micah grunted.

His reaction didn't seem to bother Chris, who stifled Micah with a searing kiss that left them both breathless. Micah settled his hands on Chris's hips, and Chris rested his hands, still full of the gifts, on Micah's shoulders. They spent several minutes reacquainting themselves with each other. It was a long time before they came up for air.

"It's good to see you too," Micah said.

"I've been wanting to do that all night."

"Was it worth the wait?"

"Very much." Chris kissed him again, and then again after that.

It threatened to turn into something Micah wasn't prepared to do in a classroom—for a whole host of reasons—so he pulled back. "How about you come over on Friday? No class on Saturday, so we don't have to worry about finishing up early. Uh...I mean..."

Chris laughed, his eyes crinkling a little. "It's a date. Shall I bring anything?"

"Just yourself."

Following another round of kisses, Chris picked up his bag and opened the door. "See you Friday," he said before he stepped out.

Micah watched him go before gathering the empty bins and his laptop. "It's a date," he said quietly to himself, and then he grinned.

CHAPTER TWENTY-FIVE

DO UNTO OTHERS

IT WAS Chris's turn to bring the flowers—a variety of carnations, interspersed with baby's breath and tied with a red satin ribbon. Micah smiled as he accepted them and leaned in for a soft kiss. This was an aspect of dating life he'd never experienced. Not through his twenties, when relationships were no more than cold beer and warm bodies. Not when he was still too ill to be a good lover. And not even with Cat, for whom traditional courtship rituals meant very little. Micah was surprised and yet somehow not to discover he liked it.

He thanked Chris by way of pulling him close. He inhaled Chris's woodsy scent, and he was pleased to see Chris had worn the tiger's eye earrings. Micah kissed him, and his stomach made delightful swoops as Chris kissed him back. Micah wanted very much to press him up against the counter and never stop, but there was dinner in the oven. Regretfully, he pulled back, but he didn't resist the last, quick peck Chris delivered before they parted.

Chris helped him set the table while Micah pulled food from the oven. It had never occurred to him that if he could do it properly, he might enjoy cooking. Now everyone seemed eager to give him their favorite recipes to try, and he'd tucked them into a file to work through one by one. Since none of them were meals for one, he would have plenty to bring to Jones and Alonzo or to freeze. Tonight, though, he'd made something just for himself and Chris.

They sat at the table, and Micah contemplated lighting candles, but it felt too clichéd. Instead, he waited quietly while Chris said a silent prayer, his hands folded on the table and his eyes closed. When he was through, he looked up at Micah and smiled.

"This looks good. Thank you."

"Of course." Micah served them both. "Maybe this is a bit heavy a subject, but I still want to hear more about your queer theology. I gave a copy of the book to my brother—the last minister standing—to read. Don't know if he has yet, though."

Chris chuckled. "Hopefully he'll be able to learn something from it." He unfolded his napkin and laid it in his lap, taking a while before he answered Micah's query. "I suppose it would help if you knew something about both liberation theology and queer theory. They're not the same, but queer theology has its roots there."

He talked, and Micah listened. He was fascinated by Chris's passion. Micah rarely expressed his enthusiasm for his job overtly, but he understood the fire, the drive to excel and find new ways to reach his students. Clearly Chris felt the same about his faith and reaching his congregants. It wasn't enough to change Micah's mind, but it was plenty to give him insight into who Chris was.

"Listen to me, going on like that." Chris laughed. "I hope I haven't bored you to tears."

"Not at all. I'm enjoying hearing what you have to say."

They cleaned up from dinner and went to sit in the living room. Chris had brought the book with him, and he opened it on the coffee table. There was a picture of the resurrected Christ, with Doubting Thomas touching the wound in his side. Micah's stomach jolted. That story had always been a source of shame for him. There was no room for doubt, only devout faith, blessed for belief in the unseen. Micah looked away.

"What's wrong?" Chris asked, laying a hand on Micah's quaking knee.

He rested a finger on the picture. "This. I was made to feel inferior for my uncertainty." A tremor ran through him, and he tensed as he waited for Chris to respond.

"That's not what this story means at all. At least, not to me." Chris shifted away a little. "Can I show you something? It's...very personal."

"You don't have to if you'd rather not." It was Micah's turn to offer comfort, though he didn't know the reason for Chris's visible unease.

"I want to."

Slowly, hesitantly, Chris drew his shirt over his head. Micah's gaze swept down his bare chest, from the curve of his collarbone to the sparse dark hair to his round, pink nipples. Beneath them ran two faded scars, one on either side. They were similar but not identical to Pam's scars from when she'd had cancer. Micah continued his perusal to Chris's now-exposed navel and the trail of hair disappearing into his jeans.

Chris pointed back to the picture. "When I was in seminary, I was looking for other trans clergy. There aren't a lot who are out, but there are more than you'd think. I came across a Catholic priest—yes, really." He smiled at Micah's obvious surprise. "Father Shannon Kearns. On his website, he suggested that the wounds in Jesus' side in this painting are similar to the incisions from top surgery. It meant a lot to me, as I'd only recently had my own."

Micah looked back and forth between them, seeing what Chris meant. As painstakingly as Chris had removed his shirt, Micah unbuttoned and rolled up his left shirt sleeve. He turned his arm over so Chris could see the marks. He didn't purposely share them, though he didn't go to any great lengths to hide them, either. Now, he wanted Chris to look at him in the same way Chris was trusting him.

Lifting one of Micah's shaking hands, Chris pressed his lips to the scar. "'Put your finger here, and see my hands. And put out your hand, and place it in my side.' This, Micah. This is our liberation."

The next moment, they were kissing. Glorious and beautiful and consuming, the thrill of their joined lips infused Micah. His senses were full of Chris to the exclusion of all else—his scent and his taste and the feel of his mouth. Micah shifted, and Chris moved with him to lie back against the arm of the couch. Chris put a hand on Micah's shoulder, tangling the fingers of his other hand in Micah's hair. Micah pressed his palms against Chris's sides, unsure whether he enjoyed having his chest touched but wanting to feel Chris's warm skin. He thought about what it would be like to simply undress and make love right then and there.

Micah did what he'd wanted to do earlier and ran his tongue along the shell of Chris's ear, all the way down to the earring. He kissed the lobe and nibbled it with his lips. Chris made a subtle rolling motion with his hips, and they panted through their kisses in concert. Micah knew he would need to stop them soon. They hadn't even talked about whether they were going to have sex. He wanted Chris, but not like this. Not like frantic adolescents, and not like—

He gasped and sat up a little, laughing. Chris propped himself on his elbows, giving Micah a quizzical look. Micah closed his eyes and tried to catch his breath.

"I'm sorry for stopping us like that," Micah said.

"It's all right. What in the world is so funny?"

Micah shook his head, and another swell of laughter bubbled out of him. "I am so sorry! All of a sudden, I felt like I was back in my teenage years, and I realized I apparently have a thing for couch sex."

"What?" Chris shook his head, but he was grinning. "I was going to say maybe you weren't ready, but that seems not to be the problem here."

"No, I am. This—what we were doing—was how almost all my first times have gone. I want to have something with you that belongs to us." He laughed again, more softly. "Is that too ridiculous of me?"

"No, not at all." Chris cupped his jaw and drew him back in for another steamy, albeit shorter, kiss.

"Did you want to stay the night?" Micah asked. "Even if we don't continue this?"

"I would love to." Chris gave him a devious smile. "I did bring a bag, but I left it in the car."

Micah stole another kiss. "I should probably let you get it then. So you were hoping?"

"Of course I was."

They stood, and Chris pulled his shirt back on. Micah grabbed Chris's coat from the closet. Chris stepped outside, and Micah paused to watch him for a moment, shivering in the gust of cold air before Chris shut the door. He wasn't sure where they were going, but he liked the idea of figuring it out together. It had been a long time since he'd felt like this. He'd had good and satisfying sex since Cat, but it hadn't had the same emotional impact. Here, with Chris in his house, it was all part of their slow slide into the bond they'd formed.

Chris reentered the house and dropped his bag at his feet while he shed his coat. He handed it to Micah and said, "I don't mean to be a mood-killer, but we probably ought to talk about this."

"We could do it upstairs," Micah suggested. "Where it's comfortable."

They ascended the stairs, and Chris set his bag at the end of the bed. Micah allowed him to use the bathroom first. While he was gone, an odd feeling crept over Micah. It was strange to have another man spending the night in his home—in his bed—and stranger still to do the ordinary rituals he would do any other night: turning on the bedside lamp instead of the overhead light, closing the curtains, turning down the sheets. Those felt domestic, the tasks of long-term lovers.

Micah smiled at the memory of nights like this one with Cat. It no longer brought him the same kind of grief it had even a month ago. He could allow the thoughts to pass freely through his brain without triggering waves of sorrow and longing for what he'd lost. The realization hit him hard, and it made him dizzy with excitement. He steadied himself on the dresser and held on, riding the thrill of making new memories as well as the anxiety that always accompanied sex for him.

That was where Chris found him when he came in from the bathroom. "Micah?" he asked, sounding concerned.

Micah looked up. "Come on in."

Chris came farther into the room and put a hand on Micah's shoulder. "Are you all right?"

"I—" Micah put a hand on top of Chris's. He wanted to tell him it wasn't about him. Letting out a breath, he said, "I was thinking about how happy I am to be here with you, that's all."

Chris ran his hand up and down Micah's arm. "Me too." He let go and went to the bed. "Is it all right if I stretch out?" he asked.

"Of course. I'll be right back."

Micah took his turn in the bathroom, spending as little time there as he could so as to be back in the room as soon as possible. When he came back, Chris was lying on his stomach, his arm tucked under the pillow and his head turned to face Micah. Something inside Micah shifted, and he admired the way he looked relaxed and comfortable. It looked and felt right to have him there. Chris scooted over so Micah could climb in beside him.

"Hey," Micah said.

"Hey."

Micah reached out and ran his finger over Chris's short beard. He embodied a kind of self-assurance Micah wished he possessed at times. Chris embraced all aspects of himself and bore none of the shame Micah had taken in. Glad to be there with him, Micah breathed in Chris's scent, warm and dark. Without thinking, Micah had moved closer to him until their faces were close enough to share a breath. They tangled their legs together, and Micah closed the gap to kiss him. Chris responded, closed-mouthed yet sensual.

"Is this what you want?" Chris asked. "It may not be worship for you, but it does mean something."

"I won't be sure until we try." It was the best Micah could do to convey his uncertainty not over sex but over everything that went with it for him.

"I can live with that."

Chris leaned in again, and the kisses were soft and sweet this time. Micah felt out of practice, all elbows and knees and sharp angles. It didn't seem to bother Chris at all. Neither of them took it further. Micah was overwhelmed with the enjoyment of the moment. There hadn't been any halfway with his previous lovers, not even Cat most of the time. Here he was with Chris, turned on and with an attractive man in his arms, yet with no need to go beyond kissing and holding each other yet.

It might have been hours or only minutes in which they were absorbed in one another before they both mutually agreed on breaking their embrace. Chris rolled onto his back, his smile gentle and inviting. Micah adjusted both his position and his pajamas.

Chris said, "We can keep doing this, but I can't promise I won't want more."

"I'm already there. It's up to you."

"Are you sure?"

"I am." Micah paused, wanting to say the right thing but not knowing what it was. "I've been with a lot of guys, but I was drunk most of the time. I wanted sex, but I didn't want to feel anything or ask too many questions of my partners. Then I was with Cat for nine years, and he was comfortable directing us because of his disability." He propped himself up and looked down at Chris. "I'm glad to be here with you now, but I'm out of practice, and I don't know how to ask you what you like in bed other than awkwardly just saying it."

Chris snickered and wriggled closer, and Micah settled in close, draping his arm across Chris's waist. "Then I'll tell you. I love having my clit-dick sucked or played with, and I'm happy to do the same in return. You can touch me anywhere you like, including my chest. But I don't like penetration of any kind, at least not in me." He looked Micah in the eyes. "I'm a top on the occasion I like it at all."

"Oh, thank god."

Laughing, Chris tugged a little on Micah's curls. "You're all right with that?"

"Hell, yeah. I'm comfortable either way, but I've always preferred to bottom, and it's not that important anyway." Micah said. "Look, it's probably not a good idea to bring up sex with my dead spouse right before we get it on, but I think it's fair in this case. His disability made any kind of penetration off the table. Why do you think we had a drawer full of sex toys?" Micah snorted a laugh.

Chris's chuckle sounded more relieved than amused. "Good to

know. I don't think I'm quite ready for that step tonight, but I'll keep it in mind for another time." He kissed Micah briefly and backed off, waiting.

The thought of having more nights like this in the future was exhilarating. Micah bent forward and pressed their lips together, and this time Chris opened his mouth. Their tongues tangled, and anticipation swirled in Micah's belly. He pressed his hips against Chris's, his cock lined up with Chris's thigh. Chris parted his legs to let one of Micah's slip in between. It was exciting, and Micah wanted more.

Chris had on a tight white t-shirt that emphasized his lean yet soft body. Micah slid his hand underneath it, working his fingers up until he found one of Chris's nipples. He toyed with it as he rolled his hips to get some much-needed friction against his hardening cock.

Sitting up a little, Chris pulled his shirt off and tossed it aside. When Micah hesitated, Chris said, "Is it all right if I show you what would feel fantastic right now?"

He took Micah's hand and lowered it between his legs, slipping it under the waistband of his sweatpants. Micah groaned when he felt the hard nub under his fingers, and his breath caught when Chris moaned and rocked against his hand. Micah leaned down and kissed him again greedily. Chris pushed his hand inside Micah's boxers, curling his grip around Micah's length and sliding it slowly up and down.

Micah closed his eyes, reveling in the sensations. He allowed Chris to bring him to the edge, then he pulled away and withdrew his own hand. He shed his clothes and waited until Chris had yanked off his pants before diving back in to kiss him again. They rolled on the bed, writhing and panting as they took each other closer each time before backing off.

Wanting more, Micah pushed Chris's legs apart and slid down his body. For a while, he simply looked, admiring. He followed the trail of dark hair down Chris's rounded belly to the tight, neat triangle just above his clit-dick. Micah's gaze stayed there for a long time. It was gorgeous, full and swollen and glistening with Chris's fluid, peeking out from soft folds. Even without touching it, the sight made Micah's excitement mount. He hoped he would be able to hang on until he'd brought Chris to orgasm with his lips and tongue. Gasping both with pleasure and at his own thoughts, Micah lowered his mouth.

He took Chris in and moaned with delight at the feel on his tongue. He loved that he could fit its entirety into his mouth, appreciating the texture as he gave an experimental suck. Chris's back arched, and Micah backed off a little. He focused entirely on what he was doing, delighting in changing his motion and pattern. In no time he had Chris squirming under him, drawing his knees up and thrusting upward with his hips. Micah glanced up to watch as Chris tipped his head back against the pillow, his face twisted into a grimace as he let go and cried out.

Micah pulled off, loving the flush of Chris's skin and the way his muscles tensed and relaxed. The sight nearly sent him into his own climax, but he held back. He had to know if he could give himself over to Chris, trusting himself in his hands. Micah crawled up the pillow and lay next to Chris, waiting for him to come down from his high.

It was a while before Chris opened his eyes and turned to look at Micah. "What a mouth you've got."

Micah chuckled. "So I've been told."

They kissed a bit more, and Chris's hand drifted down to toy with Micah's cock. He kept his touch light, and the teasing had Micah rolling his hips in an effort to increase the pressure. Chris didn't do anything to hurry up or to slow down, keeping at the steady, gentle pace. Micah closed his eyes, focusing on the feel of another man's palm against his flesh. He indulged the familiar anxiety for only a moment before he opened his eyes and gave a soft sigh. No, it wasn't holy for him, but Chris had been right—it meant something.

"What do you want to do?" Chris asked.

"Anything," Micah replied. He shuddered with want. "May-maybe a bit faster." When Chris changed his easy pace and light grip to something more firm and rhythmic, Micah thrust into his hand and groaned. "God, yeah. Like that."

Chris angled so he straddled Micah's leg and pressed against his hipbone. The sensations were overwhelming—the skin-to-skin contact and the steady motion rocking their bodies. He sought Chris's lips and joined their mouths, both of them making quiet, needy sounds. Chris rubbed against him, riding his leg. Micah felt the connection between them as they moved together almost as one. There was nothing but the two of them, captivated by each other and the rising tide of pleasure; all else faded away.

Chris's thrusts became faster, sharper, until his voice broke into a choked-off shout. It was too much for Micah, and he tumbled over the edge too, his muscles jerking and hot jets splattering against their bellies. He spasmed again, his knees shaking. Micah gasped, his vision still blotchy when Chris collapsed into his arms. They lay pressed together, breathing labored. Micah's heart beat so hard and fast his ears rang. He let what had happened between them sink in while he breathed slowly, calming down.

They separated to tidy up. When the two of them and the sheets were sufficiently clean, Chris climbed back in beside him, and Micah flipped the light off. Chris curled around Micah, and Micah folded him into his arms. Chris's beard brushed against Micah's chest, prickling a little on his sensitive skin. It had been a long time since he'd been able to let go like that, caught up in the moment between himself and another person. Everything about it was full of wonder, almost larger than life. He wanted to laugh and cry and sing all at the same time, and yet he was too sleepy to move.

Not too sleepy to grin into the darkness, though. *Be present. Be joyful.* Micah had, and it was good.

EPILOGUE

THAT THEY MAY HAVE LIFE

MICAH STRAIGHTENED his collar and ran a little gel through his curls. He stepped back and peered at himself, angling to get a better look. He debated wearing a tie for the third time. Deciding he was presentable enough, he descended the stairs and pulled his jacket from the hook on the wall. He slid his feet into his shoes and opened the door, intending to take in some fresh air while he waited for Jude.

The weather had turned crisp, and he breathed in the scent of burning wood from a neighbor's fireplace. Later, he would find the strings of Christmas lights up in the attic. It was still too early for a tree, but the first Sunday of the season was as good a time as any to start decorating. For the first time since he was a child, the thought of cut-out cookies and mistletoe made him smile. He looked forward to learning what Chris's traditions were.

Something brushed against his leg, and he looked down into wide, green eyes. "Meow."

"Thomas!" Micah exclaimed. "Well, hello there. It's been a long time."

"Meow."

Micah had a sudden urge to hug the orange beast, but he settled for crouching down to scratch Thomas behind his ears. "I've missed you, rascal," he said.

Thomas's expression plainly conveyed, "Of course you have." He rubbed against Micah's knee, oblivious to the ginger hairs he was leaving on the dark trousers.

"You want to come in and have some breakfast? I probably have a can of something left."

Micah stood and opened the door, and Thomas stalked inside, wiggling his rump and glancing back. Micah opened the pantry and took out a can of food. He'd thought about getting another cat, so he'd left everything set up. But his free time had been occupied with dinners on the lakefront and cozy evenings and tender lovemaking with Chris. Finding a new furry companion had been at the bottom of his list of priorities for the last three weeks.

Now he was glad he hadn't done it. Thomas hopped up on the counter and gave Micah cool, damp kitty kisses, making him laugh. "Are you here to stay this time?" Micah asked, though he was fairly sure he knew the answer.

Thomas's rumbly purr vibrated against Micah's hand. He stretched into Micah's touch before deciding he'd had quite enough. He leapt from the counter and wandered into his room, sashaying and twitching his tail as he went. Micah grinned after him.

The doorbell sounded, and Micah answered it to see Jude dressed in much the same style she always wore.

"Ready to go?" she asked.

"As I'll ever be," he replied.

The drive was quiet but not uncomfortable. Micah parked, and they walked in together. She'd asked him to accompany her to Chris's church for her first visit, and he'd agreed. There would never be a time when he would believe again, but he could support his niece in her quest to find what worked for her. Not to mention it would be a nice chance to surprise Chris, who wouldn't be expecting him.

The interior was not yet fully decorated for the season, but all the linens were blue. The advent wreath was up, ready to be lit. Micah and Jude slid into a row at the back. Across the aisle, a family waved to them. Micah didn't know the younger children yet, but Jude did, and she waved back. The older child had the deer-in-headlights look of a student seeing his teacher out of context. Micah exchanged a knowing smile with Jude.

The service began, but Micah only paid half attention, keeping his eyes out for Chris. During the opening song, he took his place next to the other pastors at the front. Micah wasn't sure if he was preaching that morning or not; he had no idea how such things were decided. It didn't matter. Micah had a good view whether Chris took the pulpit or not, and he liked what he saw.

There was music and candle-lighting and things that were both familiar to Micah and not. He surprised himself that he could sit through it and not feel an urge to run from the room. He didn't plan to attend often, but he thought he might be able to manage until Jude felt comfortable going alone.

Chris stepped up to the pulpit and opened his Bible to read the morning's passage. Something from Isaiah, about beating swords into plowshares. As Chris read the last verse, he looked up. His gaze met Micah's, and his mouth fell into a surprised O. He faltered on the words, but he righted himself quickly.

"Let us read the Psalm responsively," he said, and as he did so, he kept his eyes on Micah. A smile formed on his lips, which Micah knew was meant for him.

Micah closed his eyes, listening to the alternating voices of Chris and the congregation. *Advent*, he thought. He remembered Chris saying it was the church's new year. A beginning, even though it was near the end of the calendar year. A chance to start fresh and to speak of things to come. That sounded just about right.

Micah was ready.

It's been quite a journey with Cat over the last three and a half years since I began writing about him. While drafting *Passing on Faith*, I meant it to be a single novel with a happy-for-now ending. I intentionally left it ambiguous. Micah was likely to outlive Cat, but we could imagine them riding off into the sunset and hope we were wrong after all. Only Cat didn't seem to want the story to be left there. He insisted first on his own story, and then he demanded that I let him go.

I've long wanted to write something about loss and grief. I know a bit about it, having loved and lost many people over the years. But that sort of heartache is difficult to capture. Everyone experiences it differently. In order to write this novel, I had to face some of my own deep feelings about death and being the one left behind.

In late September or early October of 2007, my spouse was at school for open house and I was home with our two children, ages two and four at the time. I had just put them to bed when the phone rang. It turned out to be my spouse's younger brother. I explained that my spouse was not at home but that I would leave him a message. My brother-in-law, who was not particularly shy about mocking people who he thought were being somewhat dense, told me he'd called for me. I could almost hear him rolling his eyes that I hadn't figured it out. Still confused, I asked why. It turned out I'd entirely forgotten about my birthday.

We talked for a long time about books and television we both liked. He made some recommendations and asked me how I was enjoying the comic he'd sent me. Eventually, the conversation went deeper. We'd always enjoyed talking, but that was the first time I recall him telling me anything so personal.

I should explain here that my brother-in-law had hemophilia and multiple other health problems, as Cat does in the novel (and that's where the similarities end). When we'd barely known each other, he was already showing me how to do an infusion with clotting factor. I was a nursing student at the time, and he thought I'd be interested in learning. So it's not that he was awkward or embarrassed or avoided talking about his medical issues. This conversation was different. We were talking about dying.

He mentioned how difficult it had gotten for him to make it through the New England winters. I hesitated, but then I asked him about it—about how a person knew when they'd had enough. He said, "You just do."

Less than a month later, he was gone.

I'm convinced he knew his time was nearly up, and that was part of why he was reaching out to me. I was both willing to listen to his musings about death and dying but also not make it the only thing we talked about. I'm not sure if anyone else in the family is aware that he'd called me or what we'd discussed. Until now, it was always a private moment between us that I felt no need to share.

It's been ten years, and I still miss him. It's been over sixteen since my mother died, and I still miss her as well. The way spouse's family and mine handle grief is vastly different, and both have given me greater understanding. I don't think someone's death is the sort of thing you "get over" and "move on" from.

You simply continue to live every day the best you can. That is what I hoped to capture with this novel: that it is not only all right but good to bring those we've loved and lost with us into our future. Loving one person, even after they are gone, does not mean we cannot love many other people. Loving other people does not mean we must put aside the dead and pretend they were never with us.

My hope is that in some way, reading about the complex relationship between love and grief will help someone to process, to heal, to feel whole. No matter what it looks like for you—and everyone is different—you are not wrong or broken or alone.

Many thanks, and much love to you all.

Acknowledgements

A lot of work went into this story. If I had to list every single person individually, the list would be over one hundred people. That's not an exaggeration.

Many thanks to my writer friends who patiently listened to me babbling about my plans for this novel and made suggestions. I've incorporated as many of them as I could. Thank you for reading the snippets I posted on my blog and leaving me encouraging notes.

Heartfelt thanks to those who took the time to share with me their insights about life, death, faith, the church, disability, and mental illness. Your openness was more valuable than you know, and your stories are so important. I'm glad you were able to trust me with such intimate parts of yourselves.

Enormous thanks and appreciation for the work that Father Shannon T.L. Kearns and Brian G. Murphy have done in making queer theology accessible to the mainstream. You can visit the website at www.queertheology.com for more information and resources.

Blessings and thanks to the many, many LGBTQIA Christians I've known over the years. You've all been supportive and kind through my own spiritual journey, and there aren't words to fully express my gratitude.

Love and thanks to my family. You've been patient with my dinnertime ramblings, my frustrations over plot points that weren't working, and the agony of naming yet more characters. I especially thank my daughter for providing me with a "Just Don't" sign during times when I needed to write undisturbed.

Thank you to my incredible team of beta readers. Your uplifting comments kept me going through edits on my draft, and your insights have helped shape this into the novel it is today. I don't know where I'd be without you.

Thanks to my amazing, caring, and wonderful publisher who took a chance on Micah and Cat and allowed me to continue their story in the way I (and they) felt it needed to be told. Thank you to the editors who have lovingly guided the polishing of the novels into something I can be proud of.

And of course, thank you to readers who have stuck with Micah and Cat and all the others from the beginning. Thank you for asking what happened next. I hope that even though it was sad at times, I was still able to provide both closure and that longed-for happily ever after.

Keep reading, keep writing, and carry on.

About the Author

A.M. Leibowitz is a queer spouse, parent, feminist, and book-lover falling somewhere on the Geek-Nerd Spectrum. They keep warm through the long, cold western New York winters by writing about life, relationships, hope, and happy-for-now endings. Their published fiction includes several novels as well as a number of short works, and their stories have been included in multiple anthologies.

In between noveling and editing, they blog coffee-fueled, quirky commentary on faith, culture, writing, books, and their family at **AMLEIBOWITZ.COM**.